ALSO BY BEN SCHRANK

Miracle Man

CONSENT

CONSENT

A NOVEL

BEN SCHRANK

RANDOM HOUSE / NEW YORK

Copyright © 2002 by Ben Schrank

Library of Congress Cataloging-in-Publication Data
Schrank, Ben.
Consent : a novel / Ben Schrank.—1st ed.
p. cm.
ISBN 0-375-50707-8 (acid-free paper)
1. Graduate students—Fiction.   2. Suicide victims—Family relationships—Fiction.   3. Teacher-
student relationships—Fiction.   4. Fathers and sons—Fiction.   5. New York (N.Y.)—Fiction.
6. Women lawyers—Fiction.   I. Title.
PS3569.C52913 C66 2002
813'.54—dc21   2001048338

Random House website address: www.atrandom.com
Printed in the United States of America on acid-free paper
2 4 6 8 9 7 5 3
First Edition

Book design by Victoria Wong

CONSENT

1

In the room I keep at the Gouverneur Hotel, at the bottom of the Lower East Side, in Straus Square, I've got dozens of handkerchiefs. The cotton ones have raised needlework, often in more than one color. Some have leaves in the corners, diamonds, or Hebrew words. One has elaborate curls, which I'm quite sure are sewn with golden thread. The silk ones are more elaborate, with patterns of orange flame, waves, quarter moons, or women's faces. I dry my tears with these handkerchiefs. I masturbate into them. I wipe the sweat from my forehead. And when my eyes grow red from heat or smoke, I press them lightly with a handkerchief to cool them.

I launder each handkerchief by hand. I won't let them fall further apart. I got them from my father years ago, when I was home for a holiday break from the University of Chicago and he happened to be moving out of the apartment he shared with my mother on the corner of Rutherford Place and Seventeenth Street, where I grew up. He didn't want these handkerchiefs because her parents gave them to him, a half dozen each year on his birthday, and some had grown frayed.

I need to use one now, because the warmth in here is making my eyes water, so it's become difficult for me to smile at strangers. I move quickly across this crowded living room and I feel lucky when I find enough space on a windowsill to first steady my hand and then set down my glass. I take a folded handkerchief from my back pocket and press it to my eyes. Soon I'll go and find my friend Bear, drink another scotch, and then I'll be bold and look about me, with the hope that there's someone else I might speak with here at Professor Weingarden's Welcome the Spring party.

This handkerchief is made of blue-and-gray checked silk. My father's initials, *JGZ*, are stitched in one corner. His name is Jefferson Gerard Zabusky. I'm Mike.

"Today must have been terrifying for you."

It's a woman speaking. My eyes are covered, and I can't imagine that she's addressing me. She's probably asking someone about the market, which slipped again. March is just ending and it looks like we're going to have a messy April. We've had a strong allergy season, studded with bouts of rain. The markets have done nothing but falter, and even people like me, with few or no investments, have begun to watch. But tonight, after a full day of storm clouds and thunder, amid consistent reports of our financial doom, at least the sky is clear.

"Come on, no two-day blip is going to hurt me," a man says. "We went through this in February. This happens all the time." He laughs impatiently, and the noise he makes is like a scoff. These people have taken over the rest of the window, to my right. I put my handkerchief away, blink, and look at the woman's back. The man bobs his head, as if he's trying to catch her eye.

"So no, it wasn't terrifying," says the man, "and it won't kill me."

"I didn't say it would kill you," she says.

"The worst is over," he says. "We've maintained a substantial cash reserve. Too bad you couldn't stick around to see me do well again."

At an inch or so over six feet, he's my height, but he's at least ten years older than I am and he's wearing good clothes—a black blazer and a freshly pressed white shirt. Though I've got a strong memory for languages and names and ideas, I can't be counted on to remember to dress well for parties. I'm wearing navy blue pants and my favorite shirt, which is dark as a red rose forgotten for days in a vase.

She says, "Really, I only asked if you'd had a scary day. But you're tough. I'm sure you'll do fine."

Because I'm close to her, I can hear her sigh. I like the way she sounds. She's got rust in the lower registers of her voice and she does not speak quickly. But the man is cracking. He rolls his shoulders and splays out his fingers, as if he wants to grab hold of something, of her, but he must know that he can't touch her when they're talking this way. Her back is upright and calm.

"Katherine," he says, and shakes his head, "when I don't see you for a while—I forget what an awful bitch you are." She does not speak immediately. Her shoulders do not move.

Then she says, "I'm not. But clearly, I'm also not what you were looking for. We can agree on that now."

"No, you sure as hell weren't," he says. And then I watch with this woman while he walks away, toward the dining room. She turns then, to look out the window. She bends forward with her whole body and stares down at the cars on the West Side Highway.

"Wasn't that a bit much?" Katherine asks. She doesn't look up and she isn't loud, so she must be able to feel that I'm standing close by her.

"First he wasn't smooth, and then he wasn't nice," I say. I'd like to tell her that he repulsed me, but they may have been affectionate with each other at one time, and so she might not want to hear him called repulsive by someone else, regardless of whether she knows it.

"True. He's only someone I used to date. He runs a company and I guess these last few days have been hard going. I bet his board of directors are feeling just like me, like they chose the wrong man. He isn't smart. That's partly why he's mean. I'm sorry that I saw him tonight."

"Complicated," I say. "It was good of you to be so gentle with him."

"Gentle?" she says. "I'm wrong to rationalize his behavior. I don't feel the least bit benevolent toward him."

There are lines at the edges of my eyes and these lines crinkle down when I smile. I smile now. I don't say a word.

She says, "In fact, he's married. But he keeps bothering me. I should tell him to leave me alone."

"Why didn't you call for help?" I say. "I could have yanked him away from you. I would have thrown him out of this window."

She glances around the room. She acts as if she is concerned that someone has overheard me.

"That doesn't appeal to me. If I want to throw him out a window, I'll do it myself. Why don't we go find a drink?"

We leave the dining room and approach the nervous undergraduate who Weingarden has set up behind a high table in a corner of the foyer. Katherine points, and he gives her a glass of red wine. He sets me up with another scotch. Oddly, he ignores my request for fresh ice. I don't recognize him, so I know I haven't taught him and he can't be angry with me. This makes me wonder if I'm slurring words, or if I haven't bothered to speak at all, and in turn, if either of these things is true, if I'm not entirely sober.

There's a table next to us, and I turn to it. It's thick with cocktail food: cheeses on a wood board, some fresh berries, a chopped-up pile of bread, green dip, red dip, crackers. I don't know if it's nervousness or the dip colors, but I lose my appetite immediately, which is typical. And I haven't eaten since breakfast—one lonely egg on a biscuit and black coffee in a paper cup, from a diner on Montgomery Street. Ninety-nine cents. This is why I often find myself going to bed hungry. I eat too little at the beginning of the day and then I'm left with an unquenchable nighttime hunger. I lack foresight. That's my problem. But it's just the sort of dilemma that's difficult to fix.

I take a piece of cheese that's studded with peppercorns and I eat it quickly. Incredibly, Katherine is still here. She's staying with me.

Now I've got a sticky mouth and a stunned feeling that clenches at my ribs, because she continues to smile through my second and third glance. The room isn't bright, but the rims of things have taken on a glow, perhaps because of the scotch.

"In fact," she says, "we've met before."

Because she's said this, I feel as if I've been given clearance to look at her again, more carefully, and I do. She's in a simple dark dress, with an ache of red-brown hair grazing her shoulders, and difficult eyes. So she is no longer only a still figure in a window. Her eyes are opaque. I cannot discern a dominating color.

"Have we?" I ask. I don't recall a prior meeting. I look again at her eyes.

There is a problem with such eyes: they always seem willing to be intrigued. You try to entertain them, with the hope that maybe, for some moment in your life with her, you'll be able to get beyond a fleeting interest, and somehow find out—and it's doubtful that you'll get the opportunity—more about the wonderful and truthful things that happen inside of her. They are eyes filled with imperviousness, so that though they can show amazement and pleasure, they are equally sure of their ability to show no interest at all, and by doing so they can make you miserable. They are impossible because of this combination of opacity and excitement. Though I feel all of this, I choose to ignore it. I'm talking to a woman I've just met at a party. At thirty-one, with one marriage behind me, I am no longer truly stupid and young, but I can still behave as if I am. My eyes are dark green. They are shaped like almonds.

"You don't remember," she says.

"I do," I say. "It's just—I can't recall the circumstance." This isn't exactly true. I don't remember her at all, but complete honesty can be hollow and confining—and really, just because I don't remember her now doesn't mean that I won't remember her later.

"I believe you used to know my friend Miriam," she says.

She has to come up closer to see me, because someone has turned off more lights. Behind her, Weingarden has taken over the middle of his living room. He begins to dance with Elsie, an attractive woman who was the other TA for the medieval heretics class he ran in the fall. A few more of the uninhibited join in. Weingarden winks at me and I smile back at him. I've been one of his teaching assistants and he's been my adviser for years now. He motions for me to bring my new friend and join him, but I shake my head, and he gives me a mock frown. He's always after me—trying to get me to enjoy myself as much as he does. Again, I look around for my friend Bear. Perhaps he has met someone he likes. Bear may be acting uncharacteristically, by taking advantage of the fact that his wife, Jen, is out of town.

"That's right—of course," I say. "That's when I met you."

I was briefly involved with Miriam. She was a pleasant girl with a great job raising money for the Nature Conservancy. She had two nice parents, both therapists, whom she spoke of often and admired tremendously. We ended when I could no longer pretend that the reason sex was so prolonged was that I was being attentive. In fact, it had to do with her smell, which I didn't like. It was old lilacs. She must have had a bottle of eau de toilette infused with lilacs that she used every day. Though I searched through her medicine cabinet, I couldn't find it. And I was too young or insensitive then to know to buy her a different bottle, too young to realize that if I wanted, I could easily teach myself to smell a different smell. It was an overpowering odor of lilacs, liberally applied.

I didn't speak of the smell. I only sniffed, and couldn't come. I'm sure she smelled good to other people, but not to me. It's a chemical thing, like a mixed drink, the way two people smell. When you're on top of someone and you're naked and you're carried away from the moment repeatedly, it holds you back. I look around to confirm that Miriam isn't actually at this party. We fell apart quickly, she and I. I retreated in a way that I did not bother to control, which is an attribute that I do not like having. If I could throw away the ability to recede, the way a person discards an aphorism they no longer find reassuring, I would. I think that beginning now, I will. I never did complain to her about her smell. I let it go and never told a soul.

"So, Miriam—how is she?" I ask.

"I don't know. I doubt she'll speak to me after tonight."

"Wow," I say.

"In a way I'm joking."

"Of course," I say.

I sniff the air around us, but what I smell cannot be this woman. It's the crackle of burnt air from the candle wicks. I can't get close enough to her to smell her, but she doesn't look like she smells of old lilacs. A substantial strength in her neck is suddenly visible; a ribbon of muscle expands. Her pulse points are probably so strong that she can't wear any scent at all.

"You're Mike Zabusky. You're in graduate school. That's what I know about you. That and Miriam. What would you like to add?"

Suddenly, she finishes her wine. She leaves just a little bit, enough to color the bottom of her glass. She puts the glass down and then she's got her hands holding the balls of her elbows, creating a shelf for her breasts. She's let her head go cocked to one side and it seems as if she's waiting. Not that I can see much in this light. But what she isn't doing is walking away. I'm quiet because I would like to appear smart and thoughtful, so I'm not in a rush to add more about me.

"There—I do remember—I know your name too. You're Katherine."

"Katherine Staresina, yes."

"What do you do, Katherine?" I ask.

Without turning I hold out my scotch glass to the bartender, who pours for me (adds new ice too—I can feel the clink) and manages to cause no ripple in our talk.

"I'd rather not talk about it," she says.

"Really? That's rare."

"I know, in New York and all. But it's different for me. I don't have a pretty job."

"Tell me."

"I fight crime," she says.

"You're what, a cop? No—an assistant DA?"

"More like Legal Aid. Domestic violence—DV law. I'm fairly new to it, though, and it's killing me."

"It's too hard," I say.

"Yes, much too hard," she says. "I've found that I can hardly stand it."

She reaches out and touches my arm. I hope that there's strength there. I did a few push-ups this morning. A dozen up and down and then face on the floor, hard focus, eyes rolling up with the pain, me blowing the dust that the maids leave for me to take care of on my own. I flex and I hope.

Bear comes up. He spies some clean white cheese before he sees that I'm standing with a woman. He eats a piece and holds his head.

"You beat?" Bear asks. Bear is shorter than me. He's got a large skull covered by plenty of dark wavy hair. He has a habit of pressing all that hair down, as if he hopes to push it back into his big head. He isn't more than five and a half feet tall, and he's heavier than I am. He wears a beige corduroy blazer that's snug around his frame, and a bright blue shirt.

"Actually, I think I might stick around," I say.

Bear frowns in surprise and begins to spear the best of the now rotting strawberries. I want to tell him to go leave us alone, but I do not want Katherine to take offense at my brusqueness. Then she would go away. And I want her to stay. But I want Bear to read the signs, and this is typical of him—he's feeling sorry for himself and he just won't.

"It's only that I'm in the middle of a conversation," I say. "I don't want to end it now."

"You ought to stay up late, then. I won't stop you." Bear shoves his thumb up hard between his teeth and bites at it like a frustrated character in an Irish stage play. He looks at Katherine with a curiosity he doesn't bother to mask. She continues to look at me. I don't introduce them. I make a movement with my eyes which I hope conveys to Bear that he should cool it, he can meet her some other time.

"So I'll say good night," Bear says. He's flecked with strawberry, and it takes him a moment to smile. Katherine and I have already begun to move toward the living room. The crowd hasn't thinned but there's a couch free because nobody else has become quick and intimate friends like we have. We sit down slowly and rock together and apart on the burgundy cushions, as if on waves. I've got that bubbled-in feeling, like the important thing is not to break the bubble we've blown together.

She tells me about her path, how she's been a gypsy, living in different places, trying on different cities, leaving them, and then going to other places, discovering things that didn't move her, and then traveling again. It's hypnotizing.

"But I've never worked this close to real suffering before, and it's hard to bear. I was searching for it, I wanted it, but I didn't know that it would be this brutal. I mean, I did know but—I wish I had a name for that, for knowing what you're getting into but having to do it anyway. I don't mean destiny, exactly. It's something else. Something more conscious—not like God's will. I wish I had a name for that."

I watch her and I pray for that name to come to me, but it will not, perhaps because that thing doesn't have a name. I like to name things. Giving names to impossible things is part of my work, but I don't mention this—not yet.

"The other reason I've got to leave my job is that I'm interested in the meaning of consent," she says, "and where I work, nobody wants to talk about it."

Now the room is a forest of men and women holding glasses, laughing and talking, listening to Benny Goodman. We get a quiet going and she smiles, but not with her eyes, really, because she doesn't seem to bother so much with them. As if they've got their own power supply, their own set of priorities.

"By consent, you mean, like I'd like to put my hand on your leg, so I'm asking you first," I say.

"You can do that," she says. "I'd like you to, in fact. But that's not remotely what I mean."

I touch her leg and she touches my hand. We aren't looking at each other. I watch her face as she speaks. I catch a slight downturn around her mouth. I'm circling my finger around her knee now, sliding my hand to the back of her thigh, and then up, not too fast. My erection comes blustering up through mists of alcohol and I feel very young now, almost childlike.

"You do know his work?" she says.

"Oh yeah," I say. We're talking about someone who wrote one of the books on the shelf behind her. Emile Durkheim or Max Eastman—someone who wrote something political, and smart. Emerson? Eric Foner? Certainly some figure on the left. It's improbable, but not totally impossible, that I've said something thoughtful.

"Your friend—did he know Miriam too?" she asks.

"Why do you ask?"

"Well, I'm thinking about her, and her friend Lydia, who always has that big birthday party. I haven't seen any of those people in a long time."

"She's really nice," I say, since that's all I feel about Miriam.

"I'm nothing like her," Katherine says.

"No," I say, "I can see that."

I move closer to her, but I'm still only touching her knee. Then I pull back a few inches, for two, three seconds, to gain perspective on her. I want to let her know that though I'm not entirely sober, I don't mean to kid. I do want to be close. And yet, she's gone quiet again.

Her eyes are shuttered off and impenetrable; it's not only the lids doing the trick, but the irises; there's something not giving about them. Not revealing. That's where the game lies, in getting behind or around or deep into her eyes. I still have my hand on her knee, have slipped it over to her other leg a few times, as she has emphasized some points with her own hand by covering my own. So now we're holding hands over her legs. My scotch glass has rolled away, gone clanking over the parquet floor, to rest, finally, under a low table in the corner that holds several candles, which throw off a bright, vacillating light.

Weingarden puts old Blondie on the stereo. *I'm always touched by your presence, dear.* We listen for a moment, but then he changes his mind, and goes back to old jazz, to what must be Django Reinhardt. The change is so swift that I'm sure we were the only people who heard the Blondie. Weingarden wanders over and smiles down on us. Katherine angles away from him and moves closer to me. But Weingarden stops. He's as tall as me, though he's thinner. He's in a dark blue suit that shimmers and is made of raw silk. He puts two fingers on Katherine's left shoulder and presses down. She turns and looks first at his fingers, and then up at him.

"You were able to find our friend Adam?" Weingarden asks.

"Yes. I found him," she says. "Thanks." She appears to have silenced my adviser, which isn't something that I have ever been able to do. Weingarden turns his attention to me.

"Why don't you dance, Mike? Now that you've found a pretty partner?"

"Maybe we'll dance later," I say. I'm perfectly still, willing him to go away, to not ask any more questions, and hoping also that Katherine will stay right here.

"That will be nice—I'll like that," he says. Katherine acts as if she has not heard him speak. He moves away. He comes up behind a small group of people and inserts himself, slides in among them and makes them surround him. I look at Katherine. I don't think that she has taken her eyes away from me.

She says, "When I was growing up, my parents didn't know the answers to many things, why things happen, where things come from. I had to look so many things up."

"I did that, too," I say. "And I was an only child. I was always alone, looking things up."

"I know what that's like. I have a brother, and I had a sister. But now it's different—I'm like an only child too."

I don't ask her about her sister. I know enough not to press too hard. I pull back in order to hide how much I like her. To the right of the couch there is a Chinese screen, burnished and glowing a dark red. I look at it, and at the ragged lines of a spider plant in front of it, and I place my concentration there instead of here. I won't show her how I'm feeling, not yet, no matter that I must fight what's inside of me that's clamoring to reveal itself to her. We're strange to each other, still, and I mustn't forget this.

"I missed what you just said," I say.

"That I quit my doctoral program. I've always quit everything that's organized. The only reason I finished law school was that I wasn't paying close attention to the schedule and I forgot to drop out."

"College?"

"Dropped out of college four times. Three different ones, counting the wasted semester at Duke. I won't be a lawyer much longer. I may quit at any moment, actually. This job is hurting me, as I said before. And I'm a quitter by nature."

We're sitting knee-rub close when she says this. I've quit a few things myself, but that's not what has me excited now. No, it is this new knowledge, that if she's a quitter, then every moment I get to share with her will be a moment borrowed, gained and won. Few people are as exciting to me as a woman who doesn't stay, who dares to quit, who leaves. I've been in this territory with women before, and I like the lack of control and uncertain feeling a quitter so easily creates. I like it a lot.

"Things don't hold you," I say.

"People do, though—maybe you can," she says, and then she looks down at her own knees, smiles.

"Over there's the master bedroom," I say. "I'm going there, and I want you to come with me."

We stand up and wander away from the couch, all casual and languid so nobody will watch, but of course I'm sure most everyone does. In the bedroom I kiss her. A stranger. I do not pause to wonder what she is doing. I don't worry much about my technique, either, because I know that too recently I was only the guy on the other side of the window frame, which may be all she enjoys about me, that I'm a light diversion in what might have been an unpleasant evening.

We are up against the wall, in between two charcoal drawings of naked women in the bath. I lean into a radiator, which sears my thigh through my pants leg, and for just a moment I let it burn me. Some people I don't recognize come in to get their coats. I think that they stare in wonder at us, at how close we are to each other.

"Good night," they call to us, and they laugh uncertainly. I follow their example. Katherine stops. She must not know these people either, but she pulls away from me and I struggle with my own hands and then get them behind my back. She asks me to stop kissing her.

"Stop kissing me, then," I say.

"Don't be funny," she says. Brass sconces illuminate the pictures and cast light on her profile. She's got on a necklace that is metallic to the touch but looks more like a dark brown ribbon. I ask about it. She ignores that. She considers me.

"Busy here," I say, "like Grand Central Station."

"Yes. I'm either leaving or we can try somewhere else."

I grab her hand. We go into the bathroom. The only annoyance here is a towel rack that runs the length of one wall. Behind the toilet there's a tall and thin window with a heartbreak view of downtown. The walls are covered with black tiles lined in white. The tub has legs that end in black talons that clutch white marble balls.

She turns the light on and I turn it off and then we flip it back and forth for a few seconds, and I smile and stroke her red-lion hair through the strobe light effect while she looks away. She stands in front of the mirror and touches her fingers to her face, blinks at herself. She uses her other hand to grip my arm, as if she's going to sink without me, which is what I keep telling myself so that I don't get flustered because of the incredible serendipity of the moment and back down, which is a fair and habitual fear, considering what we're up to.

"What are you writing on, anyway?" she asks.

I've got her dress pulled up and my shirt is out of my pants. We're attached chest to chest like magnets and my head is in her hands, in part because she's insuring that I don't mark up her neck with my teeth. I've got her around the middle in a way that even my hands know I'm probably a bit too drunk to appreciate. I grope her breast, her thigh, pussy mound under her dress pushed up bone hard against my hand.

"I—" I pause. "I'm doing a religious studies doctorate. Looking at the Jewish myth of the artificial anthropoid. They haven't okayed it, though. Weingarden, my adviser—he keeps saying it's not special enough, that there's something missing."

We kiss. It's more like we're licking each other. I have her hands pressed back, above that towel bar, up against the wall. I get my dick good and jammed up against her mound and I'm rubbing in a way that forces her to be revealing. I can feel how her pussy isn't at all hidden away. I catch the gasp from her. We've known each other a few hours—less.

"Artificial anthropoid?" she asks. "You're talking about monsters."

She pushes me away for a moment.

"I am. I love monsters. The one I love the best is the Golem. But I'm studying lots of different myths."

"Myths are okay," she says. "But I worry about running to the unreal. Like: powers above, if all that's possible, then what are we doing to each other down here—"

"Or you could look at it like we don't do enough running. You could say this city doesn't have enough religion."

"That's fair. Some of us are lacking, but I hope you're not judging."

"Of course I'm not," I say. "And I'm not writing about this city."

I come forward and we begin again, only this time she's not hard in any part of her and it's easier to hold her up and to only whisper. I tug at her panties and I feel them give way, drop to the floor.

"You," she says. "It's okay for you to do it. I'm safe. Do it. You're safe too. You have to be."

"I am," I say.

Our middles are naked against the tile wall. There's the glint of something in her eyes that I can't name, but it is not eyes open and aware, certainly, and it's not her eyes that say I'm inside of her. No, her eyes remain impervious. We are not connecting through them.

I press hard against her body, grow us up the wall, with her legs surrounding my hips and me jutting into her, and I have her weight and she is looking down at me. Her eyes are closed as she reaches down to kiss me. I think this never happens to anybody anymore, this thing we even forgot we were looking for at parties. I grip her ass, hold her, and then she does look at me, and comes even closer, so we are rubbing our cheeks and necks together. Right now I would love to believe that we could stay together and she'll smell of the simplest sort of sweet bedtime sleep smell, because right now I never want her to go away.

Even as I am careful to keep us from ripping the towel bar and most of the tile off the wall, as I'm half wondering whether we're knocking the pictures off their hooks in the bedroom, I have the crazy and wonderful thought that this woman won't leave me, not ever.

Then the door is banging, shaking, like in a cartoon. A glowing and piercing light comes in at the edges.

"Katherine?"

"Yeah—Leah, yes, in here."

I come away from her and she pulls down her dress. I pull my pants up even as she flips the lock. So many motions, so fast. I want her to stop moving. The door falls open, three howling faces in the doorway—good people under any other circumstances, I'm sure. But right now I wish them horrible deaths.

"We've got to go," a woman says. She doesn't sound urgent—only confident that she's doing the right thing. Me, I feel like a criminal. I look away from these people, but it doesn't matter—they're not looking at me. Katherine is handed her overcoat, which is dove gray and mussed. There's a cream-colored scarf hanging out of one pocket that looks like a little flag, a surrender flag. I reach out and pull it free of the coat. I hold it. She sees it go and only moistens her lips. She blinks long. Then, when her friends draw back into the darkened hallway, we both look into the medicine cabinet mirror. Katherine puts a finger to her lips and turns to me.

"Do you have paper?" she asks.

"No—I've got a handkerchief. Wait, just tell me your information. I'll remember it."

"Give me the handkerchief anyway," she says.

I do, while she says her telephone number.

"It's clean," I say. "I've only used it to dry my eyes."

She touches it to her forehead and to her neck and begins to hand it to me, but then she pauses. She slips it into her coat.

"See you around," she says. "You call me at home."

She comes up, and I hold out her scarf, but she doesn't take it.

"Put it on me," she says. She's faced away from me and she pushes back, so I can smell the warmth of her hair. I wrap the scarf slowly and tightly around her neck.

"I'm quite serious," she whispers. "You and I have a lot to talk about."

"Now Katherine, you've had quite a day, haven't you?" the woman says, loudly.

"I never know when to stop," Katherine says. And then, turning to me, "Let me leave without you. It's odd enough already."

So I do, and the door closes. Since I'm still in the bathroom, I sit on the tub lip and put myself back together. I look down and my clothes are on. My black shoes are laced up. I'm still here. Nothing's changed. I look out the window and wonder how I could possibly have managed any of this, after years of never even daring to hope to pull off such a feat.

"Darling," I say. "It was so good to finally meet you."

2

I'm with Bear, in the living room of the apartment he shares with his wife, Jen, in a new building on Third Avenue and Eighty-third Street. Jen's parents provided the down payment for it when they got married, two years ago. It's very clean here. The walls are painted a creamy white and there's a lot of shelving that arrived in cardboard boxes, which I helped Bear to unpack and build. Bear has set himself up nicely with Jen. He's got an apartment and the beginnings of a promising life. What I have is a room in a refurbished downtown hotel, which I got in a fluke move that happened five years ago, when I came back to New York from Chicago. I called my father to say that I was back in town for good, and he asked where I was. I told him I was in a big hotel, where the rates were low because they were going out of business.

"The Gouverneur Hotel? Jesus Christ! In the old *Forward* building?"

"I guess so," I said, but it was only after I went and looked at the restored marble slab above the entranceway that I was sure.

My father told his boss, Max Asherberg, to buy the place. Asher-berg & Co. had started as an investment firm, and then they'd become a holding company. In the mid-nineties they were profiting excessively and needed a tax loss, so owning the Gouverneur made sense. But then the place heated up with the rest of the Lower East Side and started making money. Max died of a stroke a few years later, but his company kept the hotel, and I was grandfathered, or fathered, in. So I stayed. My hotel room has little more than a bed and some kitchen appliances against one wall. There's hardly enough space for two people to sit and talk, which is why I'm spending most of Sunday at Bear's house.

We're watching the golf tournament at Pebble Beach. That is, we're watching Tiger Woods win. The announcers whisper about the pleasures of what we're seeing, while we enjoy shots of blue water and impossibly green fairways, along with occasional glimpses of rabid fans, who drop to their feet and kiss the ground where Tiger just passed. It's refreshing and relaxing at the same time. This Tiger is a hero because he only knows how to win, and he's almost like a god and certainly not like any person I've ever met. I watch Bear watch Tiger. He licks his lips and sighs.

I make an effort to refrain from mentioning, yet again, Bear's odd resemblance to Delmore Schwartz, who happens to be the topic of his dissertation. With his thick lips and springy hair, it's as if Bear's been sent from the past to remind us to mull over Schwartz yet again—and Bear's dilemma lies in how aware he is that there's not much left to write about his subject. I think this is why he loves to watch Tiger, who has a story that will continue to grow. But Bear will always be Bear, never a hero like Tiger, never more than another potential biographer of Delmore Schwartz.

Bear is from Wisconsin, where his parents are linguistics professors, but he never goes back there. Jen is from Toronto and she goes back all the time. For business, apparently. She's a lawyer. I don't quite see the need for all her travel but I guess she understands America's legal system in relation to Canada's, or something, and anyway I'm not asking questions.

"You crying?" Bear asks. He's dug himself deep into the cushions of his overstuffed couch. I'm on a hard chair to his right, with my chin placed firmly on my fist. A few empty bottles of beer sit on the glass coffee table in front of us.

"No, no," I say. "It's just my damned eyes."

Since I returned to New York, Bear has been my one and only friend. I had others when I grew up here, before my high school stint away at Deerfield, but I lost them all during the long years I was in Chicago, where I began as a college student, graduated into unemployment, and then became a travel agent. So now I have only Bear. And I love him as you love someone who reflects the little tragedy that you find charming in yourself. That is, he's having trouble moving forward with his dissertation too. But what I really like about him is that we have a gentlemen's agreement not to bore each other with our mutual concern over all that we're not achieving. We're not openly scornful of our studies, and we don't torture ourselves over our tendency toward indolence either. We're respectful of each other's work, if little else, and because of this I think it's the finest friendship I've ever had.

"If I could only do any one thing that well," Bear says. He's talking about Tiger, who just birdied from the rough.

"Even half as well as that," I say.

"Just one thing," Bear says. He watches and presses at his hair, tests the spring. It's begun to rain again, and since we're on the twenty-third floor, it feels as if we're inside a cloud. I dab at my eyes, Bear presses his head. This is the wettest April Fool's day anyone can remember.

"Still got that cold?" Bear asks.

"Since forever," I say.

"Jen's staying up in Toronto for a few more days, working on those farm bankruptcies. You want to get dinner tomorrow night?"

"Can't. My mom's in town for the antiques show. I have to see her."

"Can I come?"

"Man, Jen's out of town for a week and you nearly dissolve—you really want to sit through a dinner with my mother?"

Bear sighs again. No matter how much he resembles him, he'll never be as romantic a figure as his dissertation subject, and this depresses him far more than he can admit. What he needs is a drama, a story that will put his life into sharper focus. What he needs is a challenge.

Bear and I were the only ones to win the Koznitz Graduate Fellowship from City University the year we went in, which amounts to five years of paid-for study. Not much pay. Loads of study. I enrolled in the Religious Studies Department with the hazy idea of writing about the universality of the act of prayer, but then I took a class with Matthew Weingarden. He told me I needed something with a little more snap.

Weingarden's the one who introduced me to Jewish mysticism, which is one of his specialties. When he introduced me to the Golem, I really ran with the concept. At first, he was encouraging. Then I became interested in what are essentially bedtime stories— tales of the Golem and his master, and their misunderstandings; stories of the Golem going to get fish at the market and instead, carrying back the fishmonger and his entire stand. What I like about these stories is how they make the Golem sweet—he wants to live as a human, but he's not empathic. He can only count forever, or keep bringing fish, keep fetching pails of water until those around him are in danger of drowning. The more I've grown to like these little stories, the less I've been able to please Weingarden. Now I need to start building a proposal with some strong chapter ideas, but somehow, I've grown still.

But I love my work. I've been happy to read and research and write for years now without benefit of great insight—there's been no sudden ladder to a place of clear-cut, hard-driving thought, no revelation coming out of my fascination. Like some fourteenth-century mystic, swathed in carpet and laid out on the temple steps, trod on by the devout as they enter to say their prayers, my ribs broken, lips cracked, bleeding in ecstasy, with the Lord somewhere up and far away, making note of this martyrdom, I spend an awful lot of time reassuring myself that I'm getting closer in a way that has not yet been revealed to me.

Bear says, "Come on, Mike—I've already done the nights with a hero sandwich and a bunch of videos. I've seen every movie Russ Meyer made. *Supervixens, Mondo* everything, the whole bit. I've already indulged, is what I'm saying. Now I'm lonely."

"Welcome to my entire life," I say.

"Maybe you and Katherine can date—go to the movies a couple of times. Then you can get married and be extremely happy like me and Jen."

"Not to put too much pressure on it," I say. "Besides, I'm having trouble believing it happened."

"Believe it. Though we didn't meet, thank you very much, I did see her. You ought to call her immediately."

"We diddled each other in the bathroom of my professor's apartment."

"So I heard," Bear says. "Call her before she goes to another party."

"You've nailed my concern," I say. But we both know he hasn't. My concern circles around the sweet pain that I'll inevitably experience if I fall too hard for Katherine, if she was serious.

"I'm joking, anyway—nobody regularly goes too far in bathrooms with guys they don't know. That doesn't happy, I mean happen, anymore. She must've liked you. Another beer?"

I nod. Bear rolls off the couch and goes into the kitchen.

"Maybe she liked me," I say. "More probably, she's a train wreck." But I don't mind if she is. In fact, if she weren't, I wouldn't be worried about falling. But all I can do is recognize my pathology. There is nothing that I can actually change about it.

"You're a train wreck," Bear says. He hands me a beer and lies down on the couch. He closes his eyes and presses his beer bottle to his forehead.

"Thanks. Wisecracks like that are why I'm leaving you out of dinner with my mom."

"Great—another night of turkey-bacon-Swiss, soft-core porn, and Depression-era zeitgeist fiction. You're a hell of a friend."

"Bear, what do you call it when you feel like you're being pushed to do something even though you don't want to, and you know how rough this thing is going to be on you?"

"Destiny?"

"No, this is something different—like some kind of uncontrollable inevitability."

"Providence? *Besherte?* Why not just call it destiny? I think you're confusing those things with your utter lack of self-control," Bear says. We watch Tiger step down into a sand trap, square his feet, and bang the ball through the air and up, into the little hole. For a moment there's silence from the gallery. Then we watch the awed teenagers imitate Tiger's fist pumps.

"But isn't that awful?" I ask. "You're saying it's awful that I do that?"

Bear is perfectly still. He's managed to balance his beer bottle at the crest of his forehead. He exhales, and the open bottle shivers but does not fall.

He says, "Let's put it this way, Mike. You're my friend. I like you. But I don't envy you."

———

"Have you spoken to your father recently?" my mother asks.

"I went up and saw him a couple of months ago," I say. "He told me that profits in the small-cap sector were making him cry with joy."

Payard Patisserie is where my mother's brought me. It's a French restaurant. We've been led up a flight of stairs to a special seating area with sepia walls and a tin ceiling. I look across at her over the yellow tablecloth, which is set with china edged in gold. There's one white candle between us. Behind my mother's head there's a glowing oval setback in the wall that frames a dimly lit painting of two horses wandering down a country lane.

"That's how he speaks to you?" she asks.

"How else would he?" I stare at her. Just now, I can't think how else he has ever spoken to me. I'm not sure what else he'd have to say. I'm not sure what else he's ever said.

"I guess you're right," she says. "How else would he speak? I don't know either." And she shrugs. She was always sarcastic when she was with him, and now the only time she acts that way is when he comes up in conversation. The rest of the time, she fairly glows with the prospect of her new frontiers. She's staying at the St. Moritz with her new husband, Lawrence Gold. They're here for the spring antiques show because they're interior decorators. They're a team.

My mom, gone from Elizabeth Zabusky of Manhattan to Liz Gold of La Jolla, California. I've always suspected that she wanted to take steps in a Christian direction. And now I wonder if she hasn't begun to grow some anti-Jewish sentiment. I've tried to discuss this with her and the result was not good. "Did I ever deny that I'm a Jew?" This is what she kept asking me. "Did I ever in my entire life deny to anyone that I'm a Jew? And who took you to see *Joseph and the Amazing Technicolor Dreamcoat*? Me, that's who. Remember, your father wouldn't have any part of it." She got pretty angry. And no, I don't recall her ever denying that we were Jews. But she doesn't talk about religion, at least not with me. We can still get through a dinner, though. We don't dislike each other.

My mother divorced my father when I was still an undergraduate, before I got married. She was quick to marry Lawrence Gold, who used to license sunglass designs to Ralph Lauren's company. Lawrence made a mint and retired into my mother's business. Now they both put tremendous thought into the way things in a house look when they're positioned in relation to one another. I visited them once out in La Jolla and watched as they pondered and enjoyed the effect they got when they set out a cherry side table and put a thick gardening book next to a pewter plate next to a vase with hyacinths in it. Then they adjusted these elements and cooed at each other while they worked. In a way, I'm proud of my mom. She's certainly living somebody's dream.

"It's fine for me not to have a relationship with him," she says. "That's okay. But I expect different from you."

"I'm sure I'll see him again," I say. "We agreed to do a better job of being in touch."

"You met his girlfriend? Sarah Jane something—a Protestant surname."

"Caldwell, yes," I say. "She was there."

My mother sighs. She touches her gold necklace and tries to smile at me, but it isn't easy. She's a more attractive woman now than she was when I was young, with her hair dyed up to a rich brown and her skin looking creamy, with hardly any hints of age.

I remember a thinness in her upper lip when I was younger. Late on a Saturday afternoon I'd watch her outline her lips with a dark brown pencil while I stood in the doorway of the bathroom, waiting for my father to come home from doing whatever extra work Max Asherberg assigned to him. We would all stroll across town to eat at Keens Chophouse. I'd try to count the thousands of antique pipes on the ceiling while I munched on celery, black olives, and pickles, and all the time I wondered at the new shape of my mother's lips.

Looking at her now, in the ivory yellow light of this restaurant, it seems possible that she's had something injected into her lips to make them full. Either that or perhaps now that she's disconnected from my father, even her face has relaxed.

"What were the specials again?" she asks. I close my eyes and reel them off: celery root soup, yellowfin tuna carpaccio, stuffed French sardines, Chilean sea bass, codfish, lamb. As I've said, my memory is good. It isn't photographic; I'm nothing for images, but language stays with me forever.

"The other night Lawrence and I stayed up and watched *Young Frankenstein* on AMC, and I thought of you and your monster. Tell me its name again . . ."

"The Golem?"

"Of course, that's it. It's amazing the things I've forgotten from my own childhood. The monsters are similar. That's what I told Lawrence. He was asleep but I woke him up and told him about the connection."

"They're not the same at all," I say.

"I don't see much difference," she says. "I'll bet you've never had a risotto with Parmesan foam on top. It's wonderful. We'll ask them to make it."

"Look, Mom, if you want to know what I'm doing, you need to forget Frankenstein. Close your eyes and forget this restaurant. Pretend you're in a movie. Imagine a group of Hasidic mystics in Germany, back in the thirteenth century. Put yourself in peasant garb. It's late at night and you see into a courtyard where they're doing rituals that involve combinations of the Hebrew alphabet and the material form of the universe. They do all this, they say some names, they create a monster."

"Mute and thoughtless, just like Frankenstein," she says. She flips over the butter knife and examines its markings.

"Fine—like Frankenstein, if you must. But let's imbue him with the will of the Jewish people. Let's let God get involved, too. The Golem we create is larger than a big man, but only by a head or so. He's got *emeth,* or 'truth,' on his forehead, and the way to turn him off is to erase the first letter, so he's *meth,* which is 'death.' They use him for holy missions, to save the people of the ghetto when they get into trouble or find themselves unfairly persecuted."

"I remember last year with Lawrence on Christmas Eve, when you told us all the story of the dead babies and the bloody Passover matzos."

"I'm sorry about that."

"Unforgettable," she says. She shakes her head. I love that story, of when Rabbi Loeb of the Prague ghetto uses the Golem to keep peace in the ghetto. But when I told my mother and her husband and their friends, they found it stereotypical and distasteful. It is a bit graphic, what with the grave digging and the idea that Jews would need the blood of Christian babies to make their matzos, but it is also deeply inspirational. The Golem helped the Jews to control the unjust forces that conspired against them. The Golem is as simple and good as that.

"All the work you did with Jung, and you're reduced to this?" She sips from her glass of wine and then holds on to the glass by the stem, as if she may need it again soon, if I keep going. So I rush.

"I know. But I believe there's beauty in the reduction. Imagine this: Once the Golem becomes a hero, he grows more intelligent and dreams of being able to speak and to love, like a man with a soul. One night the rabbi forgets to remove the letter of power from the Golem's forehead and the Golem's unquenchable desire drives him wild. Even the Jews are afraid of him. Then when the monster is sleeping, the rabbi has to get up on a stool and erase the letter of life from his forehead. The Golem turns to mud and falls on him and kills him. He destroys his master."

"An archetypal story," she says. "The metaphor of the monster run amok." She looks glum, and I find her easy familiarity with my subject matter confusing. She's just the same as Weingarden in this respect. They both act as if what I'm studying were only a part of everyday life, instead of folklore. Maybe they're the ones who are looking for more complexity and I'm not. I watch my mother scan the room around me. A waiter passes by and she taps her glass.

"I'm sorry," she says, "but I can't see what you'll do with all of this, I just can't."

I know that part of what makes her good at her job is that she can listen to anybody rattle on about anything, but listening and making the effort to extract a clear understanding are quite different things.

"Couldn't you use your memory to take apart something besides folklore? What about picking stocks with your father. I hated all that, as you know, but it wouldn't hurt, would it? A little sideline?"

"I've got to like something to remember it," I say.

"If only life were so sweet that you could go along and remember only things you like. Really, Mike, I want to understand your work, because you're my son and I love you, but lately it feels as if your thoughts are running in circles. Your father and I are practical people. I don't see where all of this comes from, not a bit of it."

I smile at my mother, even as I choose not to suggest that this is exactly why I am so in love with myth. Of course my inclination to bend reality exists in opposition to my parents' practicality. And my memory has been a wonderful ally in the struggle to adjust facts to serve my needs. My memory explains how I excelled in college and how I managed to become a professional graduate student. I memorized all of Jung, most of Freud, and lots of different religious and gnostic tracts. I remember things slightly wrong, with varying degrees of awareness. My inclination to change events and theories caused or created by others has, so far, made me guilty not of lying but of innovation. I am also aware that such a malleable memory can be used another way—as protection.

In turn, my fascination with Jewish mysticism arises directly from an interest in trying to weave together disparate, even wholly disconnected ideas using strings of stories that are bound together only by our collective notion of time. Jewish mysticism has a wildly fragmented history. It is a far more extreme version of the traditional notion of our Diaspora. Doubly hidden and reviled, and yet, like so many other broken, illogical, but entirely human sets of ideas, even after many centuries of worldly disdain, mysticism lives.

If I were religious, the fragile connections that make up Jewish mysticism would be inspiring. But I'm not a religious person. I appreciate mysticism's tenacity and I continue to want to be involved with it, but only in a spirited, cheerleading kind of way.

"When you saw your father, were you able to talk to him about your work?" she asks.

"Sure," I say. "He wanted to hear all about what I'm doing—he was really interested—I guess because he's finally happy up in Roosevelt."

"I don't know if I believe that," she says. "I bet that's your hope talking, rather than your honesty. But it's good to at least have open lines of communication—for both your sakes."

My mother looks down then at her menu and begins to read carefully.

I owe my father one large debt, which stems from a kind act he did for me, which occurred when my own marriage was falling apart. He came and sat with me for a few crucial days in Chicago. Two years after I graduated, I married a woman called Alexis, who was a few years older than me. She convinced me that we should stay in Chicago and build our lives there. Back then, apartments were inexpensive, and there was a burgeoning music scene.

Alexis was the lead singer of a band called Art Collection. They sounded a lot like Sleater-Kinney, though Alexis had a voice that was more reminiscent of Siouxsie Sioux or Cait O'Riordan. Meanwhile, I had my job at Exodus Travel. We nursed each other's affection for drugs, and when we weren't looking, the marriage dissolved into what I realize now was a combination of betrayal and addiction so horrifying that it turned into satire.

Alexis left me for the bass player in her band, who was a friend of mine and lived in the apartment above ours. I fell under the influence of a drug dealer who worked at the window desk in my travel agency. I'm grateful to my father for flying into town and forcing me to laugh about the childishness of the mess I'd made with Alexis, while I sweated out all the indignity. He's a bit crude, my father—old Jefferson Gerard Zabusky. He knew just how to handle that unpleasantness.

"I'll call him again soon," I say.

"Thank you," my mother says, and she breathes hard through her mouth. "Remember what he says? *Got zol mich bentshen ich zol nit broichen mentshen.*"

"What? 'God should—' "

" 'God should bless me so that I don't need people.' "

"But I thought he didn't believe in God," I say.

"That's the joke," she says. "No love for God or people, either. You've got to help him fight against his impulses. Only in Yiddish would anyone say such a thing. You know what I say? *Nor a shteyn zol zayn aleyn.*"

" 'Only a stone should be alone'?" I ask.

"That's right—my goodness, Michael, I didn't know you'd learned Yiddish. But that language, it's too brutal. I make sure not to speak it anymore. And you shouldn't either," she says, and she doesn't smile. I watch as she looks around the room. None of the other women are smiling either. But they can't all be worried about their ex-husbands. More probably, it's this economy. It's making all of us tense, but those who wear multiple pieces of gold jewelry without irony—real estate brokers and boutique owners, dress designers and interior decorators—they're really crackling with fear.

"What reason could you have to be worried about him?"

"You don't see it? He's lonely, no matter what he says to you. It's that house, and the life he chose up there. He should never have bought it."

"What's the matter with the house? I was up there, it's beautiful. He's the luckiest man in the world."

"Wrong—wrong on both counts," my mother says. "He's lonely, and it's lousy. A shithouse." She wipes at her eyes.

3

The room I have here at the Gouverneur is pretty nice. I pay a convention rate, minus maid and phone service, since I use my cell phone for everything. This gets me down to under forty dollars a night. When I'm really broke, I take evening shifts for Blake, who works the front desk. Sometimes I'll fill out a tax form for Lisa, the maid who works the fifth floor, or I'll tutor her kid, and then she'll vacuum and change my sheets.

There was a time when this neighborhood was filled with young people, and in those years it looked like the Lower East Side would never be poor again, but recently, gentrification has slowed. Now the boarded-up storefronts hide failed clothing boutiques and bars, rather than pizza places and bodegas. Unfortunately, my father's parents' store, Louis Zabusky's Housewares and Locksmith, which was just a few blocks away, on Essex Street, won't be coming back. They closed it more than twenty years ago. Now it's a Chinese salon called New Century Hair Center.

My father worked there all through high school, weighing out pounds of nails and cutting keys for the local landlords. He was forced to work every afternoon, right after he was finished at Brooklyn Tech. Now, aside from the occasional complaint about how his parents ruined his high school career, he hates to talk about it. He grew up on Howard Avenue in Crown Heights, Brooklyn, which is where his parents went the moment they could afford to get out of the Lower East Side. He hated it there, too. He and my mother moved away from both their parents to the relative anonymity of Stuyvesant Square as quickly as they could.

Now most of the Jews left around here are Hasidic. They maintain a presence that seems almost sentimental. Sometimes middle-class Jews come in from the suburbs on Sundays to visit the Henry Street Settlement or the Tenement Museum, but that's all. I've been to the museum and seen the room that illustrates how my grandparents lived when they came here. It isn't pretty, with its bad wallpaper and uncomfortable bed, but if I hadn't lucked into my hotel room, I'd be living that way now.

If the economy continues to falter, the only people left will be the poor and the truly hip, all of us walking around in black suits with tarnished white shirts. They look a little like the Hasidic Jews, and sometimes, still, so do I. Some nights I'll fall asleep and dream that I'm still what I was at twenty-four. I've returned to being thin faced, long nosed, string haired, wearing shoddy black shoes, white socks, a white shirt, a yellow undershirt, that pervasive greasy sheen on my suit knees and ass. I wake up pulling on a thin beard that isn't there and I'll be trying to tear their black hat off my head. But I was not Hasidic back then. I was only a punk working in a travel agency, with no real religion of my own.

Save the year I was thirteen, I've never been a member of a temple, but I can read Hebrew. I've learned German, Polish—whatever a book demands. I work hard to get close to texts, since my spiritual connection does not come naturally.

The only training I had came in the form of the bar mitzvah I went through for the benefit of my father's family, now mostly passed away. My father's parents gave me a tool kit they assembled themselves, and a check for a thousand dollars, to be saved for a trip to Israel. I spent it on a Pioneer stereo with fat dials and pulsing red lights and Fleetwood Mac and Heart records. My father didn't care that I spent the money. He encouraged me to laugh at their traditions. My mother was okay with all that too.

I stand at the window and look over Straus Square, toward uptown, and Kazan Street, which is hazy with yellow streetlight. A few teenagers play a game of dice against a newly boarded-up Japanese T-shirt store. I'm not going to do any work. I pick up my phone and quickly dial Katherine's number, with no rehearsal. The number hasn't left me since I learned it, and all this time I've been working hard not to think about her, so that when I do speak to her I'll have some chance at sounding natural. She answers immediately.

"Hello," I say, "this is—"

"Oh it's you, from the other night?" she says. "Hold for just a moment, will you?"

She gets off the other line. I've got that at least. I beat the other line. I button my shirt to the top, so I'm tightened and sober. My stomach clenches around nothing—my body telling me that though I'm excited, I'm empty.

"That was something, wasn't it?" she says. I hear her rustling, adjusting furniture—a desk perhaps, or better, a bed.

"You're in Brooklyn?"

"Yes—listen, were you serious with me the other night?"

"I was," I say. I blow hot air onto my windowpane and draw the balls and talons of that bathtub.

"Because I don't want to talk to you unless you were really serious about kissing me," she says. "I don't kiss people unless there's a future involved."

"It's so nice to hear you say that," I say. "This is no joke."

"No?"

"No," I say. "When can I see you?"

"Mike—I don't know. I'm overwhelmed with work and I'm scheduled to see friends on the few nights I'm not working. So, maybe—what about next Wednesday?"

I'm quiet. I want to see her sooner than that. I don't want to give her time to resist her own inclination toward being serious.

"What about later tonight?" I ask, and I make my voice slow.

"Tonight? Mmm. Why don't you come and meet me at—no, at Chez Omar. It's just around the corner from where I live."

Eight or so minutes later I'm in a cab headed up Bedford Avenue, to the spot where Fort Greene meets Bedford-Stuyvesant. I arrive in front of Chez Omar and stand there for half an hour. This is an odd place to have chosen for a midnight meeting, as it's not a bar at all but a restaurant. But I don't worry too much about being stood up. The one thing I know about her is that she's curious.

When she does come up the street, because I've never seen her from this distance before, it's the movement of her hips inside her skirt that beats away my reserve. I'm feeling good, suddenly, and highly aware.

"I see the place I've chosen is closed," she says. She reaches forward and gives me a kiss that melts between my cheek and lip.

We step into Bier and Wasser, a bar across the street, where a few people watch as the Knicks slowly beat the Heat. She sets her purse down. It is a massive thing, stuffed full of indistinct objects, no real color left to the leather, held up by a frayed strap at the point of tearing. The purse, duffel bag—it pulses at me. I go and get us tap beer from the bartender. She says it's just the kind she would have chosen. But she doesn't taste it.

I sit down and bend forward, my lower ribs pressed up against the table. Not because she's whispering. Rather, I'm catching sight of lines on her face, a small vertical scar at the top right of her lip, smile lines between her mouth and cheek. I'm smelling her as hard as I can, taking deep breaths that are full of the underlying scent of her.

"You told me you were doing something on religious texts?" she asks. "Some sort of exegesis?"

I nod but I say nothing. I had begun to hope that she'd forgotten the moment where I revealed my Golem obsession.

"I used to think about religion," she says. "There was a point when I was filled up with Faulkner. I was working in Mississippi and reading his novels exclusively, and I started to grow really horrified at what people do to each other. Then I lost my sister. I de-cided that I only loved God. I was sure I'd become a nun, but that passed."

"What do you mean—you lost your sister?"

The space behind her is dark, so her face is framed by shadows. She looks down at her hands and then twines her fingers together. She's quiet, and it looks as if she's angry with herself for revealing too much.

"Oh, I don't want to explain that. I shouldn't have said any-thing. When I saw that I couldn't be a nun, I figured out that I could do the next best thing, and never get married."

"Never? Why not?" I ask.

"Too much awfulness seems to surround the waiting for that sort of love," she says. Then she smiles. So I smile back. I don't mention my own failed marriage. Instead, I worry if she's telling the truth. But I'm calm, and I remember that saying never to love that way is just a thing to say—it's just an early-date thing to say.

"But I could see being very serious with you," she says. "I can imagine being comfortably in love with you."

So I see that my array of indicators, which were never terribly accurate, are useless here.

"I want you to be comfortable with me," I say. She takes up her glass and sips long from it, while she watches me. It's more than half done when she puts it down.

She says, "Yes, let's be comfortable and serious and safe. I need all that, as I've just been involved in something unpleasant. A mar-ried man. I can't have that again for a while." She shakes her head and looks away from me. She exaggerates her mouth into a sneer, but she doesn't look mean or angry.

She says, "At the beginning, he didn't tell me that he was mar-ried. And now I'm paying for his lie. That was him the other night—the man you wanted to throw out of a window. I know he was less than charming then. But at the beginning—I got bowled over, I really did."

"When you grew up, did you have a car?" I ask.

What I would like to say is, I could kill that man for you. Or I hate that man for you. But that won't sound right. I'd end up sounding vulnerable and weak, when I'd like to sound strong. Cars are safe, though. Everybody has a car story, some old car they loved.

"I had a black Rabbit convertible, Cabriolet, a freakishly fast car. I bought it at an auction in—where I'm from. Tin can, though, real rattler. Hey, it wasn't *easy*, you know? He's thirteen years older, and it's just been such a mess. I mean, I ended up having to talk to his wife about it—we had to have dinner together, to save his marriage. A real pleasure, what I had to go through. I've done things in my past that I only blame myself for, but this was not one of them."

"Where's that car now?"

"I gave it to an old boyfriend, and he sold it without telling me. I see, you're one of those. You'd just as soon not listen to the tougher parts of a woman's history." But she smiles when she says this.

"No," I say, and I concentrate, and measure my words. "It's just that I want to hear more about you, and less about this man whom you no longer care for."

I cannot recall that man's face, but I remember the foolish thing he said. I would like to believe that this married man must have only been fodder for her, to keep her busy before she met me, and yet we're discussing him now. If he's fodder, I'd like her to spit him out. She sighs.

"Leah would love that, how pointed you were just now," she says.

"Leah?"

"My housemate. You called right when we got back from yoga and we were feeling so good—she encouraged me to come out with you."

"Please thank Leah for me," I say. I pick up my pint to finish it, but the glass is empty.

"But she won't believe that I'm talking like this to you, after what I just went through with him. I hardly ever sleep anymore, not that I need any sleep. I'm going to make you listen anyway. He'd been offered a job in Berlin and he was going to take it. We were going to run away together. I had a bag packed before something stopped me. I remember sitting down on my bed, a little while ago, and just stopping, seeing how absurd my situation was. And then there he was at that party, acting so incredibly hostile. Maybe what sat me down was that I was hoping to meet you."

"Where are you from?"

"It doesn't matter. Here. New York. It was just—if I ran away with Adam, I'd only be quitting one more life, running into his fantasy this time. That's not moving forward. I hated to admit all that to myself and to end it with him. The reality of my horrible job saved me, I think. It's a kind of last stand. You see, these last months haven't been easy."

"Where in New York?" I ask. "Where is here?"

"It doesn't matter. Think of a place you like but don't know well—that's where I'm from."

Her eyes well up. I quiet down and I see that she's like me in this way. She's comfortable with incomplete disclosure. There's a quiver around her mouth. Though I've been staring at her all along, it's as if I've gotten better at staring at her now, and her eyes are wet. I take up her hands.

We lighten our talk. We shift to faraway places, trips she's made to Guatemala, Eritrea, Morocco. In between the no more than two years that she's ever spent in any one place, there were months-long trips, alone or with lovers, when no one could find her.

It is past three when we stand, and the time has knifed past so quickly that I believe we've got something, Katherine and I. I just can't name it. I don't even want to try, not yet. I'd love to believe that I don't like to name things, because of all that I've learned about Jewish mystics and the danger of speaking the name of God aloud. But it bothers me that this is the only way I've found to connect with being a Jew—by being hesitant to name my passion, as if it were nearly as sublime as the search for the name of God. This is why I like the Golem. Unlike studying the lives and writings of real mystics, like Moses Maimonides or Jacob ben Jacob ha-Kohen, the Golem is just a story, and thoughts of him are easy to carry through a night like this.

"Hey," she says, "do you want to walk me home?"

We walk back slowly and stop in front of her stoop. Her street is thick with trees and because of this it is darker here than the night. Some televisions are still on, so a few rooms bounce white light against other windows and onto our faces. I watch as she takes a few long breaths and closes her eyes. I draw on the concrete with my shoe and look up at her house.

"The whole brownstone is yours?" I ask.

"Leah owns it," she says. "Bud bought a jingle. It's a funny story, but I won't tell you now."

I stare up at the house and I don't have to remember the address or the name of the street. It is ingrained in me, and other information gives way to it. For instance, where I live or what I do, none of that matters. But the Golem stays with me. Down at the bottom of the street, behind the Plymouth Fury and the oak tree, that's where he is. He stands there, mute, watching over us.

"Don't invite me in," I say. "Unless you want to."

"I won't. We're far too intense with each other already to ruin it with that." And then she closes her impossible eyes.

It's not just a kiss good night, it's a brain-scrambling embrace, and I find myself pulling her tighter because her body is rolling with me and because I've gone so thoughtless—without her I'm sure I'd stagger and fall. I slide my fingers down her back and around and touch where we were so hard against each other the other night. Now, even though we are on the street and there are so many clothes between us, I feel as near to her as I did then.

We come apart and she goes up her stairs. She says good night. I stare up at her and she looks back at me for an instant. I listen to the oiled clicks of her lock, and then she is gone.

I throw a few more dollars away on a cab. We drive fast over the Manhattan Bridge. I look behind me at the glow of the river under the bridge's electricity. Above, there's the deepwater black of the sky, and Brooklyn's just sitting there, full of her.

"You hear about the ripple?" the driver asks.

"No," I say. "What ripple?"

"Goddamn stock market's taking hits again."

"I don't get you," I say.

"Come on, you know. Foreign investors pulled out like crazy this afternoon, because the Fed finally raised interest rates unbearably high, and now we're seeing it, all because the dollar looks like shit against the yen—like we couldn't have noticed this happening all winter? So that's what the fucking pundits are calling it. Another day, another ripple. Scary when that shit happens, especially after last week's two-day correction, you know?"

"I guess. Unless you haven't got any money. Then who cares?"

"Come on now, we've all got at least a finger in it," he says. "Me, I'm up to my armpit. My stocks are fucking plummeting and the moment I get off shift I'm going to log on and pull out, and screw what the Prudential guys say about hanging tough."

He's annoyed that I can't talk with him about the market in an informed way, so he turns up his oldies station. As we arrive in Manhattan, we listen to Bette Midler sing "The Rose," a song I've always found beautiful and never thought of as old. He turns back to me when he hands me my change.

"You must be some kind of rich to not care about the market," he says. He switches the radio to 1010 WINS, where they're announcing more bad news from the street.

"I'm not rich," I say as I get out. The front of the Gouverneur is dark. I look in my wallet for the access card that lets me into the hotel.

"Yeah you are," he says as he drives away.

4

Ah, the Golem and Michael Zabusky," my adviser, Matthew Weingarden, says. "A pleasure to have you at my party, and a pleasure to see you on this fine Tuesday morning. Yes indeed. Lord, what better gift could you have brought to me?"

"No better gift than us—we're both happy to see you," I say. I pretend to pull up a chair for my mythical friend, and Weingarden is amused. I've gotten through an entire academic year without handing him a single piece of paper, and he's still answering my e-mails and letting me come in for meetings. I amuse him. We both know it.

Though it's April, heat still cranks through this building, so Weingarden has his window open. The din from cars and buses honking their way down Fifth Avenue floats up to us. I look around his office and try to frame what it is I have to say. I don't want to take more time to write, but I have to, and that's what we're here to talk about. Only, I don't want to start in on the request. He looks at me. I look away. But I scheduled this appointment, so I've got to get us started and keep us talking, and we both know that this is far easier than if I actually started to write chapters of my dissertation and hand them in.

The books behind him are all upright and alphabetical. His coffee mug sits on a brushed steel coaster on his desk next to five black fountain pens lined up in a row. A framed drawing between a pair of big windows that overlook Fifth Avenue is by Francesco Clemente. It's a picture of a brown-and-blue clown and it is inscribed "To one of the world's few truly thoughtful men, Matthew Weingarden."

Though my adviser is the preeminent authority on medieval Jewish life—rivaled only by Elaine Basch at SUNY and Yehuda Goldberg at the Hebrew University in Jerusalem—he also likes to have it known that he's friendly with artists. His most recent book, published only five years ago, was a virulent attack on the lack of aesthetic beauty in Jewish daily life during the fourteenth century. He interviewed a variety of modern artists in order to have them agree with him. And they did. In fact, everybody did. He expected a firestorm of criticism and a real duel with the one professor who consistently outshines him—Elliot Wolfson at NYU. But instead, he received only tepid reviews. There was nothing wrong with what he wrote and many professors said as much, and his text was only assigned as ancillary reading in the graduate classes of his peers. In the years since, he's decided that in order to keep his position his next attack must move far closer to Wolfson's territory. It will have something to do with the mind of the mystic.

The Golem is one of his discards. He decided that Moshe Idel had already written the definitive text, and since then the idea of the Golem has spent too much time wading in the shallows of the mainstream. But he's told me that I shouldn't be concerned about this, that no matter what I hand in, he'll force me to revise until my text fairly stinks of esoteric innovation.

"I'm afraid I've forgotten the notes I said I'd bring," I say.

"Yes," he says. "So you have."

He leans forward and offers me his lopsided grin, angled up toward his left ear. He wears his hair long and brushed straight back. He's in a thin charcoal suit and a silky gray shirt. I imagine he's looking dapper for tonight—for yet another cocktail party. He licks the outside of his right thumb and points it at me, as if I'm supposed to come forward and lick it too.

"So, a few more weeks and we break for the summer, and you'll really get going. Where will you take your Golem for vacation?" he says. His eyes are clear and he stares straight at me, and he betrays no inhibition.

"Back to the library—I'm going to get it this time, really take it apart."

"Take it apart," he says, "like an engine? My friend, it won't take you long. An engine is far more complex. Are we going to go through why, again? Or shall I introduce something new to your equation?"

He runs his hand over the papers and journals on the left side of his desk, as if he might hand over some ideas that could solve my problem. But I start talking before it comes to that.

"Well, since we last spoke, I've gotten more interested in the idea of creators going into a necessary ecstasy. Creating a creature from that ecstasy—like what happened with Frankenstein. Last night I reread *The Golem*. You know—the one that's filled with legends of the ghetto in Prague in medieval times. I want to begin again from that book, use it as my archetypal text, and then—"

"I thought I made my feelings about that book clear. It's a fake. Written in 1908. The American cheese of mythology."

"Yes," I say. "Well, of course." I look away. Weingarden likes it better when I'm on the defensive. I speak faster then, and I've noticed that he'll occasionally make note of something I've said, possibly to use as his own.

"So it's not a good idea to use it," he says. "What else?"

"I could begin with Meyrink's *The Golem*."

"Gustav Meyrink?" he says. "Again with that madman? I looked at his book since you last mentioned it and it isn't bad, plenty of hefty insight into the doppelgänger. But it's little more than fiction."

"It's got this amazing place in kabbalistic literature—"

"It doesn't. That's early twentieth century, too. It owes as much to Indian philosophy as to the Kabbalah, perhaps more. Mike, you and I know these books too well. This Golem recipe of ours needs spice. What can you add?"

"Add?"

I don't want to admit that I don't want to add anything. The Golem is finite. There's nothing to add. If I began to grow my idea I might have to discuss every single artificial anthropoid that's ever been used in religious practice. I could easily create a dissertation without end.

"Yes, add. I don't see, really, how you can be satisfied with only the Golem, as I wasn't. Lord above, Mike, it's really just a dumb universal story, a monstrous, animated doll serving man and all that. Do you really think the Golem will suffice?"

"Well, sure. This summer I'm going to look more carefully at the *Zohar*. I'll go back through all of Gershom Scholem's books and see what parallels his conservatism forced him to deny, which might stand. In addition, I'll make some links to other myths that deal with tellurian creation by human hand. I'll probably read through Martin Buber again, too, and see if I missed anything the first few times."

He stares at me. Behind him, his laptop plays a few notes from what might be a Beethoven sonata for flute. He has e-mail, but he doesn't turn to address it. In the past, he's answered e-mail while he talked to me, and now I see that was a good thing—his lack of concentration implied that I was in a less grave situation than this has become.

"What about this? Why not go back and ask what drives a holy man to create a Golem? And don't go the simple route. Don't make it about protection from evil forces and all that. Ask a bigger question—what drives a devout man to create a monster he can control?"

Instead of speaking, I lick my own right thumb and think. The footnotes for a question like that would be epic—the preliminary construction of such a psychoanalytic/religious analysis could take months. Though I doubt I'll try it, I play along. I don't want to appear lazy or unable.

"While you're at it," he says, "why not give some thought to the monster's head? Of course he's brainless and soulless and all that, because of the lack of speech, and his eyesight's none too good either—which I'm sure Wolfson didn't address—but anyway, ask the monster a question: *Who controls you? The Jewish people? Too easy. Your creator? Why?*" He stops quickly and jots down a note on the paper in front of him. Then he pulls the paper close to him so I can't see it.

"Before I look into that," I say, "let me ask, is there an instance in the Golem's folklore that I've overlooked—where he doesn't run wild and make a mess of things before he destroys his master?"

Weingarden laughs. He twirls a pencil and stares at me. We're both clicking through all the myths we know, and looking at their endings. And though his store of myths is larger, he arrives at an answer first.

"It's a good point, and though we can't ever be sure, I think the answer's no. But what's he thinking of when he goes wild? That's what I want to know. Tell me, how long have you been wrestling with this myth?"

"Four years or so? Something like that. But don't forget that I've written on other things in the meantime. I did write that analysis of Abraham Abulafia's ideas on the music of pure thought."

"Yes, that was pretty amusing. But now, these questions I've brought to you—toying with religious anthropomorphism as metaphor for desire, or control. These questions are special."

Then he's silent again. He presses two fingers to his upper lip and makes an exhaling sound.

He says, "You're the perfect person to write this paper, and I believe you know why. It's because you've got an excessively impressionable soul."

I nod. He can't be serious. He's got a tendency to say things that reach far beyond our professional relationship, and this is certainly one of them. I rub at the bottom of my breastbone, just between my ribs, where I imagine my soul might be.

"I wasn't aware that my soul was quite so visible."

"Oh yes," he says. "On days like this, I can see it clearly."

He makes a laughing noise without opening his mouth. He takes a pair of steel-rimmed spectacles out of his shirt pocket and puts them on, as if he's going to use them to get a closer look at the soul I've put on display. They look like the sort of thing country doctors and Harry Truman used to wear.

"Well, I appreciate the, uh, the mission you've given me. I agree with you, I'm the right man for the job."

And I can't believe I've just said that. But Weingarden smiles so bright and wide, and his eyes glisten behind his glasses—it's almost as if he's beaming.

"All of this about going into ecstasies, turning to the spirits, I honestly wouldn't mind if you tried it. But beyond this, Mike, really, now that we've hammered out your next several months, why not take a lover? It's been my hope that you'd find an intelligent and beautiful woman to take up your nights—then you can really get on with this work during the day."

He pauses, but this is bait that I know not to take. I coolly place my hands under my thighs and watch him. If a handsome adviser like Weingarden knows who you're sleeping with, he might very well flirt with them too, for the simple pleasure of torturing you with his power. I know this sounds paranoid, but I've heard of it happening before. I wonder how well Katherine's former boyfriend Adam knows Weingarden. Of course, I would prefer to believe that they are all completely strange to one another. But that would be naive. Instead of questioning him, though, I remain silent. He saw me with Katherine, yes, but we don't have to discuss her now. After all, my soul's already been discussed, and that ought to be enough fun for him, for one meeting.

I pinch my thighs and say, "I'll be working too hard for any of that. I'll open up my examinations this summer. You're right to point me in this direction. I won't disappoint you."

"We'll leave it here. Schedule again with me when you have something substantial on paper—or call me over the summer. I'll be in and out of town and we can have a drink. There's a paper I'm working on that I'd be grateful if you'd read—only I'm not done yet."

"Thank you," I say, "I'd be happy to read it."

"Of course, it's for the *Journal of Judaic Studies*. Even now, I can see that it's very good. So let's speak soon." He breathes out then and arches his back, rolls his neck, and starts to hum something. He's done with me.

But then he says, "So you'll do whatever is necessary to make this work of yours sing."

"What?" I ask. I'm half out of my chair and I catch sight of the frayed hem of my khakis. They've caught on a splinter in the chair leg. There's a little bonsai tree on the windowsill, with an eye-dropper next to it. He must give it a little water every single day; or worse, some other graduate student, who's far too deep in his clutches, comes and does it for him. I wrestle the chair away from my leg.

"You will do whatever you must, that's all, in order to get our refreshing questions of today answered."

"Right, of course," I say. "I'll stop holding back."

"Wonderful," he says. "Since I met you, I've been looking forward to this new beginning." He takes a pen and curls it between his lip and nose, and waggles it at me.

"Yes, so have I," I say. Though I don't especially know what I mean, he seems to, because he smiles so wide and crooked that the pen drops.

"Call in whoever's next, would you? Lord, let's hope they want to write on the psychology of modern-day rabbis or they've come up with yet another analysis of the Dead Sea Scrolls, or some other simple sanctimonious thing, yes?"

"Oh yes," I say. "Let's hope—after all, not everyone can handle an assignment like mine."

———

Because the desk I share with seven others in the graduate bull pen happens to be unoccupied, I settle down and write notes that address what Weingarden's said. I know what he's up to. He's driving me to go inside the Golem and bring out some real meaning, and then he can insert my ideas into his crossover lectures in mass-market halls like the Ninety-second Street Y. And I'm hampering his ambition by fighting to remain little more than a recorder of the Golem's habits. But I don't like to think that I'd back down from the intensity Weingarden's urging on me. So I resolve to think more about the Golem's head and less about the little stories that surround him. I begin to make doodles of my Golem—that is, I draw a puffy version of the Incredible Hulk, with eyes that are completely filled in and unknowing.

It's then that my cell phone rings, and though the caller's number is blocked, I pick it up and say hello.

"Mike, it's your father. I'm downstairs. Why don't you get down here and see me?"

"Hi, Dad—I'm upstairs here at school. Did you think I was home?"

"No, no, damnit. I'm downstairs from your school, on Fifth. I just got out of a lunch at Smith & Wollensky. Get down here and we'll visit."

"Well, okay," I say. "Of course."

Over at the elevator banks, a few other people wait with me. I know one, a silent woman in one of those purple down coats that reach to the ankles, who has been hanging around the graduate center at least as long as I have. I'm tempted to talk to her, to say, "I'm going downstairs to see my dad, who I barely ever see," because this seems novel, since most of us are usually going down only to buy coffee or go home to sleep, but I don't want her to look at me and say something like, "I have no dad," and start to cry. So I keep quiet.

My father is parked at the curb, both hands gripping the wheel of his Cadillac. His black-and-white hair falls over his forehead and he has on a shearling coat that I've never seen before. My dad—he's a brown-eyed grizzly bear in the driver's seat and the wheel's a plaything in front of him. I half expect him to tear the wheel off the steering column and toss it out to me in the street. I crouch at his window in order to find out what he wants to do. I'm startled by a deep-lunged whinnying cough that can't belong to him—his window isn't even down. I turn to look up at a horse's nostrils, and then up farther to the mounted cop who has pulled up right behind my father's Cadillac.

The light must've turned green, because other cars begin to whiz by. The window goes down. Little clouds of warm air come out at me. I shiver, because I'm only wearing a bright orange wool sweater and my khakis.

"Look at this shit," he says. "I'm about to be friends with a cop on a horse." He shakes his head.

"Yeah, Dad, there really isn't any parking on Fifth Avenue."

"Get in, then. We'll drive."

So I run around to the passenger side and I feel about half as old as I am as I hop into the car. We don't shake hands or anything.

He snakes his head out the window and yells, "Why don't you bust my fat ass, Mountie boy?" He laughs his big laugh and anybody else would be busy getting a ticket for the next forty-five minutes for stopping in a no-stopping zone and acting like a jerk on top of that, but my dad has a way with people.

The cop only smirks and makes a get-going motion. Then he noses his horse away from us. My dad speeds off and the cop waves. My dad has made a friend, just like that.

"How's business?" he asks. He turns on Thirty-fourth Street and goes right on Sixth. We begin to cruise uptown. He shudders in the hard spring wind and rolls up the windows. I take a few moments to force my eyes dry.

"Well, grad school is going fine. I don't know how business is."

"Yeah, but you can get a job off this deal, right? I mean, you'll be the nutty professor somewhere in about two years, am I right?"

"Well, yes. I'll definitely have a job in two years," I say, which is not a complete lie, just an optimistic statement.

I sit back. His car is lined in black leather and the wood paneling is polished to a synthetic shine. The vents shoot warm air at us. He plays an old CD, of his kind of music. I check the case. Kay Starr, singing "Stormy Weather."

"Where are we going?" I ask.

"Well, I've got to get home and check my screen before the close," he says. "You come along—we'll cook up some dinner and I'll put you on the train after that. Sound good?"

"I'd like to, but I can't—not today anyway," I say.

"No," he sighs. "Well." We come to a stop at the corner of Fifty-fourth Street.

"Used to be a lot of hookers on this corner. We'd have guys come in from out-of-town firms for recruitment, and we'd put them up at the Mayflower, around the corner, and get them the street hookers. Those were good times, when any idiot could make money. Now it's not so easy. I get up, I go look at what's going on, and I can't believe it. I swear what I've lost so far this year could put me out of it forever." He laughs. "Days keep going by and I make one shit move after another. Gimme your hand."

He reaches out and grabs my hand and shakes it, and then holds it close to his heart. He slams it there, up against his thick coat and his chest. I'm not really any smaller than him, just a whole lot less fat. He rumbles a sound at me that could be a laugh or a groan. I look past him then, out the window, at the people speed-walking up and down Sixth Avenue.

He says, "You remember when you were with Alexis? That woman gave you a lot of hell, didn't she, letting you get all ruined that way."

"Well, we were both going through some awful stuff. You saw some of it. I won't ever forget all that."

"Yeah, I've been thinking about how it was when you were with her. Now, with me and Sarah Jane . . . when it's real, it's hard. I don't understand it—I'm always good to her—but she'll have to work in her restaurant or take care of her father, and I'll be walking around my house *waiting* for her, like I can't even concentrate until she's in the house with me. What the hell is that? It's not what I would've thought, this kind of feeling. I didn't figure it would happen to me, so late. I haven't prepared. You know?"

"I guess," I say. I'd met Sarah Jane only once, and we barely talked. She owns a restaurant in Roosevelt, a place called Crescent Grange.

"I mean, Dad—a crush is a crush, you know that, don't you?" I say, and I try to sound easy.

"A crush? Hell, I wish it was that. I'm in love with this woman. She doesn't care about the money, or at least she says she doesn't. She's like your mother that way. Confusing. I'll drop you up here at the park, you walk back. Be good for you. You come up to the house for dinner and a sleepover, like you did back in February, okay? Call me tomorrow and we'll schedule it."

He holds on to my hand. Then he pulls me to him and we hug and bang hell out of each other's backs and I say I'll call. I get out then and head back toward my department to get my bag.

I went up to Roosevelt for dinner back in February, and though it wasn't too bad, I'm in no great rush to do it again. That's when I met Sarah Jane Caldwell. She came by for a few hours and visited with us.

That afternoon my father and I rented a movie, and after dinner we watched it in the living room. The two of them sat on the couch and I took the ugly wicker-and-leather chair he'd stuck in a corner. It was an old Harrison Ford movie, *Frantic*. My dad likes heroes.

He sipped tea that Sarah Jane made and I finished the red wine that was left over from dinner. He joked about going to Paris, how he was too heavy to chase Sarah Jane around like in the movie if things ever went wrong.

I felt old then, because my father was slow moving, and he even began to doze toward the end of the movie. Sarah Jane and I watched each other, for just a minute, while he slept. She smiled uncomfortably and nudged him awake. I remember looking around and admiring the calm of the house. He hadn't filled it with too many things. In the apartment where I grew up, there was always something he'd broken leaned up next to the front door, waiting to be fixed. I'd leave for school in the morning and there'd be a bent golf club, or a chair with the caning torn through. My mother would explain to me that he'd been on the phone with his secretary or Max Asherberg, and he'd broken something in frustration and not even realized he was doing it. On Saturday we'd take a walk together and go and have the thing repaired. But I didn't see any evidence of that habit in his new house. Instead, his new life looks a lot like how mine could turn out. I might enjoy watching *Frantic*. I might use a back pad and drink herbal tea.

The next morning, at the train station in Roosevelt, he asked me to bring up some papers or books that my professors had written so he could understand just what the hell it is that I'm working on. But if I do send him something, I know what will happen the next time I see him: he'll get upset and say that I'm using religion as a crutch, and I'll say that this isn't religion at all, that it is scholarship. No matter what I say, he refuses to understand that I'm not interested in religion per se.

5

You've got to come out and look at the sky," Katherine says. She has found me inside the doorway of La Tartuca, where I've been waiting. She's got that same huge bag, and she's wearing gray wool pants and a soft charcoal cardigan with an indecisive buttoning scheme and more than a hint of breast at the V. Her hair is a darker red than I remember. Except for earrings that might be diamonds, she wears no jewelry.

"We'll be back," I say to the host. We go out the door and into the middle of the street and we look up. Before I bother with the sky, I turn to her. She's running her tongue quickly over her lips. I take her hand.

"Now help me find the moon," she says. "It was here a second ago—there it is. Breathe it in."

I do and we look, and I probably haven't purposely looked at the moon in Manhattan ever. I turn to her just as a man in a suit rushes by. He mutters angrily into a phone. A woman in a cab is also on the phone. She stares at me and her eyes are wild. I look up and down and I sense a kind of crackling white-collar excitement surrounding us. We're on the northern fringe of the financial district, at the corner of Liberty and Nassau Streets. I look far to our right, a few blocks below us, at the cordoned-off area in front of the stock exchange, and I can see loads of them, adults in dark suits, yelling into phones.

"What's going on? I mean, it's a perfect moon and all, but that can't be what they're—"

"Didn't you hear?" she asks. She shakes her head at my confusion and says, "The market took its first really big hit of the year."

"Today? I had no idea."

"It started yesterday. It turns out foreign investors have been pulling out slowly for weeks, then the big fund managers figured the score and most everybody followed their lead. When the market closed this afternoon the Dow had lost something like eleven hundred points—and that was just for today."

"No."

"Yes," she says. "Now everybody's screaming about eleven percent. They don't know how serious it is yet, so that's why they're acting all excited. Of course, the media's going bananas."

I reach for my phone to call my dad, but then I let it go. I'll call him later. It's not as if I can give him advice on what moves to make.

"I wonder if my father's okay."

"What does he do?" she asks. She's still staring up at the moon.

"He plays the market from home."

"Well, he's older—so he's seen this sort of thing before," she says.

"You're probably right. It can't be a big deal to him."

"Mike, come on, I'm famished. We can't stand here all night."

We go back inside and the host makes us wait because we've thrown off his timing. We stand in the front of the restaurant and I take her hand in mine. I feel her next to me and we bump our shoulders and then our hips together. She says she's just been to a cocktail party for a new magazine, WHET, which will probably fold now.

"Not a good day for a launch party," she says. She shakes her head and laughs.

"How do you have time for all of this?" I ask.

"I don't. But I spent all day in Far Rockaway prepping a woman for her court appearance. She just kept crying every time we went through the story—so afterward I wanted a real drink at a big cocktail party, and Leah gets invited to lots of these things."

"Is your client ready?"

"To give testimony? Yes, but I don't know how many years I can get for the guy. I'm hoping for three, because there was already an order of protection, and he had a gun when he attacked her, and he even resisted arrest. But I don't want to talk about it. I'll fall apart if I do and that wouldn't be fun for either of us."

We're given a table in the back room. The wood floors and the ceiling are dark and the wallpaper is stained magenta. The air is ruined from the same thin feel of smokedness that comes from cheap, flickering candles that I already felt around us when I met her— that's beginning to feel like the smell of all the times when we are together.

A woman at the table next to us moans aloud. But the man across from her ignores her and only stares at the screen on his Handspring phone organizer. The woman overfills their wineglasses and she slurps wine even as she gasps. Katherine sees them too.

"They're new to this sort of thing, so they're making the most of the drama. What about you? Are you heavily invested, because of your father?"

"I suppose I am in a way. I mean—not financially—though I'm happy to see him do well. But I have no money of my own," I say. "Are you?"

"Nope. I can't save a dime. But work will get even worse. I have one client who's married to a trader and if he goes down, he'll make things worse for her. We've already walked him through divorce proceedings, but now he could claim professional instability and muck everything up. I don't even want to think about what will happen with the layoffs. You should have seen my office before I left today. It was like we were bracing for a storm."

"I can't imagine how you keep at it," I say.

"Don't make me explain," she says. "Really, don't even make me begin."

At the table across from us, the woman has begun to cry. Instead of consoling her, the man is only leaning forward and talking in a harsh whisper. I listen to him say, "Would you please cool down? I knew we shouldn't have discussed this in public." And then suddenly, he gives up. She's crying and he's stuck. He stares straight ahead and doesn't touch her. I doubt that they're thinking about the market. They're breaking up.

"I don't want you to explain anything," I say. Katherine runs a finger over the scar above her lip and looks down at the table. She takes a few deep breaths.

"Maybe we shouldn't be here together just now," she says.

"No—Katherine, it's okay. We should be here. Us being here, it's the only thing that I'm absolutely sure about."

"You think so?" she asks. And then she smiles. I only nod.

I wait a moment and then I touch her, put my hands out, run my fingers softly over her legs. I'm not trying to get her excited, but I'm close to her and then I am trying, and I grasp her thighs. She puts her hands over mine and stills them. She reaches forward and we kiss.

"Mike, you've been so kind to me. We can feel safe, can't we? This summer, I want to rent a car and drive with you, for weeks, down into the South, where it's hot. Or wait—let's go to Israel. Do you want to take me there, take your brand-new Catholic girlfriend to Jerusalem?"

"I don't know that I'd feel quite comfortable in Israel," I say, "because of the work I'm doing. My adviser was asked to leave the last conference he attended there, and I'm closely allied to him."

"Really?" she asks, and I can't tell whether the low look she's giving me with her eyebrows is doubt, bemusement, or some combination. Either way—we both know I'm lying. Though I wish it were, my work is in no way as vital as Katherine's, no matter what I say. My adviser and his opponents do little beyond attacking one another in journals, and during the rare moments when more mainstream intellectuals glance upon them, they fire missives back and forth on the letters page of the *New York Review of Books*. Perhaps this is why I take the Golem so seriously. He gives me real-world credibility. I study a warrior.

"Sure," I say. "They could be on the lookout for me."

She smiles. "Then forget Israel. Maybe I will just quit my job anyway. Quit my job and lose the saint's mantle forever and clear my head. Just think, read, spend time with you. We could rent a house together somewhere. That would be so good if we did that, Mike. Then we could save each other from all this. I want you to know that that's the kind of thing I dream about."

I kiss her hands while she talks. I want her to save me. And I want to do whatever saving her might entail.

"But wait," she says, "do you care that I'm Catholic?"

I only shake my head. Right now it's the last thing I care about.

"Do you care that I'm a Jew?" I ask. I can't really imagine that she would, but she asked first.

"Do *you* care that you're a Jew?" she asks.

I watch her face carefully and she isn't smiling, though her lips are parted and she is inclined toward me. I flash for a moment on my father, a Saturday afternoon twenty years ago, the two of us walking around Gramercy Park. We pass the temple at the southeast corner, on the way to see *Richard Pryor—Live in Concert* at the Loew's theater on Broadway and Forty-fifth Street.

We went by just as Saturday service was letting out. My dad was wearing a black leather jacket and a fedora, pushed down over his forehead. He grabbed my shoulder and twisted me around toward the temple. "What's the most important thing about who you are?" he asked. I didn't say anything. At the time, I think, the most important thing about me, to me, might have been a crush I had on a girl, whose name, instructively, was Mary Frances. So I didn't say anything. "Well, I don't know either," he said, "but it ought to have to do with what you do every day, to make your living—and let me tell you what it ain't—it ain't your damn religion, I'll tell you that. And remember," he said, "I use the word 'ain't' to emphasize my point here. You *ain't* somebody who lives by his religion."

He kept us standing there, watching all the happy reform Jews as they mingled in front of their temple. A man in a clean blue suit came and stood near us. He started to talk to a young woman, who smiled at him in a dopey way that made it appear as if she loved him. We kept standing there. "Hey, *stupid*," my father said. "Yeah, you—you're *stupid*." And then he laughed. The couple stared at him. They looked quite impassive and superior, which was obviously part of what made my dad so angry. When we walked away my dad kept turning back to glare at them.

But that moment doesn't help me form an answer to Katherine's question. I don't want to say that I don't know if I care that I'm a Jew. I am Jewish and I do care about it. But I'd like to explain the contradictions in there, and right now I'm too busy fighting the impulse to drag Katherine under the table so I can pull her pants off and tear open her cardigan, press her breasts against my face.

"It's okay if you don't care," she says. "I just want to know. These things need to come up, about whether we care. I mean, it would be an issue if we were to marry."

"I do care, it's just—it's difficult for me to explain. Do you want to get married?"

"To you, now? Yes. But more generally, not immediately, no. I only turned thirty last month. You should have seen the party. But it does come up. No matter what I say, I do think about it."

Our wine is delivered and we drink. I wonder if I shouldn't find danger in her contradictions, but then again, I don't expect anything I'm hearing now to have any real relation to what I'll understand about her later.

"You're supposed to hold back, aren't you? Isn't it early to talk about marriage, or religion?"

"Why—I never hold back," she says. "Never."

"What if that scares me off?" I ask.

"Then it's good to find that out early. I have no dark side to be ashamed of. I'm all here, all of me, in front of you. Besides, you came after me. You're not scared."

I stare at her and I'm bursting. I've got the same feeling as the twisted hilarity that comes when you tear up dollar bills.

"You're right, I'm not scared," I say. "I can tell already. I will always come after you."

I grab her finger and bite the tip. She opens her mouth. She smiles and blinks slowly at me. Food arrives, some tuna, some steak, but we're kissing. I've moved over to her side of the table and she's got one leg over mine and we're not even bothering to talk—we're kissing so hard. We're feeding each other wine. I'm kissing her neck, biting her ear; both of us are shivering because this makes no sense. But all we can talk about is how to talk less and kiss more.

Then her phone rings inside her bag and she pulls away from me. She reaches in and pulls out the phone, fast, and I would have thought it would be lost in that mess, but no. She says her name and then she listens.

"So you're sure he's there now. You saw him there? Yes. Consider it done. Janine, this is absolutely the right thing to do, and, yes, I will call you when it's taken care of, and this is completely legal and it will make things much more safe. This is a necessary step, I assure you. I'll call you later." She puts away the phone. Then she's got a Palm Pilot in her hand and she's making notes, confirming an address, logging in the call.

"Do you want to come with me somewhere?" she asks.

"Yes," I say, and no, I don't ask where, as I don't care. I put down what I imagine we owe in cash. She's already gone outside. She's found a cab by the time I join her and we jump in.

"I've got to go out to this bar in Queens. This guy, Marco Sullivan, he's at the Doray Tavern and this just has to be done now. I know it's inconvenient and unprofessional of me, but—there's something nice about having you along. Do you mind?"

I shake my head and move closer to her. By now we're speeding fast up the FDR, and around us, though all of the city's money is shifting, the city itself seems impervious, with its great cluster of midtown skyscrapers standing so solemn and brightly lit from within.

"We're serving a summons? This has to do with what you worked on today?" I ask.

"We are serving somebody, but this is a different case. I'm lucky I got that call. It'll just take a few minutes. This guy won't be too pleased, though, and this is his territory. It's safe enough, but we can't stick around and have a drink or anything."

We arrive. We pull away from our kissing, from my hand inside her shirt, my hand between her legs and up, and inside of her, her cotton underwear pushed far to one side—from our embarrassment because the cabdriver's certainly been watching. The Doray isn't some old-school Irish place or dank slum like I'd figured, not at all. It's a great big dance club, with a doorway rimmed in green neon and a bunch of young people loitering about, dressed up in resort wear that makes them look as if they're on a luxury cruise, even though they're only milling around outside a club in Queens. We smile our way past the doorman.

There's loud music playing inside, a thumping remix of an old Aretha Franklin song. Katherine checks a photo in her purse and looks around. I grab her hand and check the photo too, so that I can help at least a little. I don't see him. We're hunched up in a corner, scanning the crowd. It's dark and we rub our bodies into each other. I'm hard and through my pants I show her that. I love this part, this feeling of being swept up in another's body, the total subsuming of self; you're suddenly freed of being only you, and you get to feel peaceful, because you're connected.

I take her hands and even as we continue to look around the massive room, we begin to dance. We're good together, moving quickly to the music. Old-fashioned disco balls hang down from the dirty ceiling and spin bits of light over us. I cannot remember the last time I've danced so easily with a woman—but this is clearly a wrong wave to slip into, because then she says, "There he is."

She's instantly a dozen feet away from me, tapping a guy on the shoulder. Marco Sullivan turns around and smiles. He's a young guy in a putty-colored suit and an open purple shirt. He's balding, with a softness around the edges of his face, and his body is thick. He gives Katherine a good look and smiles, starts to groove, like he thinks she wants to dance.

I come up, glowering close. She pulls out a crumpled envelope and shows it to him.

"You're Marco Sullivan?"

"Yeah?" he says, and more than a moment passes before he stops smiling. Katherine nods and pushes the envelope into his suit pocket. She's touched him, and his face changes. The hard glare from him, followed by a look that previous to that moment I'd never attached to a name; but now, looking at it, it's obvious. It is a man looking at a woman, gesturing with his face and hands, all offensive: *Given the opportunity, you know, I'd beat you senseless.* And then the look is gone. He sees me. He sees her for the lawyer she is. It's a no-win.

"Fucking great," he says. "Janine finally got off her ass and did something, huh?" He pulls out the envelope and slaps it with the back of his hand, then puts it inside his jacket.

"I guess so," Katherine says, and she just sounds tired. She turns away.

"So this is cute, you bring your boyfriend out here 'cause you're afraid of me too, right?"

"Sure," she says, "that's right." She's already on her way to the door. I stare at him, but I'm irrelevant. He only looks at me and smiles.

"Have a nice night, you two! And you, lady, I'll see you in court."

"All right, all right," I say.

"I really can't wait. I'll smack Janine on her teeth in court too!" he yells. "You and her both! Dumb fucking cunts!" He laughs.

Then he gets in front of me and does this ugly, awkward dance step. He grabs my hand and we stand there like we're about to do a fifties twist move.

"Come on, you bitch!" he says. "Dance with me! I got moves for you." I look at him, but he only looks like some kind of specimen, someone blighted. I know to do nothing more than pull my hand and myself from him and turn and walk. He pats my back as I go, pats me good-bye. I can tell from the faces of the people that I pass that he's right behind me the whole way.

Katherine's already at the door. I'm following her, trying to get close to her but not too close, because I wouldn't think she'd want to be touched after that. I turn around just before I'm out the door and of course he's looking right at me, and he's smiling. He's still dancing terribly. He winks and grins as the door closes.

We find a livery cab and we get in, but Katherine doesn't nestle up to me. The driver refuses to leave Queens. I tell him that he has to.

"Let's drop you first," she says, and her voice is cold. "That was my mistake. I shouldn't have done that with you."

"He had quite a face," I say, but I don't go on.

"In court he'll be different, all innocent, all fucking charming. But he gets her alone, he beats her. Suave bastard, fucking smooth talker. You know what she said? He's destroying her house. She moved out and got her own place and he'll go over there, and he doesn't always hit her. Instead, he tears something apart, like he'll go to the bathroom and tear the sink off the wall, and say he fell."

"That's so sad," I say. "I would never want to end up that way."

"You?" She looks up. "Of course you wouldn't. But I hate these guys, I really do."

I say, "If only there were some control for guys like that. Like some power that comes rushing up and puts them in their place, right at the moment when they're going to do wrong."

"That's stupid," she says. "There's nothing like that."

"There's only you, then," I say. "Do you do that sort of thing a lot?"

"More than I'd like," she says. "God, this is too much. Something has to go."

We grow quiet as we drive into the city. We float down Allen Street.

"I'll get out here," I say. "But I want to see you again."

"I feel the same way, I think," she says. She lets her hair fall forward so it's in her face. It's impossible to see her eyes.

"I was happy with you tonight," I say. I'm thinking that so much of seduction is trickery, hiding the distress of where we've been, hinting that we are good together, that she should change how she feels again, and get out of the cab with me now.

"Mike—I was happy with you too. This could really mean a lot. I'm not myself tonight. You can see that," she says. She stares up at me and then she smiles suddenly. She takes her bag and pushes it onto the floor and reaches over to me.

She says, "Let's talk immediately—tomorrow—and then we can meet this weekend. Let's get badly addicted to each other. I don't think it could be helped in any case. You've been really sweet."

"I'll call you tomorrow, then," I say. She only smiles, runs a hand over my chest. And then I'm outside, and her cab is flying down the street.

I spend what's left of the evening in my room. I pour myself a few ounces of Dewar's from an old bottle and try to make some sense of what the newspeople are calling Bloody Thursday. On CNN, I watch Willow Bay discuss the carnage in a voice so thick with grim excitement that it sounds as if she's delivering sexual commands. Lou Dobbs looks more concerned, more pensive, as if someone's slowly tightening his shirt collar, or filling him with air.

I call my dad and get his machine. I leave a message. I don't think I've ever called him past midnight before but I imagine he's up, since this market warrants late-night concern. My phone remains silent. After I've finished the scotch I continue to sit, watching the announcers list the growing numbers of companies that lost vast amounts of their value. I think about Katherine. I wonder what too much means.

6

After a morning spent reading at the Jewish Theological Seminary, with a few breaks taken to call my father, who simply will not answer his phone, I take the subway back down to CUNY. My department is nearly empty, as it always is on Friday afternoons. I sit in silence at my shared desk and I try my dad one more time. Nothing. So I decide to call Katherine at work. I wait until exactly three-forty. I'm busily reassuring myself that this is the perfect time because she won't have left work for the day but she will be mellowed, finished with lunch, feeling ready for the evening, and open to thinking about me, when my phone rings. Before I can begin to hope that it's Katherine, I read the screen and see that it's my mother.

"Hi, Mom, good flight?"

"Where have you been?" she asks. This seems irrelevant. I'm nowhere special. I'm right here.

"I'm right here, Mom."

"Well," she says. I hear her crying through the phone. "I'm afraid, Mike, that—it's your father. He died." I think she means her husband. He's already had one heart attack.

"You mean Lawrence," I say, quietly.

"No, Michael, your father. He's dead. Michael, he's dead. They're calling it suicide."

Then she doesn't say anything. I don't either. We just listen to each other breathe.

She says, "Of course we don't actually know that yet. It was probably a heart attack, or a stroke, that sort of thing. Leonora Asherberg called me a few hours ago from Roosevelt. You remember—Max's wife. His girlfriend must have called her. That woman, she's at the house."

Then I am amazed that he had a whole life up there in Roosevelt, enough of a life that people would know to arrive at the house. I stand up with my mother close to me on the phone, neither of us saying a word.

"I just saw him," I say. "He was tense. It makes sense that he'd have a heart attack, because of the markets. I can't believe it—I've been calling him since yesterday."

My mother says nothing, and I fill this silence with a memory. It's morning, before school, and we're up and going through the comics in the *Daily News* together. He's joking about how much he hates the characters in *Doonesbury* and how, if he's not careful, I'm going to end up just like one of those people.

He's peeled us a grapefruit and we're both eating sections, both of us loving the sour taste, and it's good that it's so early, only just past seven, because we're not moving fast. I keep telling him that yes, yeah, I'm going to be superliberal, and he should get used to it. He growls his no at me.

My mother is still asleep and we joke about that too, me and my dad, about how she's always sleeping in. We never had such a morning, not with sunshine through the apartment window, or rain, or cold, or anything. But this doesn't mean that I can't replace the blank quality of what I know is trauma with this warm image.

"Well," I say, "what do you need me to do?"

"You'll have to go up there in the morning. There are going to be details we'll need to think through, fast. We need to be in touch. Go home. Call me when you get there. I can't fly back so soon, Mike. I don't—I don't want to."

"I'll go home now," I say, wooden as anything. "I'll go home. And then I'll go up there, just like you say."

I sob once. I feel it come up, and then it's there, and it hurts my chest more than it makes any noise. I doubt that it's appropriate to recite the Twenty-third Psalm right after hearing the news, but I don't know what else to do, so I begin to mutter it to myself, "The Lord is my shepherd, I shall not want . . ." But then someone walks by, and I switch to Hebrew, to the mourner's kaddish, which I know I shouldn't say now, but I feel as if I've got to say *something aloud* now, because somehow, standing mute in the face of grief seems horrible, like accepting a beating without fighting back. So: "*Yitgadal v'yitk'dash shemay raba, b'alma divera chireutay . . .*"

When I am done and the quiet leaps back at me, I pick up the office phone, but I don't know who to call. So I put it down, but I leave my hand on it. I remain this way, fingertips on the phone, pressing prints into the black plastic, for what feels like hours. I rest my cheek flat on the desk surface.

I know considerable time has passed when the air circulation system whirs down to rest for the night. I don't want to bear this additional stillness. So I get up and leave. Lisa, the graduate secretary, is talking on the phone. She looks up and nods at me.

"But what about my other account?" she asks.

I check my mailbox and there's a note from Weingarden: *Extremely pleased with our meeting and your new track. Look forward to having you read my paper and then to us seeing each other in high summer. Also, have a look at Wegener's film: The Golem. E-mail with any new ideas and don't forget what I said: get out there and find some fun. I hear the women are wild for you!* I stuff the note into my pocket. Guys like Weingarden, they're always suggesting a film.

"That money is gone?" Lisa asks. "It's just fucking *gone?*"

I watch her trace a nail hard against her desk calendar, scratching at the next few days. It is her distress over her finances that makes me realize that if, in fact, my father is dead, either I am very rich or, as of right now, I'm saddled with whatever debt he carried. I cannot imagine being rich, but if he had all of his money in the markets and lost it there, left it there, then I may be responsible for whatever debt he left behind.

"*Gone?*" Lisa says again, and her nail snaps. I nod at her and go. Outside on Fifth Avenue, where the people are enveloped in the evening rush, my father is not what I think about. Not at all. Instead, I call Katherine.

She answers on half a ring and says her name.

"Hello Katherine, it's Mike—"

"Mike, listen, I'm sorry, I really am, but I can't see you anymore. I just can't."

"Mike Zabusky, from last night?"

"I know it's you, but I have to do this."

"But last night—"

"That was then. There's too much trouble here and I simply can't bow out by dating somebody new . . ." She gasps, and it's beyond theatrical, to clinical. "And Adam was waiting for me in his car when I got home last night and it was all I could do to make him go home and leave me alone. Then his wife started calling in the middle of the night and Leah had to tell her off, so I haven't slept at all."

"Katherine—"

"I can't have everything. I don't deserve anything but a lot of hard work and—that's all. Something's got to go and I'm sorry if this hurts you, but it's like I said. I can't even talk to you anymore."

"No," I say.

"So this will be good-bye."

Fighting a good-bye with a "But I think I'm in love with you" would sound just like "You can't say good-bye to me, I'm insane" to any woman, or any person really, even a horse, or a squirrel, once they've gotten to the point where they can say they never want to see you again. Still, though I know that just now I'm not capable of cogency, I can try for persuasion.

"You can't deny—"

"I will admit to a pleasant physical attraction between us, but that's as far as it goes. I should have stopped it earlier. Consider this my fault."

"Pleasant?" I say. "Well, you're one hell of a person, aren't you?"

And then I catch sight of a fury growing in me like a negative body, an eel shooting black ink from my solar plexus. I'm raging, but I know this must be a disgust and anger with him, with my father, and even through this feeling I sense the hint of her wanting me to say something mean. It isn't easy, but I hang fire. Then I can't handle that, so I hang up.

I wait a full minute. I work hard to force the anger in me to be replaced with something more attractive, and the best thing I can find resembles nothing more than perplexity. When I've walked a block and filled myself up with desire and need for Katherine and nothing else, when I can tell myself that she is just overwhelmed with everything in her life that is unrelated to me and actually believe it, I call back.

"I'm sorry I hung up," I say. "Please don't do this. We were so good with each other last night—you can't want that to end."

"No, Mike. I can. Please don't call again."

"But I didn't do anything wrong to you," I say.

"I never said you did. It isn't that."

"How can you deny—"

"I'm not denying anything," she says. "I'm the one to blame, because I move too fast. This was a mistake and I'm sorry."

Another man might easily ferret out the key to getting past this rejection, but I can see nothing but a need to pull out, to regroup and think.

"So, okay," she says. She takes a breath.

The breath is like seeing an interstice of light through a high stone wall that surrounds some beautiful old house, some special spot where lovers walk, just outside the Prague ghetto. I mark the spot and go to gather tools. When it gets dark, I'll return and begin to chip away.

"So we won't talk anymore. You won't call again?" she asks.

"No, Katherine. I won't."

"Good-bye, Mike. I'm sorry."

"Good-bye, Katherine. I'm sorry too. You were wonderful."

While I walk, the thing that grows in other men when they want to win a woman's love, the thing that pulls swords out of stones and builds great temples and kills people in other armies to win the love of a woman, whatever that thing is called, not exactly courage or pride, but some more long-winded *Ulysses*-related emotion that encompasses desire, dedication, and sexual hunger—that thing grows in me. I wonder where Katherine will go after work. I hope she's figured out a way to get home early and get some rest.

I walk down near the Williamsburg Bridge, around the projects beyond where I imagine my grandparents' old apartment might have been, on Willett Street. It's past midnight. Though it's only the first week of April, there are already bunches of teenagers, young couples with baby carriages, and older people all standing quietly in the parks that surround the housing projects.

I go into a bodega and buy some food—roast beef and cheese on a roll and a couple of oil cans of Foster's. I eat and drink while I walk past the odd combination of working professionals and poor teenagers who fight for space on the stoops of what used to be tenements. I stand in front of a very clean white tile lobby that might have replaced the staircase leading up to the apartment where I imagine my father was born. Although I have seen the photographs, it's still difficult to imagine that these streets were ever filled with hundreds of thousands of Jews.

My father did nothing but distance himself from this place, so I never knew what growing up was like for him, save for the tinny flavor of his poor Yiddish, tossed at my mother whenever she decided that it was time to go visit their families in Brooklyn: *"Khob zey in bod,"* which he gleefully interpreted as "To hell with them."

My mother always responded the same way, with a sarcastic *"Klap kop in vant un shray gevald!"* or "Go bang your head against the wall and yell for help!"

My father did this once when my mother was arguing with him, but he didn't yell for help, he just screamed, *"Ver dershtikt!"* over and over again at her. This means, "You should be choked," and my mother, in response, kept repeating, *"Doorkh du? Doorkh du?"* which means "By you?" and was a dare.

Two hours later, when my feet hurt, I go back to the Gouverneur. There's nobody around. I let myself inside my room and find that it's been cleaned. The few books I keep here have been stacked up on the table, and the bed has been made with fresh sheets. The ragged brown carpeting looks vacuumed, with a back-and-forth pattern that makes it appear striped. This is a terrific piece of luck. A new maid has taken over the floor and she must be unaware of my permanent status. I lie down on the carpet and spread out my arms and legs. I can make a snow angel on this carpet when it's clean.

While I make my angel shape, I think of how to win back Katherine. One way begins to dominate my thoughts: keep it brief. I get out a piece of white laser-print paper. I find a felt-tip pen and write:

Dear Katherine,
    I understand that you had to, and I won't stop you if you have to, but please don't.

I sign the paper and put it in an envelope. I write out her address and put the envelope on top of the refrigerator for an early morning send-off.

There's a picture of the Golem from the twenties movie version (Wegener's, just like Weingarden said) on the cover of Gustav

Meyrink's book, and I stare at the picture, and flare my nostrils and glare. Then, in the other books, there are some pictures from an illustrated version of about 1911, and they look like me. One picture has the Golem in repose, and I don't even have to distort my face to resemble that one. Even a few minutes of this quiet, soulless existence feels so relaxing and completely unlike my own. Yes, I can do what Weingarden requested of me. I'll learn a lot by making his questions mine.

Here is what I write on paper:

> You don't kiss me without stopping, you don't fall into a restaurant and keep kissing, you don't allow a man to fall in love and then he calls the next day and you tell him no more phone calls, no more nothing, ever. You stunned me. I liked you so quickly. And now to lose you is what you can't do to me. You can't. You did. Find another part of your life that will let go. I want to stay.

As I write I'm left with little beyond one most unfortunate thought: If Katherine finds out that my father killed himself, she'll only want to work harder to stay away from me. She says: I've got enough problems without a boyfriend in such tragic circumstance. I hardly know him anyway. I'll send him a note of condolence in a few months, if I remember.

I will hide what happened from her for as long as I can. I lie down in my clean bed and fall asleep so fast with no room left to think or mourn what my father, this big, angry, mess of a man I knew who was called Jefferson Gerard Zabusky—over what he did.

7

In the morning, after I've packed, I take the letter from the top of the fridge. There's no stamp on it. I haven't got a stamp. I feel the sunshine coming through my windows, and I look out at the Orthodox Jews and the Chinese people who hurry up and down East Broadway. The lack of a stamp is the only excuse I need. I pack and leave my apartment. I go and get the J train, which brings me quite near to her. It's just circumstantial, my doing this. It's just convenient.

I find her block and walk up to her house. I stand there for a moment. I could put the note under the outer door. Someone might take it, though. I would never know. So, because it's rather early on Saturday and there is some chance that she is not here, and I may only reach Leah, or perhaps because I'm hoping that Katherine will reverse her reversal of yesterday and be happy to see me, I ring the bell.

Katherine appears in the vestibule. She wears blue jeans and a pink sweater. She has no shoes on. She stares through the window at me. She opens the door, and I hold out the white letter that lacks a stamp. She doesn't take it.

"This is not an appropriate way to behave," she says.

"I know, but I didn't think you were going to be here. I'm not acting outrageously. This is only a note I was going to leave for you."

"Today is Saturday," she says. "This is weird. We don't know each other as well as you think we do."

She's looking at me and she is two steps above me and even I can see that there's something else she's thinking about, some other thing that's cramping her, that's catching at her. Something that isn't me. In the daylight, her eyes are seven colors all at once.

I say, "It's not weird. I just felt like I had to write to you, after what happened yesterday."

"You're making me feel uncomfortable now," she says.

"Please take the note," I say.

"What happens if I don't?" she asks.

"I don't understand—"

And then she holds out her hand. I drop the letter into her palm. It's so light that there's a beat when I drop it. It floats.

"I have to go, actually," I say. "There's something I have to do."

"Sure. Only I was serious yesterday, about what I said. I'm not taking any of that back. I can't be in anything new right now."

"Of course not," I say. "And anyway, we hardly know each other."

"You're sure you need to give me this?"

"It isn't so much out of need. This is just a miss-you note." But I'm a liar. Of course it is so much a need and more than a miss-you note.

"Well, thanks," she says. "I won't write back, though."

She purses her lips and I imagine that she's gritting her teeth, to cover a smile or a frown. But she's not kidding. Though I'm waiting, she's not adding any qualification. She only tucks my note into her back pocket and then folds her hands underneath the bottom of her sweater.

"I understand," I say. "Anyway, I'm going to be away for a while."

"Good-bye, then," she says.

"Good-bye," I say. I take one step back down her stoop. Then I am looking at nothing, at the pink place where her hands are hidden.

"Is there something the matter with you?" she asks.

"No," I say, "there's nothing the matter with me."

"You can be pretty funny," she says. "But the way you've shown up here. It isn't cool."

She turns and closes her door. I watch her as she goes up her stairs. I walk down the block and stop in front of another brownstone, where I'm sure she can't see me. I put down my bag and stand there. I get out my phone and call to check the schedule of Hudson Valley trains.

The waiting room in Penn Station isn't crowded. I stand with the people who are gathered in front of the television monitors, which are tuned to CNN. A reporter uses the phrase "part of our landscape." I look around me and most of the men and women are nodding in agreement. There was a strong rebound yesterday morning, and the market made up some points it lost. These swings are huge, but nobody looks surprised. After all, it's become part of the landscape.

The older people here have seen these ripples before and their calm is infectious. It's a good American feeling that I take with me as I join the curving line of people who are boarding, all of us set to go up the Hudson.

On the train, I sit down next to a girl. She wears sunglasses with pretty blue frames. She stares out the window at the platform. Her hands are long and thin, and she clasps them together over her lap.

We come up into daylight and begin to move out of Manhattan. A conductor takes our tickets. The girl is also going to Roosevelt. I did not arrive in time to claim a seat on the river side, and the scenery on the land side is repetitive. After looking over the girl's shoulder at the rush of bright green trees and black rocks for what feels like a long time, I close my eyes. But I know I can't hope to sleep.

I take some loose sheets of paper from my bag and lay them down on the plastic table in front of me. If I concentrate, I can write down a story I love, and think of nothing else. So I write.

One day in the early 1500s, in the ghetto in Prague, a money-lender named Chayim Polnicheck came home to find a group of policemen waiting in front of his house. They accused him of the worst crime that a Jew could be accused of—they said that he had made matzo with the blood of a dead Christian baby. They were working from an anonymous tip that told them to go and search Polnicheck's house, and there they would find a dead baby in his basement. They demanded entrance and they went down to the basement and searched. And to Polnicheck's surprise and instant misery, they found a little baby, pale and cold as marble and stiff as wood, swathed in a piece of cloth from Polnicheck's kitchen. So Polnicheck was marched off to jail.

The other Jews in the ghetto liked Polnicheck because he was a good man who was kind to his neighbors, so they were outraged at this charge against him. Especially since the charge was madness. It's against Jewish law to use any sort of blood in the making of matzo, much less Christian baby blood. So the Jews came together and chose one man, who went to see Rabbi Loeb because he had the most wisdom of any rabbi in the ghetto and everyone admired him and looked to him in times of great distress. The man told Loeb what the trouble was. So then Loeb sent him away and he sat up in his room and he grew very sad at the state of relations with the Christians and at all the hard times the Jews in Prague had to bear. This time he was determined to solve the problem.

My hands are beginning to strain from the unnatural feel of writing at such length by hand, but every time I stop, thinking crowds in, and I'm arrested by the physical sensation of being with my father in his car on Sixth Avenue, the two of us hammering away at each other. So I keep going.

Loeb took a nap, and when he was asleep, a young man dressed in elegant clothes, who carried a cane made of brass, visited him in his room, which was locked from the inside, so Loeb knew he wasn't being visited by any mere mortal man. The man told him about a secret recipe. He said that if Loeb went up to the attic of the temple with two trusted assistants and said a certain group of prayers over a combination of earth, air, fire, and water, then a Golem would arise. This monster would help the Jews save Polnicheck.

So Loeb took his two most trusted men, and they went up and walked in circles, three times, backward and then forward, and they threw fire and then water at dirt they'd collected. And from this mixture a man was created who was twice as big and strong as them, but who could not speak.

I check to see that the girl is not looking, and then I try again to draw the monster. The thing that I create is no Hulk, but only a bloated baby with too many muscles and a small head. I crumple the sheet and stuff it into my bag.

The three men stood in front of this monster and were amazed at him. He breathed great gobs of air and his cheeks were purple. He moved about the attic in a lumbering, childlike way. It was as if he were learning to do everything for the first time. When Loeb commanded this monster to be still, he was still. But he was mute. And he looked as if he was made of clay. Loeb told the other men that they had created a Golem, an avenger of the Jews. And the men stared at Loeb and they quaked in their boots with fear, but then they went and fetched clothes from a tailor they knew that had been made for two men who stood on top of each other in a circus act, and they brought these clothes to the attic.

They dressed this Golem in the gigantic clothes and he walked around and Loeb found that he did whatever Loeb commanded him to do, and nothing else. Loeb told him to stand watch over the ghetto each night, and so he did. He walked the streets and he watched over everyone. He hid in the shadows and he had no need of anything, not food, or water, or friendship.

I close my eyes and imagine the rest. But now it's only like a real memory. It comes on me in a few moments and jumbles together, no matter how hard I fight to make it run in sequence.

I see poor Chayim Polnicheck awaiting his sentence in jail. Then one night, very late, the Golem watched as Claussen, a Christian butcher, snuck into the ghetto. He went right up to Rabbi Loeb's house and broke into the basement. The Golem followed him inside. He saw the butcher remove a dead baby from his cloak and place it in a trunk. Just as the butcher was making his escape, the Golem seized him and tied him up.

The Golem burst into the hall and Loeb encountered him. With signs and gestures, the Golem explained what had happened. So Loeb told the Golem to bring the butcher and the baby to court the next morning, where the butcher would confess to planting the baby—both this one and the one at Polnicheck's house. In the morning, the Golem burst into the courtroom, carrying the frightened butcher and the baby. The butcher confessed to his dirty work, and said he'd been put up to it by Lemper, an evil Christian count who owed Polnicheck a lot of money that he hoped he wouldn't have to pay if he could make sure he stayed in jail forever. So there was uproar in the courtroom. Polnicheck was freed. And all the decent Christians apologized to the Jews for the behavior of the count and the butcher. And Rabbi Loeb was happy, and he took the Golem home with him to help with the chores, and to guard over the people of the ghetto.

And then the speed of the train and the rush of cool air overcomes me, and though it is not what I want, I fall asleep. But before my head grows too heavy, in order to insure that I do not touch the girl next to me, or fall onto her chest or lap, I slip my hands under my thighs and let my head drop toward the aisle.

I feel a bump at my knees.

"Hey there," the girl says.

"Yes thanks, I'm okay," I say. "I've been dreaming."

I feel something colder than perspiration behind my ears and I reach up to brush it away. She is still there. It's suddenly embarrassing, this look we're giving each other. She's seen me sleeping through discomfort. I try to smile at her, to at least be disarming. She only takes her knapsack from the seat, tries once again to maneuver past my splayed legs, which I am too slow to straighten.

"Aren't you getting off in Roosevelt?"

And I say yes, yes of course I am, and I grab my bag from the overhead rack and follow the girl off the train.

I take a cab from Roosevelt station. We drive through town and then move slowly past what must be called rolling fields. We pass horses and grazing cows, and then we suddenly turn right on Arrabarack Road. We drive for another half mile, and then we stop. I could walk back to town if I had to.

We pull up in the driveway next to my father's Cadillac and it's noon and still very bright out, and not too warm. I give the driver ten dollars and he leaves without saying a word. I do not have keys to this house, so I drop my bag next to the door and walk around to the back.

My father died in a big house. He owned about a dozen acres of land, most of it behind the house, facing west. It's a four-bedroom arrangement upstairs, with the living rooms on the bottom floor. There's a little plaque that says the house was built in 1857. It's sheathed in white shingles. There's a porch in back, painted a bluish gray. The shutters on the windows are that same color.

I stand on the porch and look over half an acre of grass mown shiny and smooth. I look down through bramble and brush, through trees, to views onto other fields, so many lying fallow.

I hear a car come up to the front of the house. Then there's the sound of another car, and another. So I walk around the way I came. I do not find cars but trucks, three of them, parked in a line.

Sarah Jane Caldwell gets out of the last one. She's a tall woman in overalls and a canvas jacket and boots. She has her hair tied back.

"Hello, Mike," she says. "I thought you might be here." She walks up and stands a few feet from me.

"Mike, these people are from Trauma Scene Restoration. Your father's friend Leonora paid for them to come. The police were here yesterday. His body has already been removed. The police know me, so I was able to take care of it. I talked with your mom. Now these people, they're going to clean up downstairs, down in the basement where this thing happened. Rope, he did it with rope down there. And then they'll do the rest of the house. I'm sorry. This must be awful for you."

"Do you have the keys?" I ask.

She hands over a set of keys to the house, which I take. I stare at her. Because I have seen her only once before, it's difficult to tell whether she's been crying or if her eyes are red because of the spring wind.

"I'm sorry that I can't stay here now," she says, "but I've got to get back to my restaurant. The police will come for you. You're going to have to identify him. Then there will be the funeral, which Leonora will help to handle. Then, of course, we can talk."

She moves forward again, but I step back and her arms are at her sides, and it is as if she never reached out at all. Then she turns and goes back to her truck.

The trauma scene people move around me and go into the house. One appears to be the leader, but it's difficult to be sure, since they're all in white jumpsuits and masks, as if we're at a waste dump. The other two carry in buckets and mops, along with sealed boxes of cleaning supplies. The leader stops in front of me.

"We won't be long," he says. "These outfits and everything are just a precaution. There's nothing toxic here. You should go right in. We're just going to give the place a really thorough cleaning."

I nod and follow these cleaners into my father's house. In the living room, I sit on the couch. There's a stereo in one corner, with a few dozen CDs piled up next to it. He had Sarah Vaughan, Billie

Holiday, Peggy Lee, Kay Starr, Ella Fitzgerald. Then there's John Coltrane, some Miles Davis, Benny Goodman, Stan Getz. The CD in the player is Nancy Wilson's *But Beautiful*.

I walk down to the basement. This part is very clear. He hanged himself in the basement, from a rafter, with a length of rope that'd probably been sitting on its shelf, year after year, harming nobody. I don't know which beam he used. I can't tell. A woman is down here. She calmly mops the concrete floor. She does not look up at me. Perhaps he vomited, or shat, released himself all over the floor. I haven't any idea, and I will not ask. This woman must have the most horrible nightmares.

The trauma scene leader tells me that the woman who comes to clean once a week, Josie, found him yesterday morning. She called the police. They took him away. When I was young, he'd hammer on my chest to make me tough, and I was encouraged to bang him right back. My mother didn't think I'd survive these lessons in how to grow tough, which is why I went away to boarding school. Later, when I'd visit for vacation, I'd watch him yell at Wilma, his secretary, when she forgot to have papers delivered to him at home, and then he'd punch at the plaster walls of our apartment until his hands glowed red.

The police drive me to the coroner's office way down in Poughkeepsie, where I show my driver's license and say yes, that's my dad. I sign papers. They explain that there will be no autopsy, because it isn't necessary, and anyway, Leonora Asherberg requested that there be none, because Jewish law forbids the mutilating of the body, except in extreme cases. And this isn't one of them. This is pretty amusing, since my father was always talking about how much he disliked the divisiveness and sanctimony of religious law.

The police drive me back to the house. I listen to them talk about college basketball. Duke could win the whole thing all over again, any day now.

8

His phone rings, and I let it go. My phone rings and it's my mom.

"So you're up there?"

"Yes, I'm here," I say.

"Well, I called Leonora and she's going to come over for a little while. It's not good for you to be alone in that house. She's no prize, and you know that, but it's better than being alone. We're going to have the funeral on Tuesday morning, and I'll be there then. Lawrence and I will fly in on the red-eye."

While I listen to my mother's travel plans I power up a Bose radio that sits next to the fridge. I press play. *I'm alone because I love you. Yesterday's sunshine has turned to rain.* I eject the CD. Kay Starr.

"Great, so everything's all set," I say.

"You're not listening at all. Perhaps you're in shock."

"Well, maybe. It'd be good if there were some people here. I don't think I've seen Leonora since the firm had box seats to the Yankees when I was six. She kept telling me that if I didn't sit still, Ron Guidry was going to lose his concentration, and I've got to see her now? What about George?"

"He'll be up for the funeral too, but probably not before."

She goes on to talk about who else will come, in addition to my father's brother, George, long retired and living down in Gainesville, Florida. She's spoken again with Sarah Jane Caldwell, who will bring food to the house.

"Mom, what was the deal with all these fifties siren singers? The house is full of them. Why was he such a fan?"

"Well, you know I used to sing, and he loved a woman's voice. That's what we all liked back in high school—those voices."

"I understand," I say. "I'd been wondering."

"Mike, don't let Leonora intimidate you."

"What do you mean?" But even as I say this, I hear several rapid knocks on the door.

"She's here—I'll talk to you soon," I say, and get the door.

Leonora is the wife of Max Asherberg, who was chairman of the firm my father worked for until he died a few years ago. Now she lives alone in a big house somewhere near here. I understood that my father would occasionally go there and they'd have tea. They'd become friends, my father said. I open the door and I have no real memory of her, save for how much she ordered me around at that Yankees game. I look behind her and see that she drives a dark green Mercedes, a very slopey two-door model.

"I loved your father so much!" she says. She throws her arms around me and hangs for just a moment. Then we kiss on the cheek, a light brush where I feel her soft skin against mine. It's a cool pressure, all powdered makeup and age, excepting the tremors, which must underscore how she's feeling.

"I'm so glad you've come," I say.

"Let's sit down," she says.

She's already past me and into the living room, where she takes a hard chair and places it directly in front of the sofa. She hunches forward and puts her elbows on her knees.

"Can I get you anything?" I ask.

"No, please just sit down, Mike. I want to talk to you."

I sit down on the couch. She peers at me.

"Can you stand it?" she asks.

She's wearing a brown and gray Chanel outfit and she carries a gold purse. Her hair is pulled back tight, the way Diana Vreeland used to wear hers, and her cheeks are pink. Her eyes, though, her eyes are old. Not in the crinkled skin around them but in the filmy quality of her iris and pupil. When she sees me staring, she focuses, and that's when I see I'm wrong—her eyes may be old but they are like the rest of her, and not tired at all.

"I guess I've had no choice—it all happened so fast," I say.

"We can handle the rest of it together. As you know, we'll have the funeral on Tuesday. He'll be buried in the graveyard that's affiliated with my temple, near Clinton Corners. I checked to see if he might be buried with his own parents, but sure enough, it's exactly the sort of detail he didn't handle. There's no more room there."

"Too bad," I say.

"Yes it is. So, we'll do it here. He'll be buried in a simple shroud and there will be no viewing of the body. In fact, we're going to have the whole funeral right at the graveyard, to save any problem with my temple. There's one more thing. He'll have a plot near the outer limits of my cemetery, at least six feet from anyone else, because he was a suicide, you know." She stops, perhaps to see if I object to this. "My temple would not bend on this point."

"That's all right," I say. He'd want it that way, to be off in the back somewhere, near the fences, with the other misfits.

"It's such horrible timing for you and me, Mike. I can't stay with you tonight because I have to go to Bard. I donated funds for a new library where one of the halls will be named after Max and me, and I have to be at the dedication dinner. It can't be helped. But I wanted to see you first."

"Thank you," I say. Then I'm quiet. A sudden, icy feeling creeps up my spine and across my shoulder blades just as I begin to recline on the couch. I sit back up. I will need to keep up a better guard against comfort, because whenever I begin to feel okay, this house rises up around me.

"I'd take the money back if that slick little Botstein hadn't moved so fast and built the building. After this past few weeks I could use it. Who knows what will happen next? And now your father's gone, too. I can only stay for a few more minutes, you understand. Your father was supposed to come with me. He was supposed to be my date."

"I'll go with you," I say. I'm sitting on the edge of the sofa now. There are rooms in this house that I have not seen yet, and I do not want to see them tonight.

"That's out of the question. You're in no condition to do that."

"Look, I know he didn't like to keep a lady waiting. Please. I'd rather not be alone."

She stands up and goes over to the window, but there's nothing to see. It is already dark out. I stand too. She shakes her head at what's happened here, and runs her hand over the shape of her hair.

"No, you shouldn't be here alone. So go and find a tuxedo, if you really think you're up to it."

I go upstairs, which I haven't done yet. I walk down the hall, past the closed guest bedrooms and through an open door, into my father's bedroom.

The bed is carefully made, with an expensive black-and-green quilt he must have bought at a country fair with Sarah Jane. Through the disinfectant the trauma cleaners have blanketed over every surface, it doesn't smell very good. But this is not a sick person's medicinal odor or the musty smell of old people. No, the cleaners were quite adept at cleaning away all the human smells. Instead, they've left me with the thin, metallic smell of old change. There's a bucket full of the stuff in the corner, an actual old tin bucket he must have found in the basement, next to the rope. The bucket is nearly full and the room reeks of old quarters and dimes.

I root around in the walk-in closet and find his tux. It's big and sort of crabby around the edges, as if it'd been dragged through too many cocktail parties and benefit dinners, so there's shrimp cocktail sauce and Lord knows what else rubbed into the sleeves. I find his yellowed tuxedo shirt along with a thin black tie that he probably used in high school and a pair of shiny black slip-ons that are cracked at the bridge.

I do up his bow tie and remember how he taught me to do this years ago, with his hands around my neck, him looking at the tie in the mirror and me looking at his face, thinking, That's my daddy, but (though he did do that and I did have that thought and I was nine and felt full of wisdom) the only thing I see in the mirror while I do up the bow is the dusky night behind me and his fallow field, glowing. What big windows you have, I think. I didn't build it, he'd say. I just knew enough to buy the goddamned place.

"Ready," I say to myself.

I go downstairs and she looks up at me. She's talking with someone on her phone, murmuring, and then she smiles when she sees me. She says her good-byes into the phone and keeps the smile. But the way she looks has more to do with the way somebody smiles at a friend who's in the hospital who has no idea how sick he is. It's grim, and I feel sad when I realize that once you're far past seventy, you have to use this particular smile quite a lot.

We go out to the car and I tell her that I can drive, but she ignores me. I stand near her and watch as she struggles to pull the car keys from her purse. This takes one moment too long, and we both can't help but fill the time with thoughts of what's happened.

"But your father!" she says. And that's when she falls against me and cries. One beat, two beats, and a soft heaving cry from us both, and then she lets me go. The car is a stick shift and the power and low center of gravity are not wasted on her. I hold my stomach in place as we burn down the country roads.

She says, "I want a simple tombstone for him. I always remind myself, as it says in the book of Proverbs, 'The rich and the poor meet together in death. The Lord is maker of them all.' "

We pull up in front of the new library. A blissed-out college student takes the car. I help Leonora with the steps and we're in a brand-new library check-in area that's all red walls and warm light. I feel like this is working, like this is such an improbable place to be that it will actually save me from reckoning with the night. We're immediately engulfed by dressed-up old people holding low-octane drinks. Leonora's got friends and I shake hands with them all.

We make our way to the check-in table and I find his name written in script on a sticker: *Jefferson "J.G." Zabusky.* I press his name onto his suit, and that makes me feel measurably unhealthy. I'd even forgotten that his business friends called him J.G. I never did. We mill about and I throw back a scotch and water, which I don't taste.

I wonder if I can steal a moment to go through their collection of books on Judaism. Weingarden's latest is sure to be here, and I could check it and see what he says about mystics and mourning— but no. The book that dispels the myths of the character of the mystic hasn't been written yet. I keep forgetting that that's the one I'm supposed to be helping him with. That's the one he's working on now.

We're seated quickly, and our attention is directed to the stage. Awards are rapidly handed out. So it's not really the library dedication. It's an awards dinner that's supposed to drum up additional dollars to pay for rooms in this new library before they officially dedicate it. A woman comes around with some incredibly bad white wine. I stare down at it.

A fat, smiling man with longish gray hair gets up to accept his award. I listen as he says, "I told Peter Norton that there were hundreds of millions of dollars to be made from his software and he nodded, got incorporated, and now look what happened! Then he mentions his spanking new baby, says he'd love to have her attend a school like this one, but get the libraries ready for the technology of the future, he says, and this time I'm the one to nod, and now look what happened!"

I feel the group's emotions turn on me. The news has worked its way around the table. They've gotten over their initial stunned feelings and now they're thinking it's bad form for me to have shown up here.

A new man begins to make a long joke about there being no refunds for tonight's event, in light of recent turns in the economy.

He gets an appreciative laugh. I wonder if all of my father's money is gone. I suppose there's someone I should ask, but then I realize they'll come to me. If he went bankrupt, I'll find out soon enough. Our salads are delivered during a quiet moment, when, evidently, we are supposed to make conversation. Leonora puts her hand on my arm and she really is smiling.

"Michael, did I overwhelm you before? That's just how I handle crisis, with organization. I can't help it. But if you don't know my style, it can seem abrupt."

"No no, you were fine. These things must—I'm glad you've taken care of so much. But can I ask you something?"

"Of course, Michael. Honey, of course."

I look across the table at an old man who has a gold pen in hand. He writes what must be numbers on a cloth napkin while another gray man peers through his reading spectacles, nods at his conclusions, and frowns.

I say, "The thing is—you seem shocked but somehow you haven't acted like you're all that surprised that my father would do this."

Leonora bends her head and eats her salad, first a few purple lettuce leaves, then a cherry tomato. There's more whispering around us. Onstage, the fund-raisers bustle around and get ready to hand out another award.

Leonora says, "Those of us who don't live by the markets can never really understand how people like your father and my husband feel about them. They have no remove. That may be why I don't appear shocked to you, but I am doing far more than grieving."

Onstage a new fat man says, "And then I sat down with a man and he said I have a company that's going to be important in global peace maintenance and I said I believe we should invest in the rebirth of that company, and ladies and gentlemen, that was fifty years ago, and today that company is—yes, Lockheed Martin. We are invested in the business and arts leaders of the future." The crowd begins to cheer. Leonora claps, so I do too.

"That man is such a charmer," she says.

"It wasn't just the markets," I say. "My father had no remove from anything. You know that."

"Yes," she says. "He moved impulsively. Max always said that when he made money, that was why."

"What else did Max say?"

Leonora turns and stares at me. Max has not been gone for so long, and I'm sure that no one interests her as much as he did.

"He said that your father fought with the markets like a rooster in a cockfight. Max simply wasn't able to make a man like him chairman of the company. He was too passionate, and no good at managing others. That's why he cut himself off from everyone and ended up alone out here."

"But he wasn't alone. He was with Sarah Jane."

"I loved your father," she says. "Not many people saw him the way I did. He was tough, sure, but he had a good side, he really did. He handled two things badly: women and religion—no, three. There was the money. What he did with the people in town is of no consequence. He sometimes said that he wished his life had turned out differently, but it was the markets that controlled him. There's no doubt of this. He did have a fondness for you, Michael. I believe he loved you. And that's the last thing I have to say about any of it."

"But what about—"

"He was truly a fine man," she says. "A little lonely at the end, but in middle age most men are." She closes her eyes for a moment and puts her hand over her mouth. Then she says, "We can't ever understand these things, Michael. Really, *yeder mentsh hot zayn eygene meshugaas.*"

She sips her ice water. I watch her, and I'm amazed that she wants to cover what's happened with a platitude.

" 'Every person has his own madness'?" I ask. "Fine, then. My father lost his fight with the market and went mad, and committed suicide. He crumbled, and now I'm here to clean up. The last time I saw him he said—"

But then I stop. I can't remember anything he said during the last time I saw him. He was driving. He was having trouble with the markets. I can only remember my hands banging on his chest.

"I'm involved with a woman now," I say. "The first woman I've really cared for since my marriage. But it's still early and I'd hate to have her think that I might behave like my father."

Still, Leonora does not look up. I'm fairly flowing with anger, but she's so cool she refuses to respond. My father is like her husband. They are shut cases and no matter how much she loved them, there's no sense in crying for them twice.

I say, "I hope that those who love me will be able to stand by and save me if I ever fall down into such a rage."

And that comment, finally, is a big enough push. Leonora turns and faces me. She does not move, and then she blinks a few times and twitches her nose back and forth, as if she has noticed a scent that is familiar to her.

"Funny," she says, "the way you're trying to blame others for what you don't understand—I can imagine your father handling trauma the same way."

"Don't tell me that," I say. "Please, that's not a thing I want to hear." And then crazy Leon Botstein hops up onstage, bow tie flapping. He jokes lightly about how valued we all are, how much he loves us, and then he thanks us. He's truly revered, and people clap and call out to him. Then, right on cue, the moment dessert is off the table, the great group of us begin to jump up and move toward the exits, as if we're all far younger and this is our recess.

9

Sunday at dusk, Bear meets me in the lobby of the Gouverneur. We go over and play basketball at the Vladeck Park courts. It was far worse than lonely in Roosevelt, and there's little to be done there until the funeral, which isn't until Tuesday. So I came back here.

We warm up, but there's a mid-April chill in the evening air that keeps us stiff. This results in a rather desultory game of one-on-one. Of course, Bear is also careful because I am a freshly made tragic figure. He wouldn't want to elbow me in the face and force me to wear a black eye to my father's funeral.

"There was a note in your mailbox from Weingarden—he wants you to call him," Bear says.

"Yeah, I think I saw it. He's following up on a meeting we had."

"You want me to tell him what happened?" Bear asks. I take a pass from him and throw the ball at the basket, and miss. He grabs it back and lopes it in. There's no net, so we stop and watch to see if it sails through.

"You could. He wants me to troubleshoot some paper he wrote—but that's not for a while yet," I say. Bear stops and he looks at me.

"Come on, Mike—that's not all he wants."

"What do you mean?"

"Hey, you know I've been watching. He wants you to drag through all that junk about Golems that he can't be bothered to handle," Bear says, and shakes his head. I take a shot and miss. I've always suspected that Bear's a little jealous of the good relationship I have with Weingarden.

"That's not quite how he presented it, but that's what advisers do," I say. "They give you their junk. You know that."

"Nah," Bear says. "You've got a special deal with him. Kiss you or kill you, that sort of thing. He likes you too much."

The sun falls behind us, so there's a defiant red fire around the rims of the dusk. If there are Jewish spirits in Manhattan, this playground is where they lurk.

"Any word from your new lady friend?"

"Katherine—nope, she said she didn't want me to call," I say. Our one-on-one dissolves into an unspoken game of horse. I sink a shot from the foul line. Vastly unusual. A heavyset Hasidic kid walks onto the court and motions for the ball. He's in black suit pants and an untucked white shirt, and he's wearing a pair of red All Stars. Bear tosses the ball to him and the kid begins to shoot, consistently missing layups. I lean against the fence while Bear passes the ball to the kid, again and again.

"One more?" the kid asks.

"Take ten," Bear says. Then, "You going to call her anyway?"

"What would you do?"

"Well, if she said not to call, you probably shouldn't call." Bear nods a yes, to himself. "I heard about her a little, from Jen's friend Lydia, who knows everybody."

"Yeah?"

"She's smart is what I heard. And she knows a million people. She's somebody who could have any career, you know? Not limited like us. I mean, people talk about her."

"This means I shouldn't?" I ask.

The kid sinks a basket. He makes a noise in his throat that represents the cheer of a crowd. Bear catches the shot and the kid runs up and grabs the ball from him.

"No, Mike, you can think about her, it's just—what was it like up at your dad's place?"

"Unpleasant," I say.

"Last night I lay awake, trying to imagine how it must have felt up there. You must've not even addressed it. That's the only way I could imagine, was no way. Are you going to sell the house?"

"Bear, he's not even buried. But I did try to address it. At night I went into the basement where it happened and I just stood there, and the pressure was pretty bad. I stood outside the house for a while after that."

"A hospital kind of death is probably easier. Really, I was thinking about it and just about any other way is easier."

Bear walks away from me. He begins to block the kid, who explodes with a bunch of moves. It's as if Bear's blocks have flipped a switch in the kid, and he comes alive. He begins to drop in an array of funny shots. He rolls backward, comes around, gives himself an alley-oop, makes one skyhook after another, and all the time he's sweating and puffing.

"Mike, do you think—maybe you should be in touch with some other people who have had things like this happen, you know? Get some structure, some counseling, like that?"

"No, I don't need anything like that. I'm just damned sorry about Katherine, about how it didn't work out. I really liked her."

"Will there be money for you when all of this is over?" Bear asks.

"Probably not. There'll be bills. That's what I'm realizing. You're right about the house. I'm going to have to sell it to cover whatever he lost. Unless he did it for some other reason, and he was flush, and I've completely misunderstood everything."

"Not likely," Bear says.

"No."

We stare at each other, and he frowns at me. I stuff my hands in my pockets and lean up against the fence. It's gotten pretty dark.

"You don't know how lucky you are to be married to Jen," I say.

He shakes his head. "She left again this week. I swear to God, she was here for five days and she wouldn't look at me. I'm beginning to suspect she's cheating on me with some bankrupt farmer."

"I doubt that," I say. "She's got too much style to bother with anybody but a smooth operator like yourself." But Bear must not like hearing that, because he only shakes his woolly head all over again.

"You gonna fucking play, or what?" the kid asks because Bear and I aren't moving. Bear tosses him the ball. The kid goes back to missing his unblocked shots. Bear and I stand off to one side. I watch cars pass us, an indolent group coming from the Manhattan Bridge, finding their way into the city. Sunday night, a few minutes after eight. Absolutely no rush. I shiver. I'm thinking about Katherine. I don't say her name out loud, though, because Bear is like other people and he doesn't want to hear how much I was moved by her, especially not now, not with what's happened. He said to forget her, but I can't. I know it's wrong, and so I try to bury my memories of her far below the moment where I raced up and out of my father's basement and into his field and watched the dark outlines of the house from fifty feet away.

"I'm going to check out some counseling for you. Man, you're looking thin. You want to take care of yourself. You don't want to starve."

"I'm already starving."

"It's my ball, it's my ball!" the kid yells. And then he's running away with it, his round face still turned to us. He is one vengeful-looking kid.

"Fucking kid stole my ball," I say.

"Worse things could happen," Bear says.

"That doesn't make it right."

———

I wait inside his house for my mother and Lawrence to arrive. We're supposed to drive to the cemetery together.

When my father's mother died, my father held my hand through the funeral. He had to get up and say something at the temple, and he took me up to the *bimah* with him. He didn't say much but he was clear, and he made everyone know that he'd loved his mother and that now all of that love would stay in the family and pass through to me. I was eight, and I watched as all the old people in the audience cried and smiled at me, as if I could hope for nothing better than this sweet speech. My father stood there and promised his mother that she'd always be proud of him and of what he did with his family. Afterward, at the cemetery, everybody came and hugged me and said what a wonder and a gift it was to have such a caring father. Even at the time, standing there gripping the sleeves of the too-big blue blazer I'd been given for the occasion, I remember being moved by all the sentiment.

To fill a moment of waiting with this memory feels only right, though it didn't happen that way. But it feels far better to recall such a fiction than to let the damned basement and its reality creep up into the rest of this wonderful house and into my head.

Better to be re-creative than to dwell on events as they actually were. We did go to her funeral. We sat in the front row and my father cracked his knuckles the whole time. When he'd cracked them till he couldn't crack them anymore, he grabbed my hands, and with a grin best described as devilish, he cracked mine.

When the nineteen-minute service is over Rabbi Joe Vrieslander hands me the ceremonial spade and I begin to dump clots of dirt and rock onto his coffin. The first spade isn't great, because the rocks in the dirt bang on the coffin's lid and the noise feels brutal, like a sudden hail on the roof of a car. Then I'm forced to hand the spade off to my mother, and then to George, who does a poor job and partly misses the grave. But then I grab the spade back, and I just go at it. First I cover the dark wood coffin with a layer of dirt, and then I slowly fill in around the sides. It's a small brass spade and if I kept working with it, this task would probably take me most of the day and into the night. But luckily, when it's apparent that I've gone beyond ceremony, one of the younger guys from the grounds crew comes over and gives me a real shovel.

The crew has a backhoe with them, half hidden behind a tree. Eventually I'll need to stop shoveling. But not just yet. I work my shoulders and make the dirt rain down fast and hard.

By now my shoes are heavy with mud and my blue suit pants are stained a cool brown. My clothes are ruined, but it's okay. Leonora already made me tear the left side of my jacket because I'm in mourning for a parent. That wasn't easy. I had to take the thing in both hands and really pull, and when I finally managed it, I tore too far and now the whole left lapel of my suit flaps open and it's easy to see inside to the canvas and the white cotton batting. I keep going. This earth is good stuff, fresh and fragrant, full of worms and clots of old weed, and before I know it, no part of the coffin shines up at the sky.

The core group of people stick around to watch. But the over-stuffed limousine from the city, which carried his friends from Asherberg & Co., fills up quickly while I work. I've hugged Wilma, my dad's old secretary, who's still with the firm, and I shook hands with a bunch of his lunch buddies. One guy simply could not stop crying and he ended up hugging me for way too long, which I didn't understand until another, much older guy came over and whispered in my ear that the guy lost all of his clients last Thursday and he'd be fired soon.

I wrote a speech and brought it here with me, but when Rabbi Joe wondered aloud if I had anything to say, I only shook my head. The speech isn't much more than an anecdote about how we used to walk together on Friday evenings when I was very young, ten or eleven, after dinner, down through the East Village and then along Eighth Street and into Washington Square Park, both of us admiring the NYU kids. I dreamed of becoming them, while he checked out the hot girls in their crocheted tops and short suede skirts. We'd both get Häagen-Dazs double chocolate chip cones. He'd tell me stories about growing up in Crown Heights. After working through the afternoon at his parents' store, he'd hang out with his gang, American Kings, who greased back their hair and wore leather jackets. But there were only eight of them, and other gangs picked on them because that's what gangs do, and American Kings was a good target since they were a bunch of Jews and the other kids hated them.

He told me about how they used to get drunk with the bums in Prospect Park who lived near the old zoo. Once they all got together and stole a car, drove it to the Verrazano Bridge, picked it up, and threw it in the water. I wrote some other stuff about how we'd read the Bible together on Fridays after our walks, and how our Bible study prodded us to discuss how awful it must have been for the Jews to spend all that time as strangers in a strange land. We agreed that as American Jews we didn't always feel that way anymore, but in some unnameable way we always would. But the combination of the true part about his gang and the walks we used to take and the utterly fictitious Bible study made the whole thing sound bloodless and stupid and completely unlike him. So I didn't read it aloud.

When I'm done I turn and look at our group of eight, who have gathered near the cars, where they wait for me to finish so we can all go back to the house and sit shivah. There's Sarah Jane Caldwell, Josie, George, Leonora Asherberg, Rabbi Joe Vrieslander, and a man named Richard Ashton, who lives next door to my father's house, who calls himself an inventor. Then there's my mother, who holds hands with her silent, wonderfully dapper husband, Lawrence. When I get close enough, I apologize for having kept them all waiting.

Back at the house, Leonora makes sure that we've all washed our hands and eaten one of the traditional eggs that Sarah Jane Caldwell brought, then she sits for a while next to Rabbi Joe. The two of them stay off to one side, and they're quiet. The rest of us take our cue from them and only murmur, "Can I get you more coffee?" and things like that. On the way in Leonora told me this hushed style of conversation is part of sitting shivah. And then, just as we're all quaking and full of rules, she motions to Rabbi Joe and they get ready to leave.

She comes over and hugs me, and she's not as stiff as I'd have thought, but she keeps space between us, since she doesn't care for me anymore.

"Take some time for yourself now, Michael, and sit. Watch the nature around here. Think on this: In the old Yiddish of Eastern Europe, where my people and your father's people are from, there were only names for two flowers, the rose and the violet, and there were no names for wild birds. We worked all the time then. Think on that, Michael, on how far we've come."

What I hear her choose not to say is if you need anything, call. In addition, I see that she has chosen to only allude to our shared Yiddish, rather than actually speak it to me. I stare after her. Good-bye, you scabrous old rich lady.

Sarah Jane Caldwell continues to sit in the living room while I speak to my mother and Lawrence. They've decided that since they're on the East Coast again, and upstate, they'll spend the rest of the day antique shopping; but even though they know I'm aware of this and they've rented a minivan, we pretend it isn't true.

I stand with my mother, who keeps running her hand down my upper arm and then gripping my elbow, again and again. She stares straight ahead as she does this, and she puffs out her lips. My mother doesn't touch me often, and I'm not sure she's aware that she's doing it now.

She says, "Your father and I didn't have anything financial together, Mike. Not anymore. But tomorrow, or soon, you'll have to go through and figure out what happened to the money."

"Where do you think it is?" I ask.

"The truth?" she asks, and then she frowns. She waves at the air that surrounds her, as if to keep it at bay.

"Why not the truth?" I ask.

"I think he was bankrupt. I think he was completely cleaned out, and that's why he did it. I've been going over this, and there is no other explanation. But cleaning up won't be that simple. There's this house to handle, for one thing."

"Who's liable?"

"Liable?" she says. "Let's just talk each other through this. We'll discuss it when I'm back in California, over the next few weeks. Not now."

We both know that in the office he made out of the library, which he called his command center, there are stacks of notes and papers that explain what happened. We turn and see Lawrence standing in the doorway to the kitchen. He holds on to the back of a chair with both hands.

"Mike," Lawrence says, "you know about my two kids, the one in Portland and the other teaching down in D.C., and well—it's a shame, Mike, that we don't all know each other better. We ought to have a holiday together soon. They're both married, and you'd like them, Mike. You'd like their husbands too. I'm sure of it."

"I'd enjoy that a lot, Lawrence," I say. "Mom talks about your kids all the time. We should visit together. That's a good idea. I'm happy that you were here today."

And then he nods his head hard and fast. His jaw is set and he hugs me, and when he's close, he whispers, "Your mother can't be here any longer. She can't bear all this. When we're alone, she won't stop crying—you understand. You call me, we can talk about it." Then he walks out the door. My mother looks after him as she hugs me. And then she follows him.

Sarah Jane Caldwell sits on the couch. She's in a black wool suit, and she wears the tortoiseshell sunglasses she had on at the funeral. She is immobile, her feet crossed at the ankles, sitting forward on the couch, watching me. I take the straight-backed chair that Leonora used when we spoke a few days ago.

Someone has opened the windows that face onto the field. A ripping cold breeze fights its way in, and there's plenty of light. These windows face west. Outside, midafternoon sun blazes down on the healthy grass. I pour coffee for both of us. Our cups sit on coasters on the coffee table, an expensive mahogany item that she might have chosen.

"Thank you for the food," I say. She's brought a bunch of things in addition to the traditional eggs that I suppose she thinks Jews like: bagels and muffins and some spreads—cream cheese, tuna fish, salmon salad.

Sarah Jane doesn't exactly smile. She only looks calm. She's kind of an attractive-looking Wasp, probably in her early forties. Or she may be one of those Christian people who adamantly say, "I'm nothing," and then stare hard at you, daring you to contradict them. One of those. That's what I bet she is.

"He didn't leave a note," she says. She sighs out of the corner of her mouth.

"Nope. Tell me, were you going to marry him?" I ask. I don't ask because I thought that might happen—I ask for something to say.

"No, we never spoke of marriage." She pauses. "You didn't cry today."

"I cried yesterday," I say, too fast.

"Of course," she says. "You'd cry in private, like him. What will you do about this house?"

It's annoying that everyone feels free to ask that. It seems that with a suicide, the grieving period is coopted too.

"I'm keeping it," I say. We both know, I think, that I can't be sure if that's something I can actually do.

"I thought so. No point in selling it now. Nobody will be buying real estate like this for quite a while. The days of a dozen acres and an old farmhouse a few miles outside of Roosevelt going for a million four are over." She stands. After a moment, I stand too.

She says, "I'll see you in town. Come by Crescent Grange anytime. I'll make you a sandwich and we can talk."

"That's it?" I ask. "That's all?"

She's quiet, and then she speaks quickly. "I'm afraid it is. I don't know what was happening last—this past Thursday. Your father and I weren't in touch then."

"You broke up with my father?" I ask. "That's not how he talked about you when I saw him. It didn't sound like it was over."

"Come on, Michael—it's always more complicated than that. He may have been waiting, but I wasn't coming back."

Then she doesn't say anything. She only turns and walks to the door with the comfort of somebody who knows a house well. She stands in the entranceway and looks back at me.

"There used to be a little table here that I liked," she says. "But I think he must have smashed it. He was always smashing things up."

"Yeah, he did have that habit," I say. And I see how close she must have been to him if she knows that, if she can speak so comfortably about such an awful habit.

"It was comical," she says. "I'd be on the phone with him and I'd say that I couldn't see him, that I had to take care of my father, and I'd hear a crash and I would be worried that he'd hurt himself, but all he'd done was ripped a chair apart because I couldn't meet him that night. I mean, the man was fifty-eight. Was he like that when you were growing up?"

"He was. My mother was always trying to protect the furniture from him."

"God," she says, and shakes her head. "I often thought of buying him a punching bag."

"We tried that. He didn't like it. He said it only felt like a game, and if he was angry in the first place, why would he want to play a game?"

Sarah Jane says, "We'll talk soon—when it gets warmer. I bet you'll be out here then. I'm sure he wanted you to have the house. He did talk about you."

"What did he say?"

She is already opening the front door and walking to her truck. She looks back at me.

"Oh," she says, "he was very kind."

I play a Peggy Lee CD and clean the house. I call a cab. I lock the front and back doors, and then I go out and stand at the end of the driveway while I wait for the cab to come.

10

It's the beginning of May, and I haven't been back to his house in more than two weeks. I did call to have his mail forwarded, so the town of Roosevelt knows me, that I'm who they need to talk to. Now I receive at least one letter each day requesting that I handle some financial aspect of his life. They want to pass on the property taxes that he didn't pay, the road tax, the water tax. All of the things that he let go are now my responsibility. Someone has sent a flyer from the Gloria Lawson Real Estate Company on Main Street in Roosevelt. The suggestion is clear. Northern Granite Bank wants to talk, too. They courteously suggest that I should contact them. Then there are more mundane requests. I pay the bill that was sent by Edward Healy, the man who mows the grass, because he sent it with a condolence note.

I should ask Leonora if she knows of a good lawyer who can handle my father's estate, but I don't entirely trust Leonora. And my father disliked lawyers, so he stayed away from them and never used the same one twice. My mother suggested that I might not want to retain a lawyer at all. If my father was completely bankrupt, there will be no money to pay the bill, and it's not fair that I'd have to suddenly start handling even more debt than I may already have. I've been living on a fellowship for so long, just depositing the check, paying the Gouverneur, and then grinding my money down to nothing over the course of each month—I've forgotten how involved other people's finances can be.

Weingarden sends me an e-mail that tells me that he must not know what has happened to my father.

It reads: *Any luck?*

The more I read about the Golem, the more I'm confounded by Weingarden's request. There is no profound answer to "Why?" that is attached to the Jews' desire to create an artificial man. There is only a simple need for protection—a wistful yearning for the safety that is largely absent from real Jewish history. And I was supposed to investigate what happens in the Golem's head—to better understand the thoughts and feelings of a thoughtless monster. I suspect that such a monster would dream of its maker.

As Manhattan grows warmer and I continue to read, I wish that I had been unambitious and decided only to create a compilation of tales of the Golem, and made my dissertation out of their unifying themes. Weingarden's questions demand a retelling, a reification of a series of actions that always lead to tragedy. He's asking me to do real work, to find the few lines or sentences that explain anthropomorphic desire. And we both know that the desire goes without saying. So that sentence, or key, may not exist.

I write back to Weingarden to say that my father has died and that while I am reading and making notes far faster than I was a year ago (this is a lie; I have very few notes), I'm not ready to present anything to him. But I say that whenever he is ready, I'll be happy to read his paper.

In return, he writes only this: *Unmeasurable condolences. I'll be in touch.*

Bear calls. He tells me that it's Jen's friend Lydia's birthday, and though Jen is not in town, he had no other plans, so he went to Lydia's party alone.

"Mike, I didn't know anybody, and I'm headed home. But Katherine was there. I thought you would want to know."

"Thank you, Bear," I say. I nearly drop the phone. I'm already looking for my wallet—I'm going into the bathroom to brush back my hair.

"Don't do anything stupid, okay?" Bear asks.

The place is called Judge's Bar. It's one of the older bars, from the early eighties, before the time when the Lower East Side exploded. It's small, and housed in a former drugstore on Ridge Street, not too far from where I live. But I've never been there before.

I see her just as I arrive. She's far down at the end of the burnished bar. She is talking to a man and laughing. It isn't dark here, because the walls are white and they are clean. The floor is a colorful mosaic, which I like. They're playing something new by Mary J. Blige, a reprise of her duet with Method Man. Alexis and I used to love Mary J. Blige. I wonder if my father would have liked her. Yes, I think. He would have liked her very much.

As I walk toward Katherine, Miriam turns and catches my eye and calls out to me. Miriam of old lilacs. We kiss on the cheek. She asks after my work, and I ask after hers. I still feel warm toward her, but in the same dulled way, where I do not see her sexually. When I was with her in restaurants or bars like this one, I always felt sleepy. While Miriam and I talk, I watch Katherine watch us.

"And I'm sorry about your father," Miriam says. She has a warm smile. This was one of the many aspects of her that made me sleepy. Her blond hair is pulled back from her face.

"That's the saddest thing," she says.

"Yes," I say. I only nod. I believe her when she says she is sorry. I'm quite sure that everyone I have ever met in New York knows that my father killed himself. There's nobody who wouldn't tell a story like that, and nobody I know of who wouldn't want to hear it.

Miriam asks, "So, Mike, are you rich now? I mean, wouldn't that be something? Or was bankruptcy involved?"

I smile at her, and I don't get angry. I'm well aware that within such a question lies the cruelty of someone who used to love you, who you never loved. They can say whatever the hell they want. Because you already hurt them. Because they should have been meaner when you were with them, because had they been mean, even just occasionally, that bit of disdain would have served to let them detach from you more easily and to avoid the sharpness of the pain that occurred when you, you fucking bastard, when you receded, when you walked away.

"I'm sorry," Miriam says. "Of course, you don't have to answer. Mike, this is Liz. I don't think you two have met before."

I shake hands with Liz as Miriam looks on, but she's introduced me only as a way to let me go, and I do. I say that it is good to see both of them and I move down the bar. I can feel them look after me. It's not as if Miriam ever met my father. We never were that close. I reassure myself that it is not as if there is any shame in having a drink in a bar only a few weeks after a family tragedy. Lots of people must do it. And now I am one.

I stop a few feet past Katherine and I look away from her, toward the back of the place, where there is a painting of a cleft in the earth that must be the Grand Canyon. I place my hands flat on the bar and I watch them until they are not moving.

"Hello, Mike," Katherine says. She taps me on the shoulder. "This is a nice surprise."

"Yes," I say. "It's a coincidence." I smile.

She is wearing a skirt made of the darkest red satin. She introduces me to a man, John, who she says she knows from a job she used to have. Although it is quite warm, John wears a blazer. He's a thin man with gray eyes and a hungry face. He hugs himself, and occasionally he rubs his bearded cheek against the shoulder of his blazer. After he nods to me, he keeps nodding to himself.

"We were just talking about Katherine's work," he says. Although John is close to Katherine, she opens the space between them at the bar, so that she's simply standing between us. They are not on a date. Katherine is acting as if she knew she would see me again. She's not surprised at all. Perhaps she saw Bear. Maybe she remembered him and expected me.

She says, "No, I don't always feel as if I can go on. I don't always look inside and find reserves I didn't know I had, though that sounds nice, to imagine that."

John says, "You really should keep at it. If you do this work for a few more years you'll have enough for a book. I can already see it—a real systemic indictment. Katherine, you could make it quite dramatic; you might be able to bring about nothing less than a substantial paradigm shift."

"A book," Katherine says. She turns to me. "I hadn't thought of writing a book. You think that's a good idea?"

"What book?" I ask.

John says, "I've been saying that Katherine could get a book out of her job—a report from the front lines, that sort of thing. She could be the one to readdress America's policy toward domestic violence. She's already gotten a great start since she's in the trenches. She can provide plenty of anecdotal material, to get people reading."

"Oh," I say. John is framing Katherine's face with his bony hands.

"You're the one to write it," John says. "Write your proposal now so you'll have it ready for after this no-money time. Then they'll be looking for new ideas and there will be a real market for that angle."

Katherine is looking around. Her eyes flash on John, on me, and then away. I look down the bar, at Miriam and her friend. They are surrounded by people. It is very crowded near the door, where they are. Someone begins to sing "Happy Birthday" to Lydia, though I'm not sure which person Lydia is. The two bartenders join in.

Katherine says, "It's a good idea, John. I can write about how all this is ruining me romantically and at the same time maybe I can bring about legislative change. Then I can just be a pundit. After a few more years of this, of five phone calls a day from new clients, each with a story more horrible and devastating than the last— that's what I'll be good for. I look forward to that comparatively shallow time. You were smart to think of it."

John smiles. He's satisfied and now he has to go. He's meeting someone. He was happy to run into Katherine. It was nice to meet me, too. I say good-bye. We look after him together.

She whispers to me, "I don't want to write any damn book. All these people think that if you're doing something, it's just because you want to write a book about it, and they're wrong."

"What did you mean," I ask, "about ruining you romantically?"

"Isn't it obvious?"

"Okay," I say. "Yes."

Then we're quiet, and I try to only look at my hands. I don't want to say that I've missed her so much. Or that I dreamed of her smell and the colors of her eyes. I don't want to rush, or scare her. She slides her hand near mine, and then takes it away.

"Mike, I'm sorry about saying that I couldn't see you. I shouldn't have been so abrupt. The truth is that no matter what, I knew I'd see you again."

I listen to her and the experience affects me like a smell, in that her voice is surrounding and does not have beginnings and ends. Then she takes up my hand and places it over her own. I begin to bite my lip. I have to tell her. I cannot smile and she sees this.

"I know about your father," she says. "I'm sorry."

"Yes," I say. "He died. Thanks. It's been—I've had a difficult time lately."

"I should tell you about my sister," she says, and the timbre of her voice is low. "When I heard about your father, I promised my-self that when I saw you again, I would tell you."

"Tell me now."

"No. But do you want to see her picture? She died when she was eighteen and I was twenty-two. Just when I returned to New York the first time, before I went away to Dublin."

She swings her big bag up onto the bar. She hands me a new copy of an old picture of a girl. The girl is laughing and her long black hair is thrown back. She's leaning against a refrigerator and there are other people's hands near her. She is clearly at a party, with a bottle of Corona in one hand, a cigarette in the other. It's probably around high school graduation—that summer. She has the kind of sharp-edged, wide-eyed look that I used to mistake for innocence and that still gives me a pain when I see it.

"There she is. You can keep people with you. That's my point. I think it's all right if you do that. They don't have to go away."

"I haven't got that far in my thinking about what's happened," I say.

"Her name is Christina," she says. "She was so beautiful."

I look again, fast, and when I look up I catch on Katherine's shuttered eyes. I stop looking at the picture and I only stare at Katherine.

"She is," I say, "but she's different from you, from how beautiful you are."

"I don't even know what you mean by that, and anyway, you shouldn't be so flirtatious with me," she whispers. And then she puts the picture away. Now the whole party is at the far end of the bar, near the door. And we are alone down here.

"I haven't said this aloud before," I say. "My father committed suicide."

"I know," she says. "It's gossip. It travels. And my sister was murdered. There it is. That's the truth. Perhaps it isn't good to have such a nasty bond between us, but now I guess we do."

"I'm sorry about your sister."

"Let's not talk about her now. I showed you her picture. That's enough. But you—I felt badly about what I'd done, both before and then after I learned about your father."

We bend our heads in toward each other and I look down through the bar stools and past our shoes at the patterns on the floor. I glance quickly at Katherine and she is doing the same thing. We are like birds, with our heads pressed down into our breasts.

"My father," I say. "He—when I met you, just after I met you, he was supposed to go to some benefit dinner but because of what happened I went instead and I had to take this really old woman who was supposed to be his date. They'd made the plan months before. So it was horrible and surreal and I was in his tuxedo and this lady was, like, eighty. Anyway, I was upset that I didn't get to see you after those few times and I guess on top of everything I looked lovelorn, so she asked me what was the matter."

While I talk, it begins to feel as if it did happen this way. If I can create real and good feelings with Katherine now, by simply reconstructing a conversation that happened during a less happy time, that only makes me feel as if what I'm saying is even more true.

I go on. "We got to really talking, about love and relationships and everything, and she said all this beautiful stuff about you and it was as if she knew you, how you got—not scared—but how you weren't ready, back then with me. Then she said to just hold on. You know? She had this whole heavy thing about how one shouldn't go through life walking away from people and regretting it, and how you shouldn't lose people. Then she was really sad about my father and I held her and she cried for a while. She begged me to try again with you. And I had to tell her that I didn't know how."

"Did she say that she had regrets in her life?"

"She talked about all the great loves she'd seen and the ones she'd missed. She told me a story about a woman who found a man again after she'd seen him through the window of a passing train during World War Two. She waited for him forever, because she knew it was right between them. When I talked to this old woman, time began to seem like nothing. I promised her that I'd at least get you to talk with me."

Katherine comes closer, and she takes my arm and holds it, lets me rest my hand on her hip. Her glass is empty, but when the bartender comes down the bar and looks across at us, she does not order anything else. She looks at me.

"I'll talk with you," she says. She takes her overflowing bag from the floor. She wants to go.

It's drizzling when we get outside. We run through the streets, up Delancey and away from the Williamsburg Bridge, grown large and looming behind us like a pair of huge waving hands, and we keep running, past the sneaker stores and the Burger King, the subway stops, cars flying along at sixty and headed toward that shaking bridge. We run past the newly shut-down stores and bars that line Orchard Street, past the teenagers and the cops, and then we find a cab on Allen Street, and we go to her house in Brooklyn.

In the cab she puts her head on my chest and acts as if she's going to sleep there. I stroke her hair and she rubs her cheek against my shirt.

"When you said I was beautiful before—do you really think so?" she asks.

"Yes, of course," I say. "I've never known a woman who was as beautiful as you."

We arrive in front of her house and she works at finding her keys. I stand next to her and look up at this place. I've been here twice before, but I've never been inside.

"Leah sold a song that got some radio play to Budweiser, and they turned it into a catchy jingle. She really got paid well. But she knew she'd be broke again, so she bought this whole house and we live on the parlor floor."

"That's amazing," I say. "I didn't understand before, but now I see. Bud bought a jingle."

"Yes. I'd hum it for you, but for some reason it won't stay with me, even though Leah plays it over and over again. She beats herself up with the success of that song. Now she's depressed and she stays in her room. Isn't that a stupid problem?"

She opens the door and we are in a vestibule that's painted bright orange. There's a poster on my left, a blowup of a film still—Steve McQueen arguing by the side of a road with Ali MacGraw. Beyond us I can hear a series of breathy noises, accompanied by some music.

"That's Leah. Now she's playing guitar while she watches porn.

God, she just gets more bizarre." Katherine giggles. "We won't go in and meet her just now."

"No," I say. "I wouldn't want to barge in on her."

Katherine's bedroom is really the front parlor, with bay windows giving out onto the street. A large brass bed stripped of any shine is set directly across from the fireplace, which contains a white wicker basket filled with dried flowers.

Katherine goes to a closet. She gropes around and finds some white drawstring pants.

"Look away," she says, and she slips her skirt off. But I don't look away, and we stare at each other. She puts the pants on, and I don't move. I sit in a chair by the window and watch. I listen to a car drive by too fast, a sudden roar that disappears just as quickly. I look up and see that the ceiling has been poorly spackled and is painted a rich orange, with hints of blue at the borders.

"I'm going to wash my face. Look around if you like. Go through my stuff." She smiles and leaves the room.

I stare at a large photograph of a couple who must be her parents. It's a close-up on their faces. They are dressed up and they stand at the bottom of some church steps. They look about our age now. They are wide mouthed, laughing.

I sit in one of two mismatched armchairs. The one I've chosen is brown velvet. The other is blue cotton. Their legs are scuffed and knocked, and the stuffing feels like it won't spring back when I stand up. A thick tree stump sits between them. The stump is just the sort of thing a boyfriend would bring into the room. I kick it.

Some fashion magazines lie in a messy pile under one window. A bright green leaf encased in a mound of clear glass sits on the windowsill. A few postcards are slotted into the frame. One is of three naked men, built identically, all smiling into the camera. I pull it free and turn it over: "Lover, I miss you so much I'm multiplying. See you in a few days. Mike." It's from three years ago. Mike— there's already been a Mike. I close my eyes. Who is he? I can turn him into nobody. He was some lightweight, half-gay young man who made overtures that Katherine found sweet, back before they were old enough to seriously consider their involvements, so that his overtures were only like some sexually weak, paper-thin butterfly kiss on a cool night. He was only somebody she passed time with, who she wasn't serious with, who had to send funny postcards to keep them both interested even when he was gone from town for only a week. They knew it wouldn't last. When it ended, it wouldn't hurt. I hear her coming back into the room and I find that I'm rocking in the armchair, quietly chanting nice old Mike out of the room.

Katherine comes back in. She pulls her hair up from her neck and swirls it around, makes it stand on top of her head.

"Are you thinking about your father all the time now?" she asks.

"No, I was thinking about being in your bedroom, how good it feels," I say. "It's still early—why don't we go and sit on your stoop?"

"Okay," she says. "Let's sit out there."

I get up and take her hand and we walk outside together. I grab her keys from the table next to the door before we go. If I hadn't grabbed them, she would have forgotten them. And we'd have to knock for Leah.

Outside, the stoop has dried and she lies down on the top landing, where I sit. She puts her head in my lap, and I let the pressure of my erection support the back of her head.

"What an odd place on one's body to feel that," she says.

She's put on a cardigan, with more uncertain buttons. I open a few at her belly, reach in, stroke her warm stomach, slide my fingers around her belly button. I do this for minutes, and then slip my hand into her pants, graze down the invisible line of hair that extends from her belly button until my hand is too far into her pants, considering that we're out in the street. I don't have a light touch. But I pretend I do.

"Let's go inside," she says.

"Not just yet." With my other hand I stroke her hair, pull her dark red hair back.

"I want to go inside right now," she says.

"Do you?" I ask. She grabs the back of my neck and pulls my head down. My chin hits my chest first, and it clanks there, my tongue near bitten. I kiss her through the pain in my mouth.

Tonight is how the rest of our lives together will be. This is not the brownstone that we will own, where our children will play, but perhaps that place is a few doors down from here, or across the street.

I steady my feet, put my arms under her, and pick her up. There's a creak in the front of my knees, but my hamstrings hold up. She sings out, breathless and high, but she knows enough not to struggle free, as that will send us both tumbling down the concrete steps. She grips me hard. She opens the door while she is still in my arms. We go into her room.

We undress each other on her bed. The sheets here are much thicker than mine, and because there is still a nighttime cool breeze, she takes out a comforter. The bed is high and old-fashioned. We're at least three feet off the ground.

We try, with what little grace we can muster, to pull each other's pants off. When we have succeeded, we sit up and look at each other. She cups one breast, the tips of her fingers pointed at me. I kiss her nipple and feel her fingers on my chin. I hold her shoulders and press her back. Her eyes are closed, which is somehow not a great change, because still, still, her eyes are not ever open to me. Then we embrace and we do not kiss. We only drive into each other.

And then I take off her underwear and she takes off mine. We roll onto our sides. Her hips make her half as high again as me. We begin to rub at each other.

"Oh! It's so big. Your dick is so big!"

"You think so—"

"Shh, yes. I said it the other night too, when we met—you don't remember."

And I believe her, though I know that she is lying and only saying something grander than the truth. My dick is about average.

But to hear her say this thing is uncontrollably exciting, is like a hit of nitrous in its sudden, brain-flutter high. Yes, you *can too* lie to make things better. She's like me in this way, and it makes me feel even closer to her.

"Hold my hands back," she says. "Hold me down on the bed and fuck me and just listen to me."

She begins to say the kindest things. She tells me that she wants to be with me always, and her voice is warm and low. I want to stop the sex and only listen to her but she is urging me on, to grip her wrists tight and hold her while she struggles—and I am watching her and she is arching up to kiss me even as she fights me. I come outside of her so hard that if I were not so shocked at the degree of my own pleasure, I would faint.

"You're amazing," she says. "So amazing."

Afterward, I can't tell whether she is holding me or I am holding her. Somehow, and I don't even try to believe it because it is so rare, we are holding each other. I smell her shoulder, lines curved round and down into her breast.

Now I can't believe that we've gone this far and I know so little about her, about her friends and her family and the boyfriends that came before me.

This room has only a little dust. The glasses of water on the bedside table are far from the dust in the corners and I'd have to pour the water on the dust and say bunches of prayers seven times each that I don't even have properly memorized and then I'd have to walk around in circles and there would be lightning and fire. And I would not be able to find any holy men at this time of night anyway—and even if I did gather all of these things and go through the ritual, then I'd only have the Golem, bright red and gulping air like an exhausted netherworld soldier. Still, so much of me wishes I could create him. Then I could feel safe, for both of us. Because then we would be protected and I would be the creator and nobody else's monster.

"You make me so happy," she says. I look over at her. I'd thought she was asleep.

"Oh yes?" I ask.

"Maybe it's because of all that's already gone wrong between us. I know you would never hurt me and you make me feel so good."

"It's true. I would never hurt you. But now here we are and I don't even know where you're from."

"Where I'm from?" She puts her wrist into my mouth and I hold it, lightly, with my teeth. I can feel her bones and arteries, her beating pulse on my tongue.

"You have to know?" She looks at her hand and she tugs at it, and I grip her with my jaw, just a little tighter. She exhales and smiles at me.

"I like the way that feels," she says. "Okay. I grew up in a white brick house on Seventieth Avenue in Forest Hills. My sister—I already told you. I have a brother too. Mark. He's a guidance counselor and a songwriter. He works in an after-school program at Saint Valentine's. That's the church where my mother works. He was always religious—but after my sister was killed he became rabidly, passionately devout. He's obsessed with being good. He makes me want to quit my job, just to keep the balance right."

"Then that's what you should do," I say.

"I can't quit," she says. "My brother's kind of crazy. We argue all the time. So my past is boring. You'd hide a dull past like that too."

"Katherine," I say, "thank God it's dull."

"Are you saying I'm dull?" And though she is kidding, or she appears to be, she flashes her eyes at me and her fingers creep to my throat. It's a pretty exciting reaction. It's really something to see. Her hands are surprisingly hot and then I feel that both of us are this way—our bodies have not cooled down at all. She keeps one hand on my throat and she points at me.

"I'm not fucking dull," she says.

In the morning I wake her to say good-bye and she opens her eyes and looks so surprised and afraid and then she reaches out to me. She begs me not to go. I hold her, and I feel her breasts rise against my chest. I still her heart and breathe with her until she calms down. I put my face down close to her ear.

"Push me down, Mike. Push me down into the bed."

I begin to kiss her and press all the weight of my upper body down onto her.

"Go slack. Crush me."

I pull the sheets away and she is naked and warm. I'm in my jeans and shirt, my shoes on, my hair combed, and I lie down on top of her. I'm heavy, with my head against hers, even our ears pressed and hurting against each other. I think I can hear her lungs constrict, as if her whole body has to go down and fight for air.

"I like you, Mike," she says. She is gasping with the weight of me. I look at her hands, which she's made into tight fists. There are lines of pulsing blue in her forearms. Her eyes are closed.

"It's too much for you to crush me like this. I can't breathe," she says. "God, I really like you so much, I don't know what to do about it. We're still so new to each other, but I can't wait to see you again."

11

Bear says, "Look, Mike, I'm serious. This is about something that I think Jen did to me."

Bear has just turned in his grades for the semester. He's quite proud because he was only a few weeks late. Now, though I did not teach this past spring, so I have no accomplishment to celebrate, I'm joining him in his celebratory drink. We sit in Bryant Park, behind the public library, on a bench. Grolsch beer is sponsoring a showing of *King of Hearts* on a twenty-foot-high screen that's been erected at the west end of the park. The movie will begin as soon as it's dark.

We stare at two gigantic green Grolsch bottles on either side of the white screen. The young people gather in the grass and spread out their blankets. There are hundreds of them.

We're drinking Budweiser, which we have hidden in paper bags. I'm sure that Katherine has watched movies here. She probably went from blanket to blanket, sipping wine, saying hello to friends. In the last few days we've talked on the phone when we haven't been together.

"Jen didn't do anything bad to you," I say.

"No, man, come on—I'm serious," he says.

"Okay, I'm not trying to belittle you."

A policeman walks by and eyes our bags. But he ignores us. We won't cause any trouble. We're not going to stay for the movie, either. We're just having a drink after work. Jen is out of town again. Katherine is working late and then she has to rush to a dinner party.

"Tell me what happened," I say.

"I'll tell you the story she told me." Bear takes a breath and sips his beer. He crouches in toward me, as if he is going to make me look at his eyes through his whole story.

"When Jen came back from Toronto the last time, when they gave her a break from negotiating this farm equipment company sale, she told me about a friend of hers who's a real loser. He draws caricatures, apparently, on boardwalks in beach towns in the summer, and the rest of the time he temps there, in Toronto. He's depressive. A lost guy. Jen tells me this is a guy she knows from her high school. He's a little older, and she used to look up to him. Jen says she ran into him, in her hotel actually, and they had a drink and he told her this story. The point is, this loser guy decided that he was in love with a girl who was in Jen's class at school. The girl—needless to say—she didn't want to be involved with this depressive guy."

"Up to now, you're just retelling me a story that Jen told you, about a loser guy who loves a girl?" I ask.

"Yeah, up to now. The guy says the girl is like him—she's depressive. Her parents have moved into a cabin by a lake way up in Ontario. So she's up there, living with the parents and recuperating from some bad relationship or something. The girl and the guy end up dating a bunch of times, but they both realize that they're too messed up. They're in no condition to date. She says she never wants to see him again, and he's crushed. Then he says he had an idea. This girl he likes is into frogs. She loves frogs. So he decides to show up at her parents' cabin in a frog costume and that will prove his love for her. Then she'll understand that they should be together."

"He's a romantic," I say.

"Yeah, a romantic. He's got a Camaro convertible that some family member bought him because he convinced them that the car would lift his depression, and he plans to drive up there in his new Camaro, dressed up as a frog, and park outside and ribbit at her. There's only one problem. When he goes to the costume place they don't have the frog in stock. Instead, he rents a fox."

"A full-body fox?"

"Yes. So imagine this. A full-body brown fox, with headgear and everything, a long foxy muzzle probably, black eyes made of marbles, and brown-and-white pointy ears, driving a Camaro convertible up a lonely highway in rural Ontario. He parks outside this girl's house. He waits for her to come home."

"With the headgear on. I see it. She comes home. What happens?"

"Well, Jen says that the girl sees this nightmare and runs into the house. She locks the door, turns out all the lights."

"Rational," I say.

"But then a funny thing happens. He comes to the door. He says why he's there. That he loves her, and he doesn't even explain about the fox and the frog. Or maybe he tries to. But he's brought no clothes. He has to stay dressed as a fox."

"They embrace."

"Right, and then they make love in the back of the Camaro, with him still mostly in his fox costume."

"She gave in to him, even though she knew he was crazy. She was charmed. That's what's upsetting you. People will do that, though. Women will be charmed that way."

Though I can see that Bear hears me, he looks straight ahead. A young couple sits down next to us. They have gourmet sandwiches in white paper bags, and bottles of springwater. They spread napkins over their laps and begin to eat delicately.

"No. It's not that. It's that I'm sure it was Jen who slept with him. You know how sometimes somebody will tell you a story and they're saying it about somebody else, but you know it's them."

I turn and look carefully at Bear. I was about to laugh. But he has painted himself into a story corner, and my laughter won't help.

"Bear, you're saying that Jen told you a funny love story that shouldn't have made you think about anything except that people are strange, and now you're saying it's her story, that this happened to her?"

"There were clues, there were loads of clues. She described how the fur must have felt. Her parents have a cabin. She visited them there a couple of trips ago. This is how these things begin. She's trying to pull us apart. I can see it."

"Bear, how's your proposal going?"

"Terrible. It's going terrible. If I make it too popular Bachmann told me there's a chance he'll make me submit it to mainstream publishers, and then I'll have to write it really well, and then I get a job. If I make it too dull, Bachmann won't read it, it'll never get published by anybody, and I'll still have to get a job. God, the worst of all would be if I have to get a job teaching high school up in Toronto somewhere, so Jen can be close to her family. I hate Canada."

"You don't think these two things are related? Jen and your dissertation? The way you made up a story based on what you heard?"

There's a test shot on the white screen where the movie will play. A flash of blinding white, as big as a house. Then we get a blast of music, Ike and Tina Turner, "River Deep, Mountain High." People get ready to move to the music, but then there's silence again. A ripple of settling goes through the crowd. People begin to lie close to each other.

Bear says, "No, not at all. I didn't make up any story. I just think she had an affair. That's all."

"Don't you think this is just the worst summer?" the girl from the couple next to us says.

"Yeah," the guy says. "My office atmosphere has been like death for days now." She lays her head on his shoulder. He loosens his tie and closes his eyes.

"How's it going with Katherine?" Bear asks.

"Good, I think. It feels really good, but I've got to be careful, because she said no to me once already and I don't want to scare her off again now. She's involved with all this stuff, like she's got these abused women who call her at home and she takes their calls and it's wearing on her, so I'm trying not to be too—intense with her. I don't want to lose her again."

"You're lucky," Bear says. He is clenching and unclenching his hands.

"No, Bear," I say gently, "I'm not lucky. You know that."

"Right—Mike, I'm sorry. It's just that this feels bad, what Jen's doing."

I say, "Look, I'm sorry that you're feeling this thing. But I don't know if it's true."

"I know it is. You don't have to be sorry. Worse things have happened to you. Jen loves foxes, you know. We have fox stuffed animals on our couch. She has a fox calendar on the fridge."

"That did cross my mind," I say.

"She drinks her coffee out of a cup that says 'Foxy Lady.' Shit. She's my wife. I can't believe she'd do this to me. I'm thinking she reversed it—he showed up as a frog. He ribbited at her. They went to the car and he covered her in his green velvet. She figured she'd fool me. Let's go. I don't want to watch this fucking movie."

We get up and two women grab our seats and look very happy. They smile and thank us and I think that if we hadn't just gone through Bear's story, we might be able to smile back, and perhaps even linger for a moment. Instead, we walk out of the park and onto Forty-second Street, where the atmosphere is much less soft. We have to take different subways and so we just stand there. Bear is pale. He rolls down the sleeves of his beige shirt and buttons the cuffs.

"I'm sorry I told you," he says. He shakes his head.

"Why?"

"You must think it's a fantasy."

"No," I say. "I don't know if it's true, but either way, you heard the story, you think it's part of your life now. I don't think that's trivial at all."

"Thanks," Bear says. "I'm going to go home right now and go to sleep and not think about it."

"That's a good idea," I say.

12

There's a tow truck out by your dad's place. It looks like they're repossessing his Cadillac." It's Richard Ashton, my father's neighbor, on the phone.

I've been sitting at the table in my hotel room, rereading Gershom Scholem's introductory essay "The Idea of the Golem" and looking for ways to fill in the blank psychological spaces left by the clear exposition of his historical style. Calls like this only make my assignment more confounding. I would like to e-mail Weingarden this minute and admit failure: *Sorry, but this is a bad time for innovative research. Right now I've got to decide if I want to fight to own a Cadillac I never drove.* But I do not want to fail, or sidestep my dissertation. Somewhere Weingarden waits for me to make my work sing.

"Don't you think that's fast?" I ask Richard, because it's the only response I can find.

"The way I see it, he must have missed a few payments prior to leaving us."

"I guess I hadn't even thought about the car."

"Mike, things fall apart in the country pretty quickly. I can clean up around the house, but I haven't got the keys to get in. Is there anyone who's going to take care of it?"

"I'll take care of it. I have the keys."

Then Richard doesn't say anything. I know what he's thinking, though: that if it's me, I'd better hop to it. It's been several weeks now. You can't just let a house stand there.

"So no one has to sign off on a repossession?" I say.

"I don't think so. Sorry to be the one to spring this on you, but as I mentioned at the funeral, I could give you a hand with the things I know about. That is, I understand the system up here."

"Well, thanks—I haven't had a chance to look at my father's papers. But I'll be up there soon to go through it all. I'll call on you."

"The bank could repossess the house, Mike. You should be reading your mail very carefully."

It is a Tuesday in early June. And it's hot. I can imagine what it will be like up at his house. I'll have to sit with several binders full of papers dense with financial figures. I have to call the bank out there. I have to unsubscribe to his services and magazines. And if I don't do it myself, I have to get out there and pay yet again to have Edward Healy mow that huge expanse of lawn. But even as I build this list, I know I need to focus on the larger issue, of the existence of the house and what to do with it.

The extended family has not let my father's death go completely unnoticed. A cousin who lives outside L.A. sends three cards of condolence. A few very old relatives in retirement homes send their own scraggly sympathies, on which they've signed their names, probably with the help of a nurse. I save them in a shoe box.

On the phone, I tell Katherine about some of these things, about how it feels to have an ever-evolving loss. I do not mention how poorly my work is going. She tries not to talk about her own work, because it gets her so upset, so it has been relatively easy for me not to mention mine. I never discuss Weingarden, because that would bring up Adam, and I do not want to think about Adam. But Katherine is not afraid to hear about my father.

"Will you go up there with me?" I ask.

"Yes, of course I will," she says. "But let's be very careful. We'll behave toward each other in an extremely solicitous manner."

"We'll make love all the time," I say.

"And we'll be cool about the tragedy. We'll just cook and talk to each other and rest, okay?"

Katherine's weekend has been freed up because a case she'd been handling was suddenly resolved. A man who was being brought to court by his ex-wife on a variety of charges, including defaulting on payment of child support and assault, had died suddenly. After being laid off from his computer repair job a month before, he'd violated her order of protection. So the woman went to hide at her sister's house. He found out where she was. He tried to climb through the fourth-floor window of his ex-wife's sister's apartment, where his ex-wife was asleep with their child. But he lost his footing and fell from the window ledge and died. He'd had a revolver with him, Katherine said. He fell four stories and when he landed, the gun went off into his body. When she called her client to discuss what happened, she'd found her celebrating with her sister and the rest of her family.

"Spiderman finally lost his grip," she said.

Katherine tells me that she laughed too, and she was able to cancel their Friday court time and take the rest of the day off.

"We'll take it easy up there," I say. "You're the most perfect person to go up there with me."

"Right now I feel like I can handle it," she says.

Katherine has borrowed an old white Saab from a coworker. We're lucky to have the car, since it will save us train fare. But there's a downside; the electrical system isn't working well, so the windows go up and down by themselves, and the stereo system and the lights cut out occasionally.

I drive fast. There isn't much traffic, though it is Friday evening. We hold hands over the gearshift.

"I haven't been in the house since the day after the funeral," I say. "But the cleaners really cleaned it. I mean, it will probably smell good, in a sort of antiseptic way. Those cleaners were amaz-ing."

"Trauma Scene Restoration?" Katherine says.

"Yes, that was them. You know—of course you know about that sort of thing."

"I do. If you can afford it, that's who you get." She goes quiet for a moment. Then she says, "Luckily, old houses tend to revert and smell like themselves."

She plays with my ear and the hair at the back of my neck. She stretches into the backseat and comes back with some purple grapes. My window goes down suddenly and I take in a great burst of the thick evening air. I love to watch her stretch and move. She's in a white button-down shirt and light blue cotton pants that em-phasize the wonderful expanse of her hips.

"Open your mouth," she says. She feeds me grapes, one at a time. She runs her fingers over my bottom lip and then she kisses me there.

"It will be fine," she says. "You're handling all of this extremely well."

I do not point out that I'm not, in fact, handling it at all. We're acting as if we're on a weekend getaway, when I should be busy clearing up my father's estate. That's self-deception, not discipline.

I veer into the slow lane and drift. She comes closer and kisses my jaw, puts her tongue to my neck. I slip my hand into her shirt, beneath her bra, and run my fingers over her breasts.

"Don't stop doing that," she says.

Katherine drops her overstuffed bag near the entranceway. She walks over to the doors to the back porch and unlocks them, but then she doesn't go out. I stand there and look out with her. When I left here I took two Adirondack chairs and faced them down toward the stream. There's a round wooden table in another area, surrounded by four steel chairs. A furled umbrella and a mildewed American flag are propped up against a round, old-style barbecue that resembles a giant gum ball and is painted safety hazard red.

"Nice," she says, and I can feel how she is trying to sound light. But then she turns and bends in toward me, and I hold her.

We walk upstairs and stand in each of the doorways of the three bedrooms. We go down to the pantry off the kitchen and look at the store of canned goods. There's nothing in the fridge but a jug of water, a few bottles of lime-flavored seltzer, and ketchup. She takes out the water.

"Pretragedy jug?" she asks. I nod. It is, probably.

"Okay for me to drink?" she asks as she tilts it back. I don't know whether to be grateful, aghast, or stunned at how cool she can be about all of this. I take the jug and drink too.

"If we sleep in my father's bed—are you comfortable with that?" I ask. "If we're in it, we'll think less about it. It can't haunt us if we're right there."

"Mike—I've seen so much worse. I feel safe with you. Really, this is no problem for me."

Upstairs, when we have settled in, we take off each other's clothes. Unfortunately, this room still smells like loose change, so I open a window. Brisk air comes in off the field. There isn't any moonlight. She is behind me and I reach out and run a hand over her belly, which feels so warm. We go to the bed. The sheets are flannel, a new set that the cleaners must have found somewhere. They are pebbled and white. Because the air is so cool after Manhattan, we are cold enough to move quickly.

By now I am ready to claim knowledge of her body, her round chunk of ass, firm belly, thick thighs, her bright breasts and pink nipples. We fuck with a hand on each other's necks, gyrating. She's on top of me and she's got her other hand on her pussy, and so do I. Both of us are rubbing at it, and we're extremely verbal, talking through all this stumble-fucking. Suddenly she lies down, urges me to roll onto her.

"Pull my hair back," she says, "so I can't get free of you."

"I'm holding you down," I say. "I won't ever let you go."

And she smiles. Her eyes go wide, and the harder I press into her, the more stunned she becomes, until she feels softer than I remember her. And then she begins to talk, and her voice is high and sweet. Again and again she tells me that she wants to be with me forever and she wants to marry me. Nothing has ever excited me more. She slows me down and we try hard to come together, when we're just exactly ready.

Afterward, we're famished because all we've eaten today is grapes. So, in the midst of the fuzzy-headed feeling our empty stomachs create, we go ahead and do it all over again.

"Mike, I'm not joking about any of this—we get through this difficult summer, we hold tight, and then I really want to be with you. Mike?" We throw off the sheets. She curls around me tightly and there is nothing I can think of but her.

"Yes?"

"It's too early and this could be a mistake and I shouldn't say it, but I love you, Mike."

"I love you, Katherine."

"Say it again," she says.

"I love you, Katherine. I love you so much. We get through this summer and we will be together. I swear. I'm the luckiest person in the world to have found you. Now you."

"I love you, Mike Zabusky. I want to have children with you."

"It's too fast," I say. I watch the quick rises and falls of her chest.

"I know. It is too fast."

"Now you say it again," I say. She laughs.

"You do everything to me," she says.

We are lying on our backs. I open and close my eyes, as if all of this will disappear and too suddenly I'll be back in New York, wandering the streets, mourning the loss of her, and plotting to get her back again. I don't like this, but I feel it strongly, that I'm losing her, even though she is right next to me and we are touching each other.

"Why did you end it with me, way back, right when we got started?" I ask.

"I was afraid," she says, in a voice that sounds overused and abstracted.

"Will you try to end it again?"

"I don't think so," she says. "I hope not. I don't like it when I'm cowardly either. But of course, it also depends on you."

She gets up and goes into the bathroom.

"I don't want you to end it again," I say, but I don't think she can hear me.

"We should really use some protection," she says. "It's ridiculous of us not to. From now on I'm going to remember to put in my diaphragm."

She closes the bathroom door. We still have some intimacy cloaks; we're still not near using a toilet with both of us in the same room together. Though I've been that way immediately with other women, and I don't doubt that she's been that way with other men. And I love her so much. I lie in bed. I hate that she's been with other men. But I hate this childish thought just as much. I'm too old for it and it is stupid but it feels fitting just now, to cut the feeling of being in love with the distance that just a little anger brings.

"I'm good with nothing, just pulling out of you," I say.

"Well, it isn't safe. I know we've been doing it that way, but we can't anymore. It's foolish of me. Anyway—my God! This tub is fantastic!"

She lets the door open. There's a little hallway with closets built into it between the big bedroom and the master bath, and she's vivid in the light that surrounds her. She's arched over the bathtub, which is round and probably just big enough for two if we scrunch up a bit. I get up and go to her, hard dick flapping.

"Please, I'm exhausted, you should let me bathe alone," she says.

She's already got the water going. The room begins to fill with steam. She finds the bath salts, the bubble bath, other things left over in a corner of the bathroom closet that must be from Sarah Jane because there is no way my father would buy such stuff. We fill the tub together, until bubbles are floating in the air.

The tub is in a bowed-out space in the wall, not dissimilar to the bay window in Katherine's bedroom. There are three windows, which look out on the stars and the field and the stream. Weeks ago, during the time of the funeral, when I paced this house, I don't think I used this bathroom at all. It doesn't smell like my father in here. Everything smells like bath soap and Katherine.

"I'll take a shower," I say. "I'll watch you from there."

I stand in the glass shower stall, blast my skin with hot water, and I watch her in the bath. I soap myself up and then wash off, begin to masturbate and then fight to stop, because, after all, we've just had sex. But she's amazing to look at and I find that I can't stop.

I get out of the shower and find a brown towel that I remember using when I was small. My father liked the scratch of old towels and this is how I learned to dry off, by taking a pummeling that turned me bright red and glowing and dry, all over, by his hand. I'm happy that he taught me how to do such a good job. Vigorous. Vigor, vigor! That's what he'd say, and I said it with him.

I drop to my knees and put my head close to Katherine's. Steam rises around our heads. She stands after a while, and we both watch the water drip down her. I find a new rose-colored towel and I wrap it around her. She wouldn't like the old towels. As I rub her, we hear my stomach rumble.

Katherine finds bathrobes on a low shelf and we put them on. They must have been presents that my father didn't like, because they are still in gift boxes. We go downstairs and heat up cans of minestrone soup. We eat, and drink short glasses of scotch at the dining room table. She takes a candle out of a drawer and lights it.

"Your father. You're thinking about him?"

"No. I'm using how incredible I feel with you to avoid thinking about him, if it's okay with you."

"But doesn't it hurt beyond your ability to control it?"

"Sure it does, yes. But I can still try."

The scotch is Glenmorangie, and it tastes very fine. For a man who didn't care for drink, my father kept quite a lot of high-quality alcohol in the house.

"I think that would make you emotionally duplicitous," she says. She finishes her scotch.

"Don't put the intensity of your grief for him into the love you've just found for me," she says. "I wouldn't like it if you chose to play this that way."

13

In the car this morning, we can't get the windows to go down. The vents spew out a warm perfumed air tinged with gray steam.

"It's *hot*," I say. "I hope this air isn't the end of us."

"I know. The electrical system in this car *sucks*." Katherine laughs. I drive faster. We're desperate to get out of this oven car and in front of some eggs because our bodies are empty, because of how stiff we are from sex, how sore. We come into Roosevelt, and Crescent Grange is right in front of us. There's parking in back and I pull in. The car feels as if it's been chugged to death.

"Do you like these sneakers?" she asks. I look at her. She's wearing a pink tank top and jeans shorts that are tight around her hips. Her sneakers are silvery and new. They look like model spaceships from the fifties.

"Yes," I say.

"They're Pumas—God, I love German design—how precise it is. Sometimes I wonder what it'd be like to live there. Don't they make me look like I'm going to float away? I love that. Aren't you famished?" she asks. "Aren't you ready to eat?"

"I am. You should know that my dad went out with the woman who runs this place," I say.

"What's her name?"

"Sarah Jane Caldwell. We may see her. She's blond and she's about forty."

We get out of the car and stand in the sunshine. She puts her arms back and stretches high, so her shirt rides up and her white belly glows in the sun. She looks so happy that I imitate her.

"Well, this place is a little folksy," Katherine says when we are inside.

"It is, isn't it?"

On the walls there are framed pictures of every sort of crescent but the crescent moon. If Sarah Jane chose the images, she was most intrigued by the circumstantial crescent, created by a half-opened can, by gouged wood, a cut fingernail. There are pictures of these things placed among simpler crescents, some painted, others drawn or carved. Many of the people who are here look as if they just came up from the city. At one of the larger tables, we hear a loud discussion of the best stocks to buy now—the cheapest ones, the fire-sale bargains.

"I guess the correction has leaked into everything," I say.

"Maybe," she says, "but we recover so quickly these days. Pretty soon everybody's going to act as if nothing happened."

Though I can feel my face flush, I do not remind her that because of my father, I will never feel as if nothing happened. I sift through my pockets, which are heavy with his quarters.

We sit down at a small table near the front windows, directly in the sunlight. A waitress who might be seventeen or even younger comes and gives us menus. Katherine doesn't open hers. Instead she waves her arms and beckons the waitress to come closer.

The waitress stays where she is. She's got honey-colored hair, lighter than Katherine's, and she, too, is wearing a tank top. But hers is blue and she is the girl I sat next to on the train, who woke me up. We recognize each other at about the same time.

"Give me a spinach and cheddar cheese omelet, home fries,

bacon, a large fresh-squeezed orange juice, a blueberry muffin, lots of different kinds of jams, and coffee, please," Katherine says. The waitress nods. She doesn't write any of this down.

"I'd like the same, only make my omelet with chives," I say. The waitress goes away and Katherine screws up her nose at me. I think that heat freckles may have grown on the bridge of her nose on the way over. They are very pretty. When I reach out to touch the freckles, she grabs my hand and bites down.

"I hate chives," she says. "They're so thin. Listen"—she's angled over, not whispering, just speaking close—"you see how the waitress is a teenage girl? You think I should go to the bathroom and pull her aside and talk to her about how good the sex gets, once you get through all that lousy high school car-and-bushes sex, and all that fraught-with-meaning college sex, and drunken sex, and then early-twenties pretend-adult sex, and just—you know—all the sex you've got to have before you get to where we are, having the great sex that we're having now? You know what I'm talking about, all the obnoxious fucking that went before?"

"Jesus, Katherine—what if you tell her all that and scare her off sex entirely?" I say.

Alexis used to talk about fucking. I didn't like it then, either. But now this feeling is not like what it was when I was young. Then, it threatened to destroy me. Now, it only holds the discomfort of a half-remembered threat that was never entirely carried out. So maybe I don't care so much about Katherine and all the sex she had before. I just hope she wasn't hurt too badly. But she's okay now. She's here, right in front of me.

Katherine flaps her hand, waves what she said away.

"Oh, I just say that sort of thing when I see a teenager who reminds me of my sister. I want them to be a little cynical, so they don't try anything stupid. Because it's just so dangerous to cultivate innocence. I hate it, that's all. I absolutely despise it because it ruins everything, and so when I see a girl like that, a girl who probably is innocent, well, I want to strip her of that quality, fast, so she'll—so she'll survive, I guess. And maybe it's just nervousness, talking stupidly sexual like that—I didn't mean to shut you down. I'm sorry. It's just me fighting with me. I know it makes some men feel funny."

"I understand—I know how dangerous innocence can be," I say.

"Do you?" she says—and she smiles the smile that is now familiar to me, the open smile that does not involve her eyes and only says, I know you're lying, or I know you can't handle what you're saying, but it's okay, I do that too.

"Sure," I say. "I know everybody is using everybody. But I bet the waitress knows it too, probably far better than me."

"Well, I doubt you dislike innocence as much as I do, but this is still a nice surprise," Katherine says.

"A good one?" I ask.

"Sort of, yes," she says. "I think that you don't want anyone to be hurt, sexually or otherwise. This makes sense after what's happened." She smiles at me, but then she is quiet.

I tell her about Bear and Jen, and how Bear suspects that Jen slept with a man in a costume in Canada.

"It's too much about him," she says.

"About who?"

"Bear, your friend. Think about Jen. She's married, she's in love. She's finished with that sort of thing, and she's not blasé enough to destroy what she built, not yet. Bear's not thinking about Jen, about what she wants. He's only thinking about himself, and he's the problem. Remember, it's my job to hear this kind of thing. You know how else I know?"

"How?" I ask.

"Because of the way you told the story. It's like you were both indulging in something. You're suspicious in the same way, and you're both wrong," and she looks down and away from me, and smiles to herself.

"It's a relief that you're sure," I say. I reach forward and so does she, and we begin to kiss across the table. We stop only when our waitress arrives with coffee and juice. Katherine drinks her juice off with one hand on the glass and the other raised, willing the waitress to wait. We're both still, watching Katherine glug her juice. She hands the glass back.

"Give me another," she says. Now the young waitress is amused, half smiling and happy to take care of Katherine. I think she likes that our recognition of each other has become a secret between us.

"The hours with you seem to have depleted my store of vitamin C. Your father's girlfriend. You think she's hiding from us?"

"I don't know. But she's why I've brought us here. I do want to see her."

We look around then, but there is no sign of her. We stuff ourselves full. There's granola and yogurt in little bowls that I suspect may have been delivered only to us. There are big plates piled high with melon, strawberries, blueberries, blackberries—and nobody else has them. Our omelets are impossibly pretty, all bright and shiny with butter. And then, when it is over, there is no bill. Our waitress only smiles at Katherine and shakes her head at us. We tip her our handfuls of quarters.

"She must have seen us," I say. "I don't know why she doesn't come out."

But Katherine is so full she cannot talk. I look around while we make our way to the door. We stand on the thin strip of curb outside Crescent Grange. Katherine is crouched down, hands on knees, gasping.

"It was so much," she says. "Already too much for one day."

The screen door to the restaurant opens and we look up the steps.

Sarah Jane comes out. She is dressed in chef's clothes, a loose-fitting pair of white overalls, green rubber clogs, and a T-shirt with the name of her restaurant on the front. Her yellow hair is pulled back. As she comes down the steps she pulls a white sweatband off her forehead and drops it into her overall pocket.

She says, "Hello, Mike. I'm glad you came by."

"Sure," I say, "thanks so much for brunch. It was wonderful. Really. This is Katherine Staresina. Katherine, this is Sarah Jane Caldwell."

Sarah Jane smiles briefly at Katherine.

"We should find some time to talk," Sarah Jane says to me.

"Yes. I'm—I'll be up here again after this weekend, I think."

"Well, you should call me then. Call me here."

"Yes," I say. "I will."

"You asked to talk, Mike," Sarah Jane says.

"So then he'll call you—he just said he would," Katherine says, and her voice is commanding. I turn and she is suddenly taller than she was a moment ago. The heat freckles on her nose pulse in the light. Sarah Jane looks at her.

"Then he will," Sarah Jane says. "That's settled."

"Thanks for brunch, again," I say.

"See you soon," she says. As she goes back up the stairs, into her restaurant, she carefully replaces her headband and does not turn around.

We get into our nightmare car. It's so hot inside that the rubber on the dashboard is blistering and the gearshift is untouchable.

"She didn't betray much emotion," I say.

Katherine, in the passenger seat, pushes the button for the windows again and again. Nothing happens. Her head drops back in agony.

"You might just say she's cold," she says. "I didn't like her. Not at all."

"I don't either, but tell me why you got whatever you got so fast," I say.

I direct us back toward my father's house and I go as fast as the curving roads will allow.

"I had this feeling from her," she says, "that she was stunted somehow, shut down. And now, of course, I feel kind of nauseated. God, this car is awful! Jesus, find somewhere to pull off and we'll just walk, this is terrible."

She's right—the car is unbearable. I'm driving with only the tips of my fingers on the steering wheel.

"Let's just get us home. She does make a good omelet."

"That's not enough," Katherine says.

I do recognize that Sarah Jane was the one who came down to us. She is reaching out. She is fighting something off and she is trying to be warm.

"Maybe she's Catholic, like you, and there was some vibe you got off her?" I ask. My experience has been that Catholics, women like Sarah Jane, they are paralyzed by a far worse kind of guilt than any Jew I've ever met. Though I don't actually know if she's Catholic.

"What? The guilt vibe? There's always that. But I spoke up because she was acting like she'd broken up with you. I found her movements hostile. I can't imagine what the hell she did with your father."

"It was probably more what he did to her." I shake my head at all I don't know. "Anyway, soon enough she's going to have to tell me about how she was with him. I don't expect the truth, exactly, but I want some explanation."

"Yes," Katherine says, "people will twist the story of what happened within hours of an event. I see that all the time. And wasn't he violent? Didn't you say he was? Throw violence in there and nobody can remember anything right. Hit somebody, and I swear to God, after that, everything is fiction."

"Really," I say.

"No, not really, but that's the sort of thing we say at my office. It lightens the day."

"I don't think my father hit her," I say.

We keep driving, past the main entrance to Bard, where I was only a few weeks ago. We'll be home in just a few minutes. We'll have to shower. I want to wash this heat off both of us.

"No," Katherine says, "when I think about what he did—one thing about violent people is that they're prone to turn their violence inward, on themselves. I don't think he hit her either."

We pull into the driveway and stop the car. It's so hot that after we open the doors, all we can do is step out and lie down on the grass to the left of the driveway. Katherine covers her eyes against the sun.

"And anyway, I didn't think your kind of Jews hit people," she says.

"Yeah, I used to think that too. I also used to think that they didn't kill themselves. And now I know different."

14

I stand in the attic, where I turn on a light that hangs just above the steps. It is a half-finished space with a dusty wood floor. There are dormer windows, three on each side. I perch in front of one window and look out. The view is quite wonderful, especially in the direction of Roosevelt's main street, where tiny lines of bright white lights can be seen in the dusk. Tree branches that are far closer sweep across the lights and make them glitter.

I reach out then and turn on another light by pulling on a piece of string that swings from a chain. In this new light, a heap of broken furniture becomes visible. I step toward the pile. Smashed chairs with torn caning lie flat against the floor. There are small tables too, with their legs ripped off and their tops hacked in pieces. I recognize a cherry desk from our old apartment that must have been broken down with the butt of an axe. Sarah Jane knew what she was talking about. The fact that this compulsion followed him here explains why the rooms downstairs are so sparsely furnished now. He was tearing apart what filled the house.

I stare at the pile and then I understand: this pile is Sarah Jane's work. Josie must have discovered him in a house filled with broken furniture. Sarah Jane came in and saw all of this too, and there wasn't time to cart it away. So she brought it up here. I pick up a spindly chair leg and bang it against a piece of that old desk. Then I start smacking the leg against a beam in the roof, and finally, after I've been banging for a while and I can see where I'm cutting into the beam with the sharp edge of the weak leg, the wood pops and breaks in two in my hand. It feels good, but not like burying him did. You asshole, I think, getting off on smashing wood.

This winter, I will chop up his mess into smaller pieces and place them over kindling. Katherine and I will make fires in the living room fireplace on a sleepy Saturday night after dinner. I lock the attic door tight and take the key when I leave. Katherine hates men who tear things apart. There's no reason to rush to reveal to her that I'm the son of that kind of man.

Back downstairs, I pass through the living room, where she is on the phone. She must be talking to Leah. She is lying on the couch with her legs up in the air, and she is laughing. I kiss behind her knee when I walk by and she motions with her chin: kiss again there, kiss behind the other knee too. And I do, and I nuzzle between her legs and she smells good, and then she's crushing my head between her thighs and giggling and pushing me away.

"What was that noise?" she asks.

"Oh," I say, "I was just trying to build something."

I go into his study and sit behind his desk. If the Golem were here I would order it to take me outside and play catch until I was totally exhausted. It would dance me around the kitchen and keep me from looking in at Katherine again. If the Golem were here, he'd help me do something with all that broken furniture.

I listen to Katherine saying no, no, no, over and again, and I must be occupied and not listening so I open the middle drawer in front of me and find several small keys, which I use to open the old oak file cabinets that sit to my left. The drawers spring open. This is where all the files are neatly kept.

I suspect an accountant could divine most of what's been mishandled in these files in a long afternoon. And I may hire one, since I cannot imagine doing this work myself. A sleeping life kept in a cabinet. Rows of yellow files hang one behind the other. Each one is labeled: *Cadillac, Roosevelt house, Life ins.* (I do pull this one out. He'd collected a folder full of pamphlets with different plans, and he'd made little checks on the ones he liked—but he hadn't chosen a policy, not just yet. Too late. I put it back.) *Health ins., Property taxes, Personal taxes, Deductions, Expenses.*

In another cabinet, everything is financial. There is *Asherberg & Co., Zabusky Personal Growth Fund, Asherberg/Zabusky Aggressive Growth,* and even a file with the title *Big Gambles,* written in small blue letters. I keep tugging these files out and then slipping them back. I want somebody with me when I go through all of this. Leonora or an assistant of hers, somebody who's trained in these matters, so I don't make errors that I won't even realize I've made. I'm sure if I reapproach Leonora with such a request, she'll forgive me for my outburst at her library dinner, because she'll appreciate my interest. Unless there is no money here. Unless, somehow, he blew through everything he had and there's no significance to these files. If that's the case, then I don't need to learn what happened. I can weave together my own set of explanations. But I need ingredients if I'm going to attach a resolution to the end of his life.

In another cabinet there are files with people's names. *Leonora, Edward, Wilma, Liz, Mike, Sarah Jane.* Me. I go ahead and pull me out, and I'm thick and I decide that no, it would be best not to go through me tonight, or perhaps ever, when Katherine comes in.

"Was that Leah?" I ask.

"No, that was Kristin, this client I stayed friends with—she's working as a hairdresser and she's got these funny stories about it. It's not very savvy of me to maintain these friendships, but I can't help it. Anyway, what are you doing?"

"I'm holding a folder that is called me," I say.

She comes behind the desk and stands behind my chair. I still have the folder in my hands. She slips into my lap and touches the folder with her pinky.

"Go slow here," she says. We turn together, in his chair, and I put my folder and Sarah Jane's on his desk. I stop and she looks around at me.

She says, "When we're old together, I don't want you to keep a file on me."

"I already started a file on you," I say, "full of things I thought about you that were wrong."

"Too late then, my love."

"Too late." I can feel her on me, and then, as I pull the Sarah Jane file toward us, I feel her shift.

"You're joking, aren't you?" she asks. "About the file?"

"Of course I am. Are you sure you want to do this with me?"

"You know what? Let's open you first."

So we do. There are pictures of me from when I was growing up. One picture is of me and my high-school girlfriend, Isabelle Meyerowitz, taken during the summer after junior year, standing in the kitchen looking very guilty. My mother must have taken it. Katherine looks at Isabelle but she doesn't say anything. Then there are a few book and music reviews I wrote for free papers in Chicago right after college. Next are some photos taken during my marriage, and a card from Exodus Travel. There's too much to take in and not enough to really accept here, as me, and I think Katherine must know this, because she chooses not to ask about any of it.

Meanwhile Sarah Jane is sitting right there. She is who we need to see. So I close my folder and push it to the edge of the desk. But Katherine pulls my mother from the cabinet, and so we look at divorce papers, or a copy of them. We spread out several photographs of her, from all through their marriage. We take a little extra time to look at the picture of her when she was about our age. She is staring out a window, and she looks as if she's listening, probably to my father.

"I haven't heard you talk about her," Katherine says. I shrug my shoulders.

"She's in California. She's okay, she looks different now, not just older, but like a different person. She really doesn't want to be involved with all of this, with him."

And so we close my mother. And we look at Sarah Jane, unopened and certainly the heaviest and freshest of any of the files.

"Open it," Katherine says.

The first thing we see is a sheet of paper. At the top, in small blue handwriting, it says: "Dear Sarah Jane, Please forgive me. I love you." Besides that, it is blank.

"Oh shit," I say. And I put my hand over the rest of the papers. Katherine does not know what to do. She can't force me to look at all this, but clearly she's curious, and so am I. I can hear her breathing.

"Come on, Mike," she says, "that could be anything. Don't be an amateur detective. Don't make up a story to explain what you see. Just look and let the papers be what they are. It might help. It could."

I turn to her. "Yeah, what if it says, 'I'll kill you if you leave me'? Or, 'I'm sorry I beat you up'? Then what?"

"I don't think he's going to say that here," she says.

"You're saying that he might have said it elsewhere."

We keep going. There's a menu from Crescent Grange, and a good review from the *Hudson Valley Times*. Then a letter from her. "Jeff, here's the recipe. I do believe that you'll take the time to make it right. I shouldn't have laughed at you. I really do believe it." It's a recipe for a roast that takes a day to cook.

"She was wrong—he wouldn't take the time," I say.

The next page is a small watercolor sketch of a few pieces of fruit. It is inscribed: "To Jeff, welcome to my town, from Sarah Jane."

"None of this is in order," I say.

There are pictures of her, and they're terrible pictures, so he must have taken them. She's smiling in a few of them, but in others she looks like she'd rather be busy doing something and not simply standing still. The more we look, the more we can feel her, and it's making me upset. Because I can't feel him, only her.

"I hope he didn't do anything too terrible—to her, I mean," Katherine says.

"Or her to him, don't forget," I say.

"If that's all that's in there, then it's okay," she says. I dig around then, and I hope she's right. There are only a few more letters, written in his tiny, cramped handwriting. They are all fairly short.

"I don't know what I'll do without you, but I can see why you don't want this." "I'm very hurt." "Had I known that you were not serious, I would not have approached you." "I'm sorry that I got so upset." "I'm sorry that I got you so upset."

"What a lousy writer," I say.

"You were more concise," she says.

"Yeah—wait, Katherine. I didn't know about any of this. I barely ever saw him. What I could tell you about him, it isn't more than you're learning right here. It looks like what she told me is true, though, that he lost control of the relationship, and they broke up. Hey, this is just like, this is like what you do, building a case."

"But we're talking about your father," she says. Her arm is cold against the nape of my neck.

"So?" I ask. There are more letters and I keep going through them, but the tone is the same, and it's difficult to tell if he sent them, or if these are copies, or drafts, or notes to himself, or just what they are.

"We're talking about your father," she says. "And it looks a whole lot worse than them breaking up. But clearly, you don't want to see that."

"But you told me not to make up a story to explain what happened here," I say.

"Fine," Katherine says. "I did say that, but I didn't think we'd see notes like these. Now I understand why you don't want to figure out anything at all."

She walks out of the room before I close the file. I take a few more minutes and I try to replace everything just as it was, with that first note on top.

"There's more here," I say. But she's gone into the kitchen and she doesn't answer.

———

Sunday, late afternoon, and we're standing in his bedroom. We have to get back because she has a full workday tomorrow and she needs to return the car.

"Why don't you leave some of your stuff?" I say. "We can come out next weekend."

She looks at me. I pull my shorts from my bag, a pair of boxers, some socks, and I drop them into the bottom drawer of a bureau. She bites her lower lip. She's got her hair in a ponytail, with long strands running behind her ears.

"I don't know," she says. She grips her messy bag and absently pushes her things down into it.

"It's okay," I say. I'm happy that I'm comfortable enough in my father's house to leave my own things there.

"I don't even know about next weekend. I'd better not."

"Okay," I say. I take my bag and put it back in my father's closet. I just drop it on the floor in there.

I wash the sheets that we used. I sweep the crumbs from the kitchen countertops. I lock all the windows and doors. I take the insurance files and the Asherberg & Co. files to the car, and I take a white plastic container full of Zip disks too, because I've made copies of everything on his hard drive, all the e-mail, all the financial programs, everything. I'm going to read it all.

It's after eight when we leave and I'm behind her as she sets her bag on the backseat. I can't help it. I press against her back. She pulls my hands to her breasts. Slowly, I unbutton her pants and pull them down, while she is faced away from me. We have sex in the driveway, in the dusk, up against the hood of the car.

All the way to Manhattan, the windows are permanently at half-mast. The air grows more and more cold. She shivers and I take off my red shirt and slip it over her shoulders. We've got to return the car to a lot off the West Side Highway and we've got to get the windows up. And all of this is made harder by the fact that we can barely stay awake.

"I can't believe how tired I am," I say.

"I can," she says. "Don't be grumpy. Mike, we learned a lot."

"I suppose," I say. "I'd feel better if the damned windows would go up." And then I press the lever and they do go up, as if they were never broken. When we arrive I find that it is difficult for me to get our things out of the back, because my hands are shaking. I pick up her heavy bag and I am delicate when I place it in her hands.

"Thank you," she says.

"Yeah," I say.

"Oh, Mike," she says. But then she doesn't say anything more and we begin to walk. We have to take different subways home from the lot, and she says we should talk toward the end of the week.

"Would it be okay if I called you later?" I ask. She is walking faster than I am, with her head bent down, and she does not turn to me.

"No, I can't talk to you tonight," she says. "I have too many things I have to do."

What do you have to do tonight? I wonder. Who do you have to see? But I think that if I asked, she'd have no choice but to pull farther away from me.

"Anyway," she says, "you can't have time for me just now." She gestures toward the bag in my hand that's filled with my father's files and disks. She says, "You've got plenty of research to keep you busy."

Before I can object, she ducks down into the subway.

15

J en, it's good to see you," I say.

Jen smiles and the corners of her eyes turn down. She's always been cute. I kiss her on the cheek. She is much shorter than Bear or me, but she moves quickly and gestures with her hands a lot, so she seems big. Bear is wearing light green Skechers and black pants. I know how much Jen is bothered by his poor style of dress.

Bear shifts his feet. "I guess we haven't seen you in a while," he says.

"And I missed my big old grouchy bear," I say.

Bear laughs and claps me on the back. He is always lighter when he is with Jen. He just loves her so much. I think about what Katherine said and it sounds even more right to me.

We stand in the doorway of the Old Walls bar, which is a place that I'd like to think only the three of us know about, tucked in among the Indian restaurants on Lexington Avenue in the twenties. Some time has passed since my father died, so it's become appropriate for me to see people, even if in this early stage we're all aware that they're only helping me to ape normality, so that I may look forward to a time when going out to dinner doesn't seem so odd.

We settle into a dark booth in the back room. I sit back and let the base of my skull rest on the oily wood. I'm in new blue jeans and a worn navy blue business shirt that belonged to my father. I'm carrying only my wallet and a pen. I feel light. Casual.

"Is your new girlfriend meeting us?" Jen asks.

"No," I say—and then a tremor comes over my face, imperceptible, I hope, but there. I reach for my handkerchief and run it over my forehead quickly, to cover it up. It suddenly feels to me as if Katherine was wrong and Bear was right. Jen has been sleeping with someone else. She seems quite calm, even radiant, and Bear is smiling.

"Katherine had to go to a dinner party," I say, "but she did say that she can't wait to meet you two. We should set something up."

Maybe she's confessed and Bear has forgiven her. He's been busy and he's forgotten to tell me. And now they're working through it. Or maybe I am projecting, because I don't know where Katherine is. I called her office today but she wasn't there. A woman who was willing to take a message said she might be in court. The reason I've said that she's at a dinner party is that very often she is at a dinner party. She's rarely specific with me about where she is, as she doesn't like the idea of me trying to keep track of her movements. And though we've talked, I haven't seen her since the weekend. It's been more than a few days. It's been a week. She's been overwhelmed with work and then she went away this past weekend with Leah, up to someone's house in New England.

"I'm sorry about your father," Jen says. She has on a string of pearls and she tugs at them while she looks at me.

"Thank you." I smile at her and then I smile at Bear. We order pints of beer from a waiter, and he brings them swiftly to the table.

"Look, Mike, Bear tells me that you haven't dealt with the insurance companies. I understand that, and you probably have a few more weeks of grace, assuming that there were no disputes with the police. But you really need to address all of this. You should check in both his health and house policies for catastrophe compensation, since this surely was a catastrophe. You could come out of this okay, you know."

"Jen—" I'm a bit shocked, but clearly, Bear has put her up to this. I have told him how slowly I'm working, how my dad feels like my dissertation. What controlled him? Who made him do this thing? At night I sit up and read his files and during the day I read everything I promised Weingarden I would read, and I'm working slowly, because when I come out with an answer, I want it to be the right one.

"Was there a will?" Jen asks. "Have you and your mother checked on that? Sometimes those things are left over from first marriages. And it might still stand."

I can imagine how it is easier for her to act professionally, especially if she even suspects that I know about her and the fox, which is certainly comical, but it's also suddenly more conceivable because it feels like a joke. If her infidelity were less unreal, she would never have hinted at it. In many ways, only a very serious person would do something as ludicrous as succumb to a fox in a Camaro convertible.

"My mother. She doesn't really have to deal with any of this, so I guess she just hasn't. We've talked quite a bit, but she never mentioned a will. And I haven't seen one. He didn't have life insurance either. I know that."

"Come on, he probably did, attached to his health policy. Do you want me to have a look at his files? I can help you and I'm happy to, whenever you want, but the sooner the better."

"Thank you, Jen. I suppose I do want that," I say. Though I had not thought that I did. "You two should come up to the house and we can make a weekend of it."

But when I smile across at them, they only look back at me blankly. And it's apparent that no, they're in no rush to come and barbecue at my father's house.

"Is it your house now?" Jen asks.

"I don't know," I say.

"You could be bankrupting yourself and not even know it.

Mike, this isn't a joke. There's a mortgage, certainly, and the bank could foreclose on the house. You'd lose all that equity. If you're not careful you could be in debt for the rest of your life."

"Really? Jesus, Jen, how could that happen? I haven't got any money. I pay the hotel every two weeks right out of my grant. That's all I've got. I don't make phone calls. If I'm hungry, I cook rice. The way I see it, Old Granite can take the house. There's nothing I can do. I'm already bankrupt."

"You should listen to Jen," Bear says. "There are ways out of this."

"With investors, there's always some money somewhere," Jen says.

"Look, I've been through his papers. My father died broke. There wasn't anything to leverage against. I don't know how big the mortgage is, or if he was about to pay it off, or whatever. He did have some stocks, but that's it. I've just been a little slow about the house. That's all."

"We're going to have to work on this," Jen says. She shakes her head. Our waiter brings food to the table and Jen excuses herself to wash her hands. I sit there, slumped down, no longer hungry for my cheeseburger.

Bear eats some fries. He says, "She didn't do it, Mike, I'm sure. Forget what I said in Bryant Park. She didn't do anything with anybody."

I look up at him. He looks so happy, even serene.

"How do you know?" I'm immediately sorry I have asked. If he says she didn't, then that should be enough. I have no right to ask him how he knows. I must own that house, I realize. I must. That house is my house. I cannot allow any other resolution, and that must be why I haven't started in on the problem. I don't even love the house. I just want it. I want to live there and make it right.

"The guy called us at home," Bear says. "I spoke to him. He sounded just as nuts as she said."

"He called and so you figure he wasn't with her? That was your conclusion?" And again I have spoken before I could think.

"It seemed logical, sure," he says. "He wouldn't call if they'd been together. Of course he wouldn't. That's madness."

"But you just said that he was nuts," and I'm whispering. If this stupid thing between them really did happen, then a lot of other stories could go wrong. I can barely keep myself in the booth, so badly do I want to call Katherine on her cell, find where she is, and run to her, ask her to stay with me once again. But an obsessive boyfriend who interrupts a dinner party will not keep her near. So instead, I put the cheeseburger in my mouth and bite down. It's too hot, so I swallow it. I might as well have opened my mouth and thrown in a coal.

Jen comes back from the bathroom. She sits down and tears into her chicken Caesar salad. Bear continues to look at me, and then he smiles. It's a sudden, cracked smile.

"Is yours good?" Jen asks him.

"Yes, it's good," he says. He's staring at me.

"There should be organizations that take care of these guys who go out and invest alone like your father did," Jen says. She cuts a piece of lettuce in half and nods to herself.

"Come on, those are rich guys," Bear says. "They don't need our altruism. Now that they've got satellites, extranet systems, and DSL lines, they go out there and they can just disappear."

"That's right," I say. "That's just what allowed my father to live that way."

"I heard that you saw him just a couple of days before he died. When you were with him—were there indications? I mean, did you know?" Jen asks. Her white skin flushes pink. She drinks long from her beer. Now that she's done the good work Bear asked her to, she wants a payoff in maudlin gossip. I understand this. It's fair. But I can't play even if I wanted to. I was only in his car for a few minutes. He told me he was having a hard time loving his girlfriend. He said he was losing control of the market. He was completely impulsive. I don't believe he knew what he was planning to do when he saw me.

"Looking back—but you know how that is—everything looks different in retrospect," I say.

"Of course, in retrospect, of course. Really, I'll be happy to help in any way I can. I mean, this sort of thing is my specialty." She picks at her salad. "This chicken," she says, "it isn't very good. I should get a plate of fries."

She turns and looks around for the waiter. Bear gives me a hard glance.

"I hope you're wrong," he whispers.

"Of course I am," I say. And I smile. "It was a foolish lapse. You know—because I'm in such bad shape. Actually, I told the story to Katherine and she said there's no way it could've happened."

"What?" Jen asks. We both look at her. Bear puts an arm over her shoulders. With his other hand, he rubs his heart.

Bear says, "When you were in the bathroom Mike was just—he was just worrying about how what happened with his father is affecting his love affair. He's more concerned about that than the money and he was saying that he's worried that this new woman who we'll meet soon, Katherine, how she might not stay with him through this time, and they might not have a future, because he's in such fragile shape. I was saying that I hope he's wrong. That they'll make it."

"Why, Bear, that's nice of you," Jen says. "Mike, I hope you make it too."

I smile at the two of them and take a long sip of my beer.

━━━

I call Wilma, my father's old secretary at Asherberg & Co. When I began to read through the files, I realized that I shouldn't be in touch with Leonora about anything just yet, since it looked like he was trading a lot of stock for her. Over the last few years, she'd become his only client. So she probably knew more than she chose to tell me when he died. But there were no printouts about the last six weeks, so I have to call Wilma to try to fill all that in. She can't believe that I'm still at the Gouverneur.

"It's just—that place is controlled by a big management company now. Newmark or ESG or somebody. I think Asherberg still owns a piece, but the link to you—I'm surprised you're still there, Mike."

"Well, they give me a good rate. They must have me grand-fathered in somewhere."

"I doubt it. Oh, I get it, you're swinging some kind of deal with them. That's smooth of you. I know how hard it is to live in Manhattan."

I remember that Wilma's been living with her mother in Bergen County for years. She never married. I look around the room I've had for so long now, and it takes on a different cast, suddenly, with my father and Max Asherberg both gone.

"Now, about his accounts . . . Let me see. Over the last several years we made a deal with your father where he became a favored client, rather than an employee. We held things for him, though we didn't maintain a pension. We did meet his margin calls, and let's see . . ."

"Didn't he also trade for Leonora?"

"Was that what he was doing? I was wondering. They must have drawn up something between them, then, because I have no records on that. Now our files won't really reflect what he was holding when he, you know. But, I do see holdings in a few companies, Atlas, ConAgra, JDS Uniphase, Lucent, Raytheon . . . I can mail you a statement. But these aren't big shares. Altogether . . . this is hardly any money."

I listen to her as she scrolls through the screens of reports and I can feel her begin to reconstruct the story as she reads about his movements and sees what happened at the end.

"Well, it looks as if . . . He wasn't involved with us during these last months, not since early in the fall. So I guess we weren't meeting margin for him after all. And if we weren't, and he was trading as big as he liked to when I was with him, that might have been a real problem during the beginning of April. I mean, everybody had to put up a lot of capital to stay in right then. That might have been the problem, Mike. Of course, I'm just a secretary here, and if you want to talk to somebody who can explain it better, Lou Kleinholz, or even Marty Richman, I can put you through to them, once the floor is closed."

"No. That's okay, I saw those guys at the funeral. I've been reading through his stuff, and with what you've said—I get it."

"You should talk to Leonora, actually, to get a full picture. What should I do with this little account, here?"

"If you just left it intact, that would be good. I'm sure I'll need it to cover the mortgage pretty soon. Actually, you know what, Wilma? When it looks like it's high to you, over the next few weeks, could you just turn those positions into cash? I'm going to need it."

"Okay, Mike, and listen, God bless you. This has been a tough time. It looks as if your father really pulled the roof down with him, and there's no reason you shouldn't be upset. I remember he told me you were in school studying religion, right? So you'll become a rabbi, and I think that's just terrific. That will help you handle this, surely."

"Well, thanks, Wilma. I'm sure we'll be in touch. God bless you, too."

I'm fairly sure that rabbis don't say, "God bless you." But that's what I say. I figured that in the short run, considering how I'm living now, it's better to lie and have good people like her be proud of me.

———

Weingarden gets hold of me on my cell. I'm happy to hear from him. I've missed him. When I answer, I'm standing down the block from the Gouverneur, staring in the window of Chiu-Kee Electronics, where they sell Hello Kitty dolls, cell phones, and baseball hats. I'd been considering whether or not to go in and buy a nine-dollar calculator so I can start counting up what I have and what I need. I decide against it before I answer. I'm so bad with numbers, and I can't justify the expense.

"Again, my condolences, Mike—this is a terrible thing," he says.

"Yes," I say, "it's been bad."

"Are you back to work yet?"

"No, not really."

"Then what in God's name are you doing with yourself?" Weingarden asks. "You ought to be keeping busy."

"Actually, like it or not, I'm having to deal with my father's estate."

"That only sounds like a chore. Now, Mike, about what we discussed a few months back, let's get started. I want you to go over to school and pick up a copy of my paper. There's a little divot in there about the Golem, and I want your input. Can I count on you?"

"Sure you can, certainly. I'll get it soon."

I lean up against a building. I watch a group of Chinese men take boxes of white cabbage from a truck and load them into a warehouse. Inside, the concrete floor is dirty and wet. The stacked cardboard boxes of vegetables leak ice and make the room cool.

"Good, and when you've read it, call me up and I'll take you out for a drink, yes?"

"Okay, absolutely. I'd like that," I say.

"Tell me, have you seen our friend?" he asks.

"Who?"

"Katherine. She is a tricky one. I hear a rumor now and then, so I wonder. Have you seen her?"

"I—" But I stop, because days have passed and I haven't seen her. Perhaps he is curious about whether Adam's involvement with her is done. He may want only to know if I've taken his advice and gotten involved with someone. In the rare instances when we discuss people, women especially, a hushed eagerness comes into his voice that isn't present when we talk about work.

"The reason I ask is that you two looked so happy together at my party. I think back on that time and I smile. If you've got someone as good as her to be with through this tough time—well, I just hope you two are enjoying each other."

His Welcome the Spring party feels like a long time ago. I find it odd that he would remember how I looked. I think that if anyone looked happy that night, it was him.

"That's why you ask?"

"Of course," he says. "Why else would I care?"

"I have seen her—I do see her occasionally," I say, because he sounds warm, and it occurs to me that he might know the answer anyway.

"That's good, then. I had wanted to know. And Mike, before you read my paper, go back through the Song of Songs."

"Right," I say, "I'll get on it."

"Don't rush. Take a few weeks. I'm hard to reach just now. I'm back and forth between the Vineyard and the city and then I'm on a panel in Chicago during the last week in June. So there's time."

"Okay," I say. "I won't forget."

16

Lara Nieves, a colleague of Katherine's, is leaving to go to the Kennedy School. She's been doing DV law for six years, and she's made a lot of friends. A dinner party is planned for her at a restaurant called Sixteen, because she needs a big space that can contain everyone who's worked with her.

"She's going to be great at public policy," Katherine says to me on the phone. "She exudes the kind of confidence that I wish I had."

I pick up a box of matches I took from the Old Walls. They're blue tipped and I light one, and snuff it out with my thumb and forefinger. I like watching the fire fight for air. Katherine goes on about the qualities of Lara Nieves. How she takes no shit from abusers or clients, and how judges and court-appointed counselors give in to her requests practically all the time.

"She's like a superwoman. Hey, Mike, you should say I'm confident, that I'm confident too."

"You're confident? Of course you're confident. But I didn't think you wanted to go back to school." I light five matches at one time and immediately singe the few hairs on the back of my hand. I drop the matches on the tabletop, and they clatter there and continue to burn. I blow them out.

"Well, going to Kennedy isn't really like going back to school, it's more of a training program for government agencies. But this isn't envy—I don't want to go there. Anyway, it'll be mostly women tonight. We're going over there now, so it won't go too late. Why don't I come by afterward?"

I tell her that would be great. It's Thursday, eleven days since I've seen her. I tell her to call when she's ready, and if I'm not at home, I will meet her somewhere else.

I push the books I've stacked in front of me aside, tuck in my shirt, pull a brush through my hair, and slip out of my room. Now that I know I will see her, I can't read.

I walk up Allen Street, past Delancey, where there are few street-lights and the rats are so thick that it's best to walk in traffic, since I'd rather be knocked down by a sleepy livery driver than bitten by a startled rat.

My father's e-mails feel as if they were written by several members of a small business, rather than just one man. He is jocular with his former colleagues. He's usually soft with Sarah Jane, but occasionally I think he forgets that he's writing to her, and business creeps into his language.

One reads:

S-J, things were ripping till noon and I was up, but then after my country walk I went back in for a big dabble, got overexcited, and gave back the day in less than two hours. Fuck me, hah? So maybe you were right. Look, I miss you. I wasn't serious about a damn thing I said. So take my call. Let me know when I can see your pretty face again.

This was written on a Tuesday, a week and a half before the Thursday when he died. I've been meticulous about keeping these e-mails saved and in order, but I can't find responses to any of the later ones. Soon I will ask Sarah Jane about this.

If I were walking with my father now, I would do what I did not do when I last saw him. I would try to explain my dissertation.

He'd react differently than my mother, I think. Here we are, walking along, me strung out and overstudied, worried about what my adviser thinks of me, killing time before I get to see my girlfriend. He walks several feet ahead of me, in brown pants and a dark blue blazer, wearing black New Balance sneakers on his feet to soothe his aching toes. He'd listen, and he wouldn't understand a goddamned thing.

"So what?" he'd say.

We'd be walking right here, up Second Avenue, and he'd take exactly that good, slow look at that tall girl dressed in white jeans and a black T-shirt, confident, shoulders back, headed toward her bartender or waitress shift. She'd look right back at him because she likes the open and aggressive quality of his glance, in opposition to what really just happened, when I was only quick and furtive with my eyes and she chose not to look back at me.

"A monster represents the soul of a people," he says. "So what? When you think about it, that's what monsters do—that's their *job*. Why the hell do you want to make it more complicated than that? And why did we get stuck with a difficult monster like the Golem in the first place?" He shakes his head, as disgusted with our Jews as ever. I scuttle along after him, as he walks even faster when he is annoyed. I'm desperate to explain about the mystic's thought process and the desire to imitate the ways of our Lord, but on this sort of warm summer night, with girls all around us wearing skimpy shirts that show off their breasts, he just doesn't want to hear it.

What I liked about our walks was that our mission was so clear. He was out to exchange looks with girls. I probably made him look like a better man than he was: a doting father, perhaps recently divorced, since I was young and was often gripping a sugar cone piled high with double chocolate chip ice cream. If we were talking, that probably didn't hurt either. The more interaction we had, the more sexually charged eye play with women for him.

"That's just it," I say. "About this difficult monster—that's just what Weingarden's asking me. Take the idea somewhere, figure out what it really means and what it can do."

He only shakes his head, in further frustration. He's not like my mother, so he isn't willing to hear more about something he doesn't like.

"Use this life to take yourself somewhere," he says. "Figure out what the hell you can do." He was always saying things like that, spouting off some American philosophy he must have learned from a shop teacher in high school.

At Saint Marks Place I consider tapering off, moving west or east, instead of continuing uptown. I could look at CDs at Kim's or walk far over to the West Village, where I don't know anyone. There's plenty of takeout food over there and I like the oak and elm trees that line those old streets. But I keep walking straight. It's the most thoughtless way to go.

The movies playing at the Loew's theater on Eleventh Street don't seem inviting. Not *Get Tough, Broken Promises, Loving Mean Ones, Shoebox Full of Me,* or even *The Agreeable Kind.* I haven't seen them, but I don't think I could watch one now.

If I were more like my father I'd go and see what the hell Katherine's up to. We'd do that sometimes, walk back onto our block and look up into our windows and watch my mother. We'd see her on the phone, or standing in the kitchen, looking at a magazine or going into the refrigerator to find something to eat. He enjoyed that, knowing that she was where she was supposed to be. We looked in other windows too, just to see what was going on, but I don't recall us ever admitting this to each other. Even when we were standing next to each other, staring.

Because I'm not going to walk farther uptown to see Bear and Jen, I turn left on Thirteenth Street. I walk past the Quad, across Sixth Avenue, and then I stride along next to the sleeping brownstones and quiet restaurants, places that have sat still for decades with hardly any change in manner or appearance.

I'll go and have a look at her. See what she's doing. I turn right again and walk uptown. I am down at the east end of Sixteenth

Street, where there's nothing but restaurants and nightclubs set in among galleries and huge storage facilities that are protected by great steel curtains. I just want to know what you're up to, see who you're with tonight.

It's this place, I think, this one, just past Ninth Avenue, the north side of the street, across from where I stand, with windows that shoot right up to the second floor, and thick black curtains swaying behind them. A few people make their way down the street toward the shining metal door. I'm dressed simply, in black pants and a black T-shirt, so I resemble the people who don't hesitate before stepping inside.

Sixteen is very large; they must serve hundreds of people at once. It is too big and generic to be expensive, and it makes perfect sense for a birthday party. I'm not showing up unannounced. That would be wrong. I just want to look at her face. I move in through the front door and it's very cool in here, even frigid. There are levels of dining up above and down below, and the clatter and bang of footsteps and glasses and knives and forks fights with the stereo system, which blasts out music that sounds French, what could be Françoise Hardy singing "Pas Gentille."

"I'm just going to look for some friends," I say to the hostess. I walk slowly between rows of couples, toward the back of the restaurant, near invisible amidst all this clamor.

Katherine sits at the far end of a table of twenty or more. A woman who must be Lara Nieves sits at the other end, surrounded by other women. The few people at Katherine's end of the table are angled away from her, toward Lara Nieves. Katherine is bent forward. She looks at a man who sits across the table from her, whose face I cannot see. They are very much alone. He has brown hair that's a bit long, and he is also straining forward. Katherine is listening. Her head is bowed down. It looks as if she is saying no, again and again. Their hands are not visible.

I stand in the middle of the crowded field of diners and I stare across at her. I think she and her friend must have parted from the larger group some time ago.

She smiles at something he has said. He raises his right hand and begins to make his point. He bangs one finger methodically against the white tablecloth. An inch of gray shirt is visible at the end of the sleeve of his black suit, but that's all. I see her bite at her lower lip and throw her head back. She wears the same ribbon of dark metal that she wore when I first met her. Then, as she relaxes, she glances across the room. I stare at her.

She fastens her impossible eyes on my face before she drops her head back down, to look again into her plate. Then she looks at the man, and again she shakes her head. She says something, and he brings his right hand to his face, where I cannot see, and makes a fist, points it at her, thumb forward.

If this is Adam, I think, then she is no longer in love with him. No matter who this is, they are, at this point, in disagreement. That's all I wanted, was to see your face. I never said that I didn't believe you.

I walk out of there. When I've already traveled several blocks south, my phone rings. Now, when it's Katherine, the display on my phone says so. I watch her name spelled out in yellow light. I'm at home, waiting for her. There's no reason I wouldn't answer this call.

"Hi, Mike," Katherine says. "Are you home? I'd like to see you."

I tell her that I am, that I'd love to see her. Then, though I'm twenty blocks away, I begin to sprint down the streets. And while I do, I call Blake at the front desk at the Gouverneur and tell him that if a woman comes in and asks for me, to please make her wait because I'm coming in the back way and I need to clean my room before she sees it.

I circle wide around to my house, all the time choosing streets that no cab would take, so she cannot run into me, and I come in the back way and take the service elevator. I call Blake again, and he mutters that she's already here.

"Two minutes, just give me two minutes," I say.

"It's no problem—I said that you were there, but you'd called down. You're getting out of the shower. So, my friend, throw some water on your face."

He chuckles as he hangs up. Blake has two wives, one in Brooklyn and one far out on Long Island. My deception is nothing to him. I've covered shifts for him many times.

Upstairs I turn on the shower and quickly wet my face and hair. I throw away the matches I burned and spray some Glade that I borrowed from a maid's cart. So my hotel room only smells artificial, and like nothing strange.

I call downstairs. And then I go in the bathroom and turn the shower up, so that it's steaming, and I stand there, until it appears as if I have just gotten out of the shower. A few minutes later Katherine comes in and we embrace, without speaking. She sits down in the chair across from me. Her eyes are rimmed with red, and she says she's exhausted. Her bag, as always, is just by the door. She shakes her head at my room.

"This is really a hotel, isn't it?" she asks.

"Yeah, I know it's a funny place. And I just found out—"

But then I don't bother to explain that in reality, there's no good reason for me to live here.

"I don't know how you get comfortable with the transience of it," she says. She looks at the walls. Nearest to us, I have a small collection of tacked-up note cards. On another wall I have the covers of Art Collection's two disks, each blown up to two feet square, a photograph of a smiling, mischievous Martin Buber, and nothing else.

"I'll miss Lara so much," Katherine says. "I always think I know how to say good-bye, and then somebody quits my damn workplace, and look at me. I get all weepy and upset. I can't let go."

"I'm sorry. I know it won't make the work easier."

"That's right, it won't. She helped me a lot. She was really like a mentor, and I guess I forget how much somebody's helping until they're not there anymore. Anyway, I'm happy you were home. I've been thinking a lot about you."

Perhaps, I think, I could have told my father that we create mute monsters to right God's wrong in creating man, because man is so fallible. God designed us to fail. Our vengeance occurs in the masochistic act of creating failures of our own. That's not a moralistic thought, and it is circular, so I may be able to use it somewhere. Weingarden would like it, as it is a kind of arrogant, blind stab at the monster's complexity. But for my father, even that analysis would be too sophisticated.

"Do you have anything to drink?" she asks.

"Some water. There's scotch too."

Between us on the table there's a copy of today's *Times,* some pencils, and a stack of my father's e-mail that I printed out. The top one says: *Lou—Got fucked yesterday—hard. Loved it. You and your wife should give it a try.* Lou responds: *I tried it but the seventies are over. Watch out now, J.G., lest you suck too long on the nipples of youth.* Then they make a lunch date.

It's difficult to imagine how my father could be this guy, and how he could be in some kind of sweet love with Sarah Jane. That's why I often feel as if he were not a man but a variety of things, a group of his own constructions. I touch my wet cheek to my shoulder and remind myself that of course we don't create monsters. That's myth. We just wake up every day and remember who we are, and we try to figure ways to get out of it. And I'd love to believe that I said that, but I didn't. My father did. Katherine comes and reads over my shoulder.

"You wouldn't believe these e-mails," I say. "They just go on and on."

"No, I would. We subpoena them regularly. I don't mean—oh hell. This isn't easy, Mike. Look, do you want to know why I had to get away, the other night, at the end of last weekend?"

"You don't have to tell me. It was tough up in Roosevelt. I just hope it wasn't—" But I stop. She must not have seen me in the restaurant. I don't need to hope out loud.

"Do you want to know, or not?" she says. And then she stands suddenly and goes and takes one of the two clean mugs I keep by the little sink. She opens my mini refrigerator but there must not be anything inside that she wants, because she turns and fills the mug with water from the tap. Then she fills the other mug and hands it to me.

"I want to tell you about my sister."

"Okay," I say. I sip the cold water and watch her.

"You know she was killed," she says. She goes and sits down on my bed and I stay in the chair. I don't say a word. It's way past midnight.

"Christina. She was murdered. It wasn't notorious, didn't make the papers or anything. It happened in the year after she graduated from high school, when I was down south, during the year after I finished at Ole Miss. Things went bad for her and she wasn't allowed in our parents' house anymore. She was using all sorts of drugs and she was stealing from my parents. She hit my mom, knocked her over a coffee table, and sent her sprawling to the floor. So my dad wouldn't let her in the house anymore. She was eighteen."

"She was homeless," I say.

"No. She moved into an apartment in Long Island City with some guys. One of them was her boyfriend. He was five years older and he used to wait outside of school for her, beginning in her junior year. He'd just wait and wait. And eventually she fell for him. He worked down on Wall Street as a runner. And he had this apartment with some friends. Back then crack was popular and they all got into it very fast—in the space of six or eight months my sister went from my parents' house and senior year at Saint Valentine's to a crack den. I was busy with the work I was doing at the Southern Poverty Law Center. I had my first grant then, and I didn't know, I didn't realize that all these things had happened. My parents didn't tell me, because they wanted me to concentrate on what I was doing."

"You mean they wanted you to prosper and they figured she wouldn't get better."

"Not so brutal as that, but my dad was very angry at her. Nobody knew what to do with her. People got upset with her really fast, because she was beautiful in a way that got them frustrated. I watched her with her boyfriends when she was young and they would want to hold her and then they'd get angry with themselves for feeling so much desire, and they'd push her away. Those boys, they didn't understand why. I felt it, though—I understood it. So of course, her boyfriend was horrible. You know, cracked up, and abusive and overprotective and jealous. She loved him."

"The equation that creates that relationship has always been mysterious to me," I say. And I hope that she'll explain it, in the way that she sees it, so I can test it against the few things I do understand. But she shakes her head.

"I know you don't understand," she says. "That's part of what I like about you. So this boyfriend, one night he didn't come home. He was the one who was supposed to be protecting her in this ruined apartment with these other guys, and he didn't come home, and she was doing drugs with his friend. They had sex. That's what came out at the trial. Her boyfriend, he came home the next morning and he figured out what happened. She was passed out and he was so angry at her, because I guess he felt like he was betrayed—not by his friend, who was a rapist, but by her. He slapped her, and then he twisted her neck back and forth, and he broke her neck. We don't know if she ever woke up."

I can feel some bile in my mouth, and I pull it back. I've neglected to eat again today. Although I'm beginning to feel stiff in the chair, I don't move from it.

"This was in the early fall. Everything went bad in only a few months. It all happened too fast and there was no time to even prove a substantive pattern of abuse."

"You came back home."

"I did. His parents got some lawyers, and he ended up with an involuntary manslaughter charge and a two-year sentence that was suspended, because they argued that he was only trying to wake her up, and they said she'd overdosed anyway, which was difficult to dispute. Even though our lawyers kept pointing out that it's hard to breathe clearly and spit up all that beer and cocaine when you have a broken neck. And of course she was filled with semen, and his lawyers even said there wasn't a rape. They said because she'd had sex, it pointed more toward her consent for the whole series of events. I got up and asked them if they'd gone and asked her, in the morgue, if she'd consented to being killed the next morning. His lawyers were good. They even disproved the time of death. At the end I started screaming and they threw me out of the courtroom."

When there is no good thing to say, and silence is an affront, too, I find that it is best to cover my mouth. Then at least I know I've displayed the wrong response. And of course, when listening to a story like this, there is no right response.

"It wasn't a passion crime, either. She was raped. And then she was killed, by her boyfriend, because he didn't trust her."

All through this, her voice has been steady and flat. Sometimes she sounds rusty, and sometimes she speaks quickly and sings a little, but there's only a flatness here. She just sounds very tired.

"The day after it happened my brother, Mark, called me in Mississippi, and he told me about it. He kept implying that I'd been too far away for too long and that this is what I got for staying away. Because after high school, I never went back home. You know that."

Katherine begins to cry. I go and sit on the bed with her. She has her hands spread flat on her lap and she continues to talk while looking straight ahead at the lights outside my window.

"This thing happened to my sister and then afterward my brother, Mark, broke my heart."

"Why would he do that to you?" I ask. But she doesn't answer. I should be able to look into her eyes now. She could reveal them to me. But even right now, as I stare right at and into them, they continue to be shuttered. I wonder if it is this hidden quality that allows her to be here with me and to also be the woman I saw in the restaurant only hours ago.

"We buried her. Because of the nature of the crime and how my family felt about her, they hid her, in the cemetery connected to Saint Valentine's, but far away from the good spots that had been set aside for us. So she'll be apart from the family. Then we sat through the trial for four months. I left again, went back down to Mississippi, and then I did my year studying in Dublin, and I didn't come home for another few years after that. My brother got a job in the after-school program at Saint Valentine's so he could be close to my mom. As if she wants him around."

"So that's why you're not in touch with him."

"I speak to him. He's a little bit mad, I think. He's fully functioning, but he—well, you'd have to meet him. The truth is I talk to him all the time. He's making me pay for when I wasn't here. I've actually got to go see them soon. It's my father's birthday. You could come and have dinner with us. That'd be good, it would make it easier for me." She turns to me and smiles, puts her hands on my shoulders.

"Don't you think it's early for me to meet them—like, if they're older, won't they take us too seriously, or—"

"I don't care about doing things in sequence," she says. "I think that kind of progression is bullshit."

She reaches down and takes off her shoes. They make a clunking noise on the carpet. Once they're off, she kicks at them. She is not wearing stockings or socks. I stand up and turn out the light.

"I'll go," I say. "I want to meet your family."

She lies down on my bed with her hands behind her neck. She's stiff there; her body is straight. She looks up at the ceiling. There's enough light coming in from the street to see her face. She isn't blinking. I lie down next to her. She turns to me, kisses my lips, lets her eyes close.

"How do you smell to me, Mike Zabusky?"

"How?"

"How does my Mike Zabusky smell? He smells like burnt linen. He smells like the puff of smoke, the sulfur when a flame is blown out. I don't know why he smells like a burned thing, but he does. His lover says she loves this, how he smells like a hearth in winter, like a warm, acrid, burnt thing."

"Acrid?"

"It's good, to me," she says. "Your burnt acrid sulfur smell can feel so good to me."

And she is falling asleep even as she is speaking, as she is smelling me. She reaches out and tastes the skin on my neck.

I say, "I think that was the smell that was part of everything that drew me to you, the night we met. Maybe it was me that smelled of it that night, not the candles. Maybe I started to smell differently when I met you. As if you changed me."

She says, "It does seem possible that we could come together and change and smell the same way, underneath."

And then she is asleep. It has grown hot in here. Her neck perspires and I kiss the place at the nape where her hair grows straight up.

I begin to suspect that I am no longer asking a question that can be answered by an understanding of the Golem. Before any of this happened, Weingarden was right to suggest that the monster can be limiting. But so much of me still loves my monster. I was in a restaurant earlier tonight, staring at Katherine, and when I think back to then, to the possibility that she might not be honest with me, my heart quickens. We are testing each other. It isn't so much about a smell.

"Mike?"

"Mmm?"

She turns to me. I've been asleep. She's looking at me. We have looked at each other so often that I've gotten used to not seeing her eyes. And so now, when she lifts the shutters, and I realize that she has done so, I also realize that I was wrong when I met her. This process of revealing is within her control.

She says, "You know, Mike, I wouldn't like it if you were following me around."

We're quiet then. Nobody says a word.

"Are you with anybody but me?" I ask.

"I'm not with anybody else. Tonight I was with people from work. But you can't ask questions like that. Don't make me leave you. I don't want to look up and find you staring at me. It feels good to know that you care, but I can't have you doing that. You know better, Mike. Don't make it impossible for me to stay with you."

"I don't understand what you mean. I know you were with people from work, earlier. I was here, waiting for you. I would never follow you around."

"Don't make me leave you, Mike. I don't want to have to."

"But we agreed, you know—I said I would always come after you."

"Yes." She pauses. She comes closer to me, and her hair falls over her face and surrounds my neck. "You did say that. Now may be a more difficult time for you than you know. You may not realize how you're behaving, just now."

"That's true," I say. "Maybe I don't."

17

Her parents' door must be unlocked, because she opens it and walks right in. But I hang back. I take in a big breath of air and try to see the place from the outside. It's clean and upstanding, with a smell of pine that makes it feel as if not a thing has changed since 1962, when her parents moved in.

"Hello, hello," Katherine yells.

The hallway is brightly lit, with photographs of Katherine and a dark-haired boy who must be Mark, taken when they were growing up. Even then, Katherine has her head tilted. She looks away from the camera. There are also pictures of Christina, but they are fewer and they end early, before she becomes a teenager. Of the teenage pictures, the great majority are of Mark.

Katherine's father comes out of the kitchen. He shakes hands with me and though his fingers and palm are coarse, his grip feels fragile. He wears green work pants and tan boots, a clean blue oxford shirt. He is quite bald and older than I would have thought, far past sixty. His name is Henry.

"Happy birthday, Daddy," Katherine says.

She gives him a shopping bag that I know is full of books on military history. He embraces her and I see his hands, laid flat along the blades of her shoulders. His cheek is against hers and his eyes are closed. Then he takes her by the hand and they pad away over the thick hall carpet and up the stairs. I watch them go and I stand alone for half a minute, and then I stand in the kitchen doorway, where I can see Irina, Katherine's mother. She's past sixty, too, and she is as tall as Katherine said. In shoes, she is taller than me.

"Mike, you come in the kitchen," she says. She speaks slowly, with an Eastern European accent. I walk into the room and Mark is sitting there. It must be Mark. He's in very pale blue jeans and a white shirt with wood buttons. He has his feet up on the table and he wears soft white Reeboks and clean white cotton socks. His black hair is carefully combed.

"Would you like a glass of red wine?" Irina asks. She's got very few wrinkles and her hair is held back with a pair of black barrettes. I nod as I watch Mark, and I wonder, can this be why Katherine is so changeable, because nothing ever changes here? Irina hands me a thick glass half full of wine.

"I'm not a drinker," Mark says.

He takes an acoustic guitar out of a black case that sits on the floor behind him. He leans farther back on two legs and he begins to strum chords. It's a big kitchen and Mark is sitting at the table where we will eat.

Irina turns away from us and checks on a pot of what might be rice. I watch Mark and he smiles at me. His pupils are small and dark blue.

Mark strums at his guitar.

"Trouble, trouble, trouble, why can't you let me be?" he sings. "Trouble, trouble, trouble, so many folks is looking for you, you don't have to bother me."

"I'm afraid that Mark is in a sad mood," Irina says. "He brought his guitar but now we can't convince him to sing happy birthday to his father."

"My usual mood, I suppose," Mark says. "When I'm like this the only song I like to sing is Katherine's."

Irina does not turn to us, and then she goes out of the room quickly. I continue to stand, with my hands laid palms down on the red tile of the counter. The table has been set. The tablecloth is made of an old piece of cream-colored embroidery. It occurs to me that the dominating smell in the kitchen must be Mark's cologne.

"Katherine's song?" I ask. "I don't understand."

"Trouble, trouble, trouble—you see?" Mark asks. "That's all she is. You should know that by now. Goodness—I know you've already had plenty of it. I can't think why you'd add my sister to your list."

His voice is calm and a little high, like his father's. I can find nothing to say. I hadn't realized that he would know who I am, or what's happened to me. I only stare at him, and then I'm saved by Katherine, who comes into the room, alone.

"What hellish things are you saying about me now, Mark?" she asks.

"Katherine, you're so wild—I couldn't begin to say the things I know in just a few minutes."

She turns to me then, and she puts her hand over mine and squeezes hard.

"See?" she asks, and juts her chin, first at Mark and then at the quiet kitchen. But I don't see. She never told me about what really went on in her house.

"Mark, I'm going to quit my job, really soon," she says.

Mark cocks his head to one side. His feet dangle in air.

"We've discussed that enough, haven't we?" Mark asks. "We think you should keep doing your job."

Katherine moves close to me, suddenly, and kisses me hard on the neck. I feel her body, the inside of her thigh against my side, and her arms pulling me closer. Mark looks away and strums on his guitar. I feel her then, saying, Look, here's why I've been difficult with you. This is why.

Mrs. Staresina—Irina—comes back in. She looks as if she's washed her face.

"What are you saying, my dears?" she asks.

There are a few crocheted oven warmers nailed to the wall, to the right of the stove. Magnets on the refrigerator have different sayings on them. They have put up their favorite *Rose Is Rose* and *Dilbert* cartoons. When the children are away, Henry and Irina must be happy.

"Jesus was just expressing his opinion," Katherine says. "We can't stay if he keeps it up."

"That's too bad, dear," Irina says. The phone rings, and Irina picks up the handset and leaves the room again.

Mark only looks down at his feet, strums the opening of "Jesus Christ Superstar," and then laughs to himself. I can imagine how the kids at Saint Valentine's might love him. His smile is so superior—it's as if he doesn't know what it is to be wrong.

Mark says, "She knows it's best for her to continue with her work. Both my sisters are so wild. I do my best to keep the one who's left grounded and safe."

"It's seven and a half years since she died," Katherine whispers to me. "But he still likes to bring her up all the time."

She sits down at the round table across from her brother and I sit next to her, because she has my hand and she will not let go.

In order to bear this, I am no longer at the dinner table. I am far above, poking around in the cosmos, trying to let my head click free to a place where I can divine some clear thought about how God perceives justice in the world. I've got to dare to think on something that high sounding in order to keep sitting here. Katherine puts her hand on my knee and squeezes tight.

Irina returns and begins dishing out rice and what looks like creamed chicken, and our plates are suddenly full. Henry sits down. He nods solemnly and smiles at me. Then he begins to eat. It occurs to me that tonight, because of me, the nod replaces prayer.

"Daddy, you must be happy that it's your birthday," Katherine says.

"Yes, I am happy," he says. His voice is pitched high.

"This is really good," I say. I have finished my glass of wine but

I don't know how to ask for more. I can't see the bottle. No one else is eating much. Irina places a plastic jug of cold water on the table. She leans against the counter, folds her arms, and watches us eat.

"Well, Mike," Mark says, "is it hard for you, trying to handle my sister?"

I look up, but Katherine turns to me and shakes her head. She doesn't want me to answer. I don't think her brother's entirely mad, or fanatical. He only seems completely absorbed with his family.

"Katherine's really something," I say to him, and I try to smile. "I'm happy to be with her."

But Mark only stares at Katherine. I'm not related to him, so I don't think he's heard me.

Katherine says, "I'm not kidding, Mark. A little while now and it's over. I'm going to quit and get to work on something with a little more glamour. Sorry, buddy."

"We've discussed this," Mark says. "We agreed that it isn't right for you to quit."

Katherine makes an angry noise in her throat.

"Find me something better," she says. "I can't stand it." She gets up from the table and walks out of the room. Her father puts his fork on his plate and he follows her out. I don't believe he's looked once at me or Mark.

"Those two love to talk," Irina says. "He's interested in military conflicts, especially those in Eastern Europe. He's been thinking about what happened in Yugoslavia, and she's willing to listen to him. I consider it one of her special gifts." Irina smiles, as if this relatively normal relationship can camouflage her son's behavior. She quickly clears their dishes from the table. She turns on the water in the sink.

"Katherine's path has been a wandering one," Mark says, quietly. "You wouldn't believe how much life she's seen."

I look at Irina and she's working noisily at the sink. She hasn't heard Mark. I lean forward. "How do you know so much about Katherine?" I ask.

"She confesses to me," Mark whispers. He sets his chair fully on the floor. He leans in and he's grinning. "On the phone, late at night. She calls me in my apartment and she tells me what she's done. We talk for hours. We pray together. We're really very close."

"So, if you know so much, do I have a chance?" I ask. There was no way to resist. If he is her confessor, then he knows everything about her. And yet, he is not so good. He is full of pride. I think he wants to share what he knows. He smiles at me and his teeth are huge and clean. They are all I can see, and his grin surrounds them, and then there's his head shaking back and forth. No.

Irina says, "Mike, you and I will go into the living room and talk. Mark, why don't you clear the table and load the dishwasher?"

Mark has his fork in one hand. He taps the fork against his front teeth and stares at me.

He says, "I'm sorry. I shouldn't say whether you have a chance or not—I don't know. But one thing I do know—my sisters both attract a lot of men. You think you're so special? You think you're the only one?"

"Mike, come into the living room now. I want to sit with you." Irina's voice is resonant and clear. I stand up and follow her out. And I don't look back at Mark. But it's then that I do feel better, because Katherine wouldn't have brought me here if she didn't think that I could handle her brother. He's not warning me. He's just jealous because she is out in the world. She has a chance to be happy and free of this family. So yes, I do think that I'm the only one.

Irina sits on the couch and she motions for me to come and sit on her right. There is only one light on in this room, a floor lamp with a deerskin shade that stands next to the couch.

"I hope Mark didn't make you too uncomfortable? I know how he can be," she says.

I shake my head and smile. I don't feel so bad, now that I see how Mark tries to sabotage his sister's life. That must be what she's brought me here to see.

"You know I was born in Poland, in a little town? Lizhensk. That is where I grew up."

"Yes, Katherine told me."

She stares at me, and she has one finger on her chin.

"There were no Jews in my little town. The Nazis took them all away when I was five or six. That was a terrible time. I look at you, I see their faces. You and I, our people are from the same place in the world. Only I did not come here until I was twenty-one. And then, when I came here, that's when I met Henry and married him. He is from here, from Forest Hills, he and his family. They are Croats, and more American than me, fifteen years more, so they told me. But you must know that too."

I nod at her. We can hear Mark in the kitchen, cleaning up. My hands are on my knees. She picks up a leather binder of photos from the coffee table in front of her. We begin with pictures of women in groups of four and five, all smiling, all in similar dark skirts and white blouses.

"Find me," she says. "Which am I?" She runs her fingers over a picture of a dozen college-age girls posed in shorts. I examine the faces. I realize who these girls are. These are the Polish people who the Nazis decided were of German descent. She looks happy because her family was spared. I keep looking at the photograph. My father really hated these people. Growing up, he and his friends, they hated the people whom the Nazis spared as much as they hated the Nazis themselves. They were the ones who went out to the fields at the edges of town and watched as volunteers dug a pit, rounded up the Jews, stripped them, shot them, and then buried them. He thought their self-satisfaction was appalling. But he couldn't discuss it with me, because then he'd talk about what it meant to be a Jew, and he hated that subject just as much.

"There I am," she says. "I'm that one."

"Your smile is really radiant," I say.

"Oh, that's nice of you to say. When you're happy, it's impossible to hide it."

She leaves her hand on the photograph of herself.

She says, "I was on the women's volleyball team. We won a lot of games and I had a good serve. That was a happy time. I was also on the soccer team, and I did archery. Wait. Quiet now, Mike—can you hear that?"

"Hear what?" I ask. I can hear Mark loading the dishwasher.

"She comes through the house. It's easy to hear her."

Katherine is on the stairs. It is dark at the top of the landing and she descends slowly, as if she is aware that we can see her coming into light.

"Dad was tired," Katherine says. "But Mike, he said that it was good to meet you, and that he had a happy birthday."

"Christina comes through and sits with me," Irina says. "She's so sorry for what she put us through. She says so all the time. We look at these books together. She enjoys that. Honestly, I wasn't a very good player. But my friends didn't mind."

Irina shakes her head and closes the book.

Katherine says, "Now we're on to ghosts. You've got to watch it with my mom. She'll have you believing just about anything. We're putting on quite a show, aren't we, Mike?" Then she turns and goes into the kitchen. We can hear her talking to Mark and then he calls out to us.

"Mom, I'm going to take the Special K and the Grape-Nuts. They're going to go bad. You buy too much cereal at once, you don't eat it, it goes bad. So I'm going to take these boxes, because I'll eat them."

"Yes, yes, of course," Irina says. "Take whatever you want."

She nods again, and she says, "It's good that Christina can visit with us here. In life, it wasn't so easy for her."

I look at her and wonder if she thinks I'm a spirit, too. Maybe I'm just visiting from Lizhensk, a Jewish friend she had back then, before we were all carted away. Again, I'm struck by my useless Golem. What would he do? Run into his house and look about— but who to attack? Who to save? He would run in circles, fall to the floor.

How big is God, I wonder, how big, to contain an evening like this? Conceive the distance around the world, multiply it by thousands. Throw a ball up into the air and concentrate on it while it travels in a straight line at sixty miles an hour around the world for the rest of your life, and your children's lives, and on and on, and then, then, you'll have some idea of how big God is, how impossible to measure. But you can try.

I turn to Irina and I pick up the book. The faces of the women in the pictures are all warm, sepia-toned, and smooth. But they stand together and they look tough. They look like women who have been through a war.

Irina says, "What about you, Mike, what are your intentions here?"

"My intentions?" I ask. And it is as if I've fallen into a kind of spell, where I am thinking and moving as slowly as Irina, and I am completely calm.

"I'm not sure of my intentions," I say. "I only know that I'm very happy with Katherine."

"I think she could be happy with you too," she says. "That you are Jewish, this is not—this is a thing I can understand. I'm pleased that she is done with the man she was with before you. Now she brings you to us. So that's good. Time to move on."

I look down at my shoes. Mark and Katherine sound suddenly sharp in the kitchen, and then their voices drop down again.

"And about yourself?" she asks. "Katherine says you've gone through a tragedy."

"Yes," I say. "My father died."

"I'm sorry—I hope you'll forgive me for talking so intimately with you," she says. "Do you want to tell me what happened?"

I say, "I don't know what went wrong with my father. I'm looking, but I haven't found the answer yet."

"Who have you asked?" She angles her head and waits patiently, as if, suddenly, we are more alike than she realized.

"I haven't asked anybody," I say.

"What about your mother?"

"They'd been divorced for a long time," I say. "He had a girl-friend, though."

She says, "When Christina died I didn't speak to the people who knew her. I was wrong, and I regret that. Why won't you speak to the woman—his girlfriend?"

We listen to Mark and Katherine in the kitchen. This is not a fragmented family. I think this family is tight and thick as a gang of mystics, of apostles, of criminals.

"I wasn't ready, but now I am. I'll go and talk to her."

Katherine comes into the room very quickly, swinging her hands through the air so they will dry. Irina turns to her and looks up, smiles, as if she's been enjoying light conversation with her daughter's suitor.

"Well, Mark's made me furious. Mike and I will go now."

"All right," Irina says simply. We hear Mark slam drawers shut in the kitchen. He bangs around for a while longer and then comes into the doorway of the living room, where we are.

"Yeah, forget it," Mark says. "I'm leaving first." He only glances my way, as if there's no need to remember me, since he won't see me again.

Katherine says, "Come on, Mike. We're not taking any damn cereal either."

She goes to her mother but they do not embrace. I watch as they place dry kisses on the air next to their cheeks. So when I come to Irina, I mean to imitate her daughter, but she pulls me close and kisses me. It feels like kissing a memory, because I can sense the tough, brutal quality of the twenty-year-old woman inside of her.

We walk out to the street and I look for Mark, but he is gone. The trees above us have kept the evening air warm and dewy. Couples are out with their young children and there are others, far older, all taking after-dinner walks. Overhead I can see hints of dark blue sky through the dense trees.

"Your mother was nice," I say.

"She's not nice," Katherine says. "Don't tell lies."

Katherine crosses her arms over her breasts and walks with her head down. We come out of the green streets of Forest Hills and step onto Queens Boulevard, where the cars move fast. There is city light here, and suddenly our conversation feels awfully sensitive.

"I'm sorry if that got too weird," she says. "I always forget how they must look to outsiders. Really, I need to get away from them, but it's as if they've cast a spell on me."

"And you've been trying to figure out how to break free," I say.

She looks up suddenly and says, "Yes. I suppose you're right. Let's—why don't we walk for a while?"

We walk a few blocks up the street, and then we make a right. This is not the way to the subway. She pulls my arm around her and we stay close, for as long as the heat allows us to bear the closeness.

"My mother asked you about your father?" she asks.

"Yes, she did."

"That's good, I asked her to do that."

"Let her tell somebody else what to do for a change?"

Katherine motions for me to stop. We are standing in front of Saint Valentine's.

She says, "You were watching carefully. It's exhausting that it's always me, so now she told you to do something instead. But that doesn't make her wrong."

We stare up at the stone church. It is a massive construction, busy with jagged steeples and shadowy places where pigeons live, doors a dozen feet high, outlying buildings all of the same dark stone.

Katherine points to the casement window in her mother's ground-floor office. When I turn to look at her, she is no longer next to me. I see her run around the side of the church. Her black sandals leave a sharp trail in the grass. I follow. She has turned another corner and gone into a wide alley behind the church, where it is dark and the ground has been swept clean. It's hard to find her figure in the dark, but then I catch sight of her, twenty feet down from me, walking backward, daring me to come closer.

"Can you catch me?" she whispers when I'm near enough to grab her. She is in silhouette, and I can see her chest rise and fall.

"Should I be afraid?" she asks.

"I'm going to catch you," I say.

"Come and get me," she says. And she turns to run, but I grab her from behind and whirl her up into the air. I set her down, onto a low wooden shed that holds garbage cans. She pushes at me with her knees. I hold on to her and take most of her weight. We're staring at each other, her hands grasping at my shoulders and back, as I pull her burgundy skirt up around her waist. I'm above her, standing, with my khakis around my ankles. I press into her and pull her off the shed, swing her around, put her back down. Tear at her bra and push back the folds of skirt.

"Tell me," I say.

"I love you so much, it's you, I know it, I swear."

"I love you so much," I say.

She smiles. "I only need to hear it from you."

"Do you hear it from others?" I ask.

"What? What did my brother say to you?"

But I only shake my head, and look up at the church.

"Nothing. He didn't say anything. Sorry, I shouldn't be suspicious."

She looks up at me then, gives me a level look where she doesn't hold her eyes back at all, and then, when I only stare right back, she pulls up my shirt and kisses my chest. I'm looking down at the top of her head, at her incredibly clean lines of burning red and brown hair.

"Can I go away now?" she asks. "Could I get free of you even if I wanted to?"

"No, you can't go. You can't get free. I've caught you in the alley and you can't get free."

"Mike, Mike," she says. She sounds suddenly urgent, even as she rests against me. She smooths my shirt, pats it back down.

"Yes, Katherine, what?"

"Nothing. I was just wondering what it would sound like if I ever had to scream out your name."

18

Because it's a weekday morning, and long after rush hour, I find that I am alone in the parking lot at the Roosevelt train station, alone and standing at the far end of row upon row of parked cars. I called Sarah Jane a few days ago. She sounded pleased that I wanted to talk, and she agreed to pick me up at the train station.

The warm air of the end of June is blown about by the wind off the Hudson, and the oak trees that surround the parking lot cast shade. I close my eyes and turn toward the water. Sarah Jane drives down to the end of the lot and stops several feet away from me. I hear Tammy Wynette singing "The Legend of Bonnie and Clyde," and then Sarah Jane turns off the radio.

"Hello, Mike," she says.

"Thank you for picking me up," I say.

"Sure. Good trip? Why don't you throw your bag in the back?"

There are wildflowers in the bed of the truck, tied together with a dark purple ribbon. I put my bag far from the flowers and then I climb into the cab.

Sarah Jane smiles. She's in her overalls and a light blue shirt. Her hair is back in a ponytail, tied tight with a rubber band. Her hand rests on the gearshift as she looks at me, but she doesn't start driving yet.

"Are you in a rush to get to the house?"

"Not really," I say.

"I thought we'd drive out to where your father is buried. You haven't been back, have you?"

"I haven't," I say. "Leonora told me that we're not supposed to go to the grave for a year after the burial, because it'll increase our feelings of guilt. That's the tradition. But let's do it anyway."

"Good. I'd been wanting to go. But I didn't want to go alone."

I look at her and I try to see what Katherine found so suspicious. She pulls out of the station and we begin to drive fast, with the windows rolled down and the wind whipping around us. I look at her face but all I see is a few freckles dusted over her cheekbones.

"The flowers in the back, they're for his grave?"

"Yes. I didn't pick them. They're delivered to Crescent Grange every other day. These came from yesterday. But aren't they great? People really respond to them."

"Did my father like them?"

"Oh. Well, he wasn't big on flowers, I don't think."

We arrive at the graveyard at Clinton Corners and find ourselves quite alone. We turn left and drive slowly up a path. She brings her truck to a stop, down low on the hill where my father is buried. It's easy to look up and find his spot. He's far away from everyone else and the sod is still fresh. The sun is high. Light comes through the oak trees and makes all the greenery glow.

I say, "It was kind of Leonora to have him buried here."

"I suppose," she says.

"If she hadn't paid for all of this—I don't know where I would have found the money. She really saved me a lot of grief."

"You don't know what Leonora did?" Sarah Jane asks.

"Tell me. What should I know?"

Sarah Jane puts her fists into her overalls and sets her jaw.

"That woman—you may as well know that she's not my favorite

person," Sarah Jane says. "Burying him was the least she could do after she ruined him."

"What?" I ask.

"Listen, it was trust that destroyed your father. That's how it always is with money managers. They won't protect themselves because then it's as if they don't believe in what they're doing for their clients."

"I don't understand," I say.

"He was manipulating a lot of stock for Leonora. He had one client: her. He was holding his money with hers, and when we had that horrible week in April, she refused to cover their losses. She wouldn't put any more money out for margin, and there was nothing he could do. I imagine he lost several million dollars. Mike, he was humiliated."

Sarah Jane stares at me. "Leonora ruined him, and if I didn't tell you, I don't think anybody would. What happened to him had nothing to do with me."

I begin to shiver. I slip my hands in the pockets of my jeans and look away. I watch her. Bad loans or falling stocks might make my father blink, but money wouldn't kill him. He'd already been poor. Much as he may have cared for her, there's no way Leonora would sway my father that far. And now I don't want to look at Sarah Jane, because I don't believe that she's telling me the truth about what sent my father into his basement.

"I'm telling you that when your father called to ask for money to cover his positions, she said no. I guess Max Asherberg brought your father up in the business, so he had loyalty. Your father must've known Leonora since before you were born. But he shouldn't have trusted her. It's business, after all. There's no place for that kind of loyalty, or honor."

I step back and sit down against the gravestone that lies at my father's feet. Sarah Jane still stands, a few feet away. I pick up a stone and hold it in my hand. She doesn't look at me, and then she takes up the flowers and fans them out over the grave.

I say, "Leonora and Max had box seats to the Yankees when I

was growing up and my dad used to take me sometimes. This was back when Thurman Munson was still alive. One time we were coming back from the game on the subway, and we were standing because it was packed like it always was. There must have been thousands of men on that train, and not too many women. My dad had one hand on my shoulder and one on the pole. It was past eleven and I was tired. I remember how I was always looking up then, because I was so short and young.

"Anyway, this one guy, a ways down the car from us, he starts making fun of these two women who are sitting down. He's drunk, and he's laughing at them, saying that they're ugly, that they better be careful or he'll unzip his pants and show them something. Of course, he was a big guy. So my father begins to get angry, and I can feel this, because he's gripping my shoulder tighter and tighter as he's listening to the guy. I start wriggling around, 'cause I'm in some pain, and I know he's not even thinking about me. The guy is getting nastier, and then my father can't stand it anymore. 'Why don't you shut up?' he says."

Sarah Jane is looking up at the trees. She's kept one wildflower from the bunch and she smells it while she looks around.

"So of course that's just what the guy is looking for and he gets into it with my father, which isn't easy, because the train is totally packed. But they knock each other around and my dad gets this guy pretty bloodied up in the face, and the guy hits my father some, too, until a bunch of young guys pull them apart. And the young guys think it's pretty funny. Somebody starts yelling for a cop, and I remember somebody else telling them to shut the hell up. I'm up against the door by then, and when we get to Grand Central, my dad finds me, and he grabs me by the shoulder and we go home. You know why he didn't like how that guy behaved? Because he was that way, I think, and he hated seeing it in other people. He shook me the whole way home, and I learned how awful being that way can be. So now I'm not lewd with women, and I start to shake when I see someone else acting lewd. I mean, I can't stand it. He made me allergic to all that, and he made me, he made me angry too."

"So," Sarah Jane says. She smiles and looks quizzical. "You're telling me that he cared for honor above everything else? I guess I knew that."

I shake my head, no.

"It wasn't honor he cared for. It was women that made him act crazy—nothing else. I found all of the stuff he wrecked, up in the attic. I read through the notes he wrote to you. My father didn't kill himself because Leonora allowed him to go bankrupt. He just wouldn't. Money wouldn't drive him that wild. He loved you. What happened between you and him? That's the one thing I don't know. The only time I heard him talk with an emotion that wasn't anger in the last dozen years was when he talked to me about how much he cared for you—and that was two days before he died. Did he hit you? Is that what this is about? Because if you're protecting me from hearing that, well, I can stand to hear it. If that's what happened, then I will apologize to you forever, but I have to hear it."

She says, "He didn't hit me, Mike. He never hit me. He was certainly rough with me. He was rough with everything. But I would never let a man hit me."

She drops the flower she was smelling. She sits down cross-legged, only a few feet from me.

"I like you, Mike. You're smart and you're thoughtful, but you need to know that your father and I, we weren't consistently together. It wasn't like you think it was. We had a few years, yes, but we weren't always close. Out here, people get lonely. He hadn't been with many women in his life. He married your mother right after college, and he wasn't one to cheat. I had to—sometimes I think he didn't understand, and he tried to decide what we were for both of us."

"He didn't understand? Did you love him? I read his letters. I know he loved you."

"I left him before he did this," she says. "I don't want to talk about how he felt about me. I've said all I want to say, Mike."

I get up then and go and place the stone I've been playing with at the top of the mound, about where his head would be.

"It's not traditional to just leave a stone that way," Sarah Jane says. "You're supposed to put it on the gravestone, but not until the unveiling, which isn't till a year from now." She's still sitting. "But of course you can leave it there. There's nothing wrong with that."

"How would you know? I thought you were Protestant."

"That's in your head. My family is from Connecticut, and I went to Choate, but I'm Hebrew to the core, or at least my mother was. My father isn't Jewish. But I am." She sighs. "That's part of what I suspect is the problem here—you're not satisfied with what you know, and you're filling in too many details."

"I have to fill them in. You're only talking about money, and it's like I've said—I don't believe that money was the problem."

"Well," she says, "that's all I can tell you."

"The things you say—they don't fit together." And I know I sound harsher than I want to, louder, and more confused.

Sarah Jane lets her head rest on her shoulder, as if she's gotten sleepy. She doesn't seem angry with me. And then she smiles, as if she sees something familiar.

"I should get back," she says. "I need to start getting set for dinner. It's not easy for me, Mike, when I think about your father. You know, when you're finished with someone—it's never when you agree it's over. Sometimes it's before and you're just taking care of business, or often, it's long after. But it's never just when you say you're done. And your father didn't let a decision like that go over easily. That wasn't his way. But I am sorry, Mike. I'm sorry that all of this is hurting you."

I watch Sarah Jane. I don't feel anger or disappointment. I just feel as if she hasn't told me the truth, and then I see that maybe when she looked at me and saw something familiar, she wasn't seeing how I resembled my father, but she saw how I am a little bit like her. I think we're both trying to make up stories to explain something that we don't understand.

"You could tell me a lot of things about my father that I didn't know," I say. "You could completely change the way I feel about him."

She says, "I wanted to do that. I've suggested one way that you might want to think about all of this, so you wouldn't have to worry anymore."

19

I walk into town, to Northern Granite, the bank that holds my father's mortgage. I called them, but they wouldn't release any figures over the phone. The whole way, as I walked along the road
enjoying the morning breeze and views of hills and trees that are
now full and green, I kept hoping that Northern Granite wouldn't
be an antiseptic little bank built for easy access to the drive-
through ATM. That's just what I didn't want—anything but that,
since such a place does not fit into the picture of my father's life
that I'm beginning to build—but here I am.

I sit across from a guy who is at least five years younger than me.
His eyes are awfully round and there are no lines at the edges. I
look at this young man, whose eyes are fresher than my own, and
I can feel my nervousness, and I know it's reading as anger, because
this young guy, this Malcolm Willgreve, he keeps his computer between us, and he doesn't offer me any good wishes.

"He certainly cornered us into giving him an excellent rate, I
must say," Malcolm Willgreve says. He continues to stare at his
screen, then looks up at me briefly and says, "Will you excuse me
for one second?"

When he departs I look around and understand what I have to do, regardless of what happens here—I have to be in touch with Leonora. Regardless of who bankrupted who, she loved him. She said so, and she wouldn't let his legacy be pushed around by a little bank like this. Especially if I tell her that they seemed less than warm toward his memory. I don't know how to finesse a business situation like this one. My father never taught me, and it's not part of the routine in graduate school, but surely I can outsmart a man like Malcolm Willgreve.

"It's been a very difficult time for me," I say when he sits back down. I watch him shift uncomfortably. I follow his eyes to an unopened container of peach yogurt that sits at one end of his desk.

"Mr. Zabusky, sir, I'm sure it has. I'm sure it has. You—we, we feel very bad about all of this. And here are the figures."

He brings out several sheets of paper and hands them across to me, along with some brightly colored pamphlets.

Normally, I'm awful at math. I have to use my hands to do subtraction. But when I see these numbers, I divide, cut them with what I've learned is still in stock at Asherberg, remember what the yearly property tax is, and then a number pops into my head. It's too high. I could carry his house for six or seven months, maybe, and then I'd go bankrupt too. I'd have to give it back.

"Let's suppose that I'd like to make an even smaller monthly payment," I say, which sounds comical, even to me. As if I'm trying to blithely pay him Tuesday for a hamburger today.

"Yes sir, the orange pamphlet is a step-by-step approach to a second mortgage. We could begin there, and then see whether that's something we can all agree on. Or, of course, well—I've been instructed to inquire of you as to whether you're sure this is a burden that you want to take on. You see, it might not be sensible to maintain a house of such value, especially if you're on a limited budget. Of course, we know nothing about your overall financial situation at this time. We'd have to get together and figure it all out, if you don't want to—that is, if you do want to maintain the house."

"But," I interrupt him, "I don't understand. It's my house."

In response to that, he only goes back to looking at his yogurt. I stand up.

"It looks as if I need to make some calls before talking more with you," I say.

"Yes sir," says Mr. Malcolm Willgreve of Northern Granite Bank. "That sounds like the right thing to do."

"Because it was my father's house and now it's mine."

"Yes sir," he says.

I smile then, and I gather up the orange pamphlet, and the blue one, and even the green bankruptcy pamphlet. I'm keeping that house. I like having it. I like it there.

I shake hands with Mr. Willgreve. When he stretches out to me, I see that he's got a tattoo shooting up from beneath his white shirt. It's a dagger, pointed at his ear. So he's just a punk. As I close the big glass door behind me, I decide that if I have to see him again, I'll do a better job of treating him like one.

———

I call Katherine. She's coming soon. I tell her what happened at the bank. Outside I see pots that I had not seen before, pots that I can fill with dirt and plants. I will make ivy grow all up and down the sides of this house if, in fact, ivy can grow around here.

"Call them back and ask to speak to somebody in a more senior position. Mike—you messed that up. They know what happened. You can easily make a mortgage on top of that mortgage. Describe it to them as some sort of a catastrophe mortgage. Oh Mike, I'll go with you. You just have to make a lot of stuff up with people like that."

"Shit," I say. "I can see how I could have done it that way."

"They don't want the house when they can have money. That house isn't worth anything to anyone but you. If he bought it four years ago, or whenever he bought it, six years ago, it's probably— today—it can't be worth what it was. My God, Mike! It needs to be reappraised before you do anything else. Wow, you shouldn't be keeping it so clean."

She is using the voice that I have heard her use when she takes care of her clients. She sounds clearheaded and bright, and absolutely sure. Leave him, she says. He won't stop attacking you. Leave him. So now I feel even more sure that I can keep this house, if I want to.

Katherine arrives late on Friday evening. I hear the door open and I wake up and I'm chilled, because I have been dozing in a chair out on the back porch. She has borrowed a Subaru station wagon from a man who she says is not worth explaining. He's just some friend of Leah's.

"Which friend of Leah's?"

"Some guy. I promised I'd return it with the tank full. I said it's not worth explaining." She doesn't look at me.

As I help her with her things, I say, "Sarah Jane told me my father was double-crossed by Leonora Asherberg and so he lost his money. He was humiliated and that's why he did it. I told her I didn't believe her."

Katherine stretches forward with her arms intertwined, and she watches me while she arches down. She must be stiff from driving. I move toward her, to massage her back and arms. She allows me to do this for a moment. But then she picks up a paper bag filled with groceries that she's brought with her, and she goes to unpack them in the kitchen. I follow.

"But when I said that, Sarah Jane wouldn't offer another explanation."

"I'm going to make us dinner," Katherine says. "That's too bad, that you saw her and that's all she had to say."

"I think she told me all that to cover up something else. Like, I knew what she was saying was factually true, but it felt like lies."

"Of course," Katherine says. "Why would she tell you what really happened between them? I mean, look at her. She wanted to feel better by convincing you she wasn't involved, and all she needed to do was make you listen to a bunch of bad stuff about somebody else. Simple."

"How do you know that?"

"Because I've done it. And in your life, so have you."

"So then she's still hiding something," I say.

"Yes, of course. We know that. Maybe it's just a small thing, but give it time and you'll find it out, whatever it is. She'll tell you when she's ready."

When we have finished putting everything away, we go and sit on the couch in the living room. She rests her head in my lap and I trace the lines of her lips. I had been dreaming about seeing her all through the day, and now it is almost too much to have her here.

"Do you mind if I run around and throw myself on the lawn?"

"What?"

"I don't think you know how happy I am to see you," I say.

She smiles and reaches up to kiss me. I kiss her back and I want to take her upstairs and make love to her and I swear that she feels it too. But then I can't be sure, as she comes away from me and goes back into the kitchen.

We make a simple pasta and sit down to eat on the porch. It is fusilli, mixed with fresh tomatoes, basil, and that's all. She has found a great white bowl in one of the cabinets and it sits between us, brimming with pasta. We have made too much. The thin red skin of the tomatoes is all I feel in my mouth as I look at her. I tear at the skin. She is wearing only a short skirt and a T-shirt she found upstairs. Her hair is tied back. I want to touch her so badly. She looks beyond me, out at the back field.

"What are you thinking about?" I ask.

"How it would feel to be alone here."

"I was just alone here. You could ask me that."

"No, I was thinking about your father. I mean, I'm always in-volved with other people, clients and friends and you. I don't think

I'm ever alone the way he was. I don't know what it would be like."

"Who did you see in the city this week?"

"That's just what I mean. I saw all sorts of different people. I can't even name them all."

"Of course not," I say, and we go back to eating. Though it is evening, and cool, I find that the pasta remains hot, almost too hot to eat. I can't understand why we are even bothering to eat, as we have never seen each other and then waited this long before having sex.

"But," I say, "you'd tell me, wouldn't you, if you—if you'd seen other men, if there were other men after you?"

She does not speak. She begins to pick the tomatoes out of her bowl and I motion to her that I'd like to have them. I put out my hands, cup them together, near her plate, and my hands are shaking. She pretends not to notice the shaking and only fills my hands with hot tomatoes. I put them on my own plate and I am making a mess. I take out a handkerchief and try to wipe my hands clean.

"You haven't seen Adam?"

"No, I haven't seen him," she says. She puts down her fork and looks away from me. "I doubt that I'll ever see him again."

I say, "I hope you're telling me the truth. You are, aren't you?"

She sits quietly. I eat a little more pasta. I take a long sip of red wine. There are wooden cases in the basement that are full of really good bottles. This one is a Château-Figeac. There's also several cases of a fine burgundy La Romanée, some Château La Fleur Petrus, and some odd bottles of old Brunello. There's champagne, Armagnac, and there's port, too. When I open a case, I look around for a note he might have left. I know perfectly well that he wouldn't be mischievous in this way, but then I didn't think he'd kill himself, either. At least he learned that during moments like this, it is better to go into another room and smash something.

She says, "If you ask me another question like that one, I'm going to leave here tonight."

There is a light blue dish filled with olives in the center of the table. The olives are colored burgundy, grass green, bottle green, yellow. I eat the burgundy, a kalamata, and then I reach out and chuck the pit onto the lawn. Katherine loves these olives. She made a special trip to Balducci's to get them. In my mouth, the taste of brine is very strong.

"Please don't say that," I say. "Don't leave. How I was feeling— it's passed."

"I should never have come up, but I felt as if you needed me. And in spite of everything, I do—I do want to be with you."

"Is it just because of what I've been through?"

"Mike, stop," she says. She sighs. "I'm in love with you. No matter what happens, that's how I feel. Don't ruin everything by being suspicious."

I reach out and touch her neck, and it is warm. Her T-shirt is loose at the collar. I wait, and then I know that I will be okay when all I want is to take the shirt off her and kiss her neck and grope her breasts.

It is as if, when she's talking, she's admitting something. She doesn't want to leave, but she's aware that maybe she shouldn't be here.

She says, "I can see how you'd be distrustful, because our period of wooing was so insane . . ."

"That's it," I say. "I'm just scared, that's all. It's because we are so intense. And it's all my fault, because I'm wrapping too much up in you."

She smiles at me suddenly, almost as if she's seen this before but is also open to a new interpretation.

"Baby," she says, "this could all be okay."

"Of course it will, now." I take her hand. We get up from the table and go out onto the back lawn, and then we do manage a few dance steps. She isn't wearing shoes. She jumps up into my arms, and I swing her around.

Of course you get freaked out and want to destroy things that make you feel so good. Sure you do. We can't stop staring at each other. We don't need any music, or food. I haven't been able to eat at all, but now I feel full.

"Let's have sex right now," I say.

I reach forward before the words have left me and tear the T-shirt off her. She gasps. We both stagger then, before falling down onto the grass, and I can no longer talk because I have stuffed my mouth with her shoulder.

Katherine comes into the kitchen with flowers that she found out in the field. She takes a tall glass, what might have been a beer glass, and fills it with water. She splays the white and purple flowers out with her fingers and puts the arrangement on the kitchen counter. They look wonderful in the bright sunlight of our Saturday afternoon.

"My father used to bring my mother white roses for no reason," I say, and I wish it were true. He must have given her flowers, even if I never saw him do it. And in my ongoing reconstruction, flowers for no reason feel appropriate.

"Yes—my dad did that too," Katherine says. "It's so important to do that. Not just when you're apologizing for something or trying to fix something, but for no reason at all. My dad barely ever says anything, but he brings flowers. In that way, he's smart."

She puts her hands out, placed together in front of me, and I hold them up. I can smell the dirt on them, and they are wet from the water.

She says, "There's food left over from last night. I can put it together—make us some lunch. Would you like that?"

"I'll help you," I say.

She opens the fridge and we find the olives and the pasta. It's hot here, now, at midday. Our movements are slow. She hands me some radishes that we must have forgotten to use, and I wash them in the sink. Perhaps there was a day when he gave her roses. It might have happened. But I never witnessed such a kindness. Still, in the time it takes for me to turn on the cold water, to feel sun on my forehead, and then to turn and look through the window and up past the trees at the sky, the scene becomes possible. By the time I've pulled the last paper towel from the roll and dried the radishes, and found a knife to slice them, I've made it true.

I walk into the living room. Katherine is standing over the stereo, looking through the CDs. She turns to me.

"I don't mind all these women singers, but God—I never thought I could get so sick of Ella Fitzgerald," she says. "I miss Leah and her music." She slides a finger around and adjusts her underwear inside her jeans shorts.

"There's plenty of jazz," I say.

She picks up a Miles Davis CD: *Dig.* She puts it in the player.

"Well, this I can deal with. I just don't want to hear any more women's voices, you know? No more singing. Any more singing and I swear I'll scream."

"Yeah, that's all he liked to hear, was the sound of women's voices," I say. "I guess I'm the same way."

"Now you're looking for parallels between the two of you?" she asks.

"Is there some reason I shouldn't?" I ask, and my voice may be a little loud.

I go over to the stereo and turn the music up. We're both standing in the middle of the living room. Saturday, the last day of June. It's hot in here, because the house sits low on the side of a valley, and it's been baking all day. There's been no rain for more than a week. So, with no moisture except for the morning dew, the grass and fields that surround us are dry.

"I'm sorry," she says, "I didn't mean that."

"Let's take a nap. Let's go upstairs and rest."

She flattens her pink shirt over her chest. She takes a step back from me.

"You go up," she says. "I'll join you in a little while. Right now, I'm going to stay down here and read."

20

"You want to know what I think you say to your friends?" I ask. "I think you say that I'm just some freak who walks around Manhattan and thinks about God all the time."

She starts laughing.

"What, why are you laughing?"

"A stone freak," she says. "Stone freaky. You know I went to Dead shows constantly after I dropped out of Duke? I spent months following them, living in a car with this guy called Loamy. Isn't that a stupid name?"

"Loamy. Katherine, goddamn. Who haven't you been with?"

"What? I—"

It's Sunday morning. She is over by the door to our bedroom, putting on her bra. I am lying in bed, naked, propped up on one elbow. We have found blankets and quilts tucked away in closets in all the different bedrooms. Now I am under the nicest one, a thin gray bedspread, with strips of red ribbon sewn through it.

"I," she says. She stops. I have shaken her. A dazzling pain extends from my Achilles and then up the back of my knee, to the soft spot that I'm always gentle with, because I've read that scientists think it's where we keep our inner clock that keeps us calibrated in relation to the turning of the earth. I reach down to bang on the muscle before it hyperextends and really hurts me. She leaves the bedroom. I hear her go down the stairs and then I try again to tend to me. I'm still stretched out, still gripping my calf. I can hear her rush back up the stairs, faster than she left.

"Mike, don't fuck me around—that kind of teasing doesn't look good coming from you, and I don't like it anyway," she says. "Yesterday wasn't good. Let's try to make today a little nicer, okay?" Her face is flushed, her mouth is small, and her eyes are brought together in a glare.

"I know. I didn't mean anything by it. It's just Dead shows with Loamy—"

"Don't make fun of me," she says.

"You're right, I won't. I went to Dead shows too, but in high school, with a girl called Willow."

"No you didn't," she says. She slows down. "Now you're lying."

"Sort of—I did date somebody called Willow."

Katherine frowns and shakes her head. She sees that I'm hyper-extended and she comes and kneads down the muscle so I can get out of bed. I stand with her help, and slowly the muscle contracts. Just like that. House afire, come the water now to put out the flame.

"Katherine, do you believe in God?"

"You're asking me now?" She smiles. She goes and stands by her bag, and reconsiders her clothes. She takes off her shirt and shorts, then her bra and underwear, and she puts on a white bathing suit.

"Yes, I do. I always have. Not much I can do about it now," she says. "I pray too, at night before I go to sleep. You just don't see me do it. You don't believe? I mean, I know you're not sure. There's no way you could be who you are and do what you do and be any-thing but not sure."

"Isn't that too bad?" I ask.

"Mmm," she says, "for now, it's how you have to be. What should we do today?"

"How I have to be? We should do something outside."

"We'll go swimming. But I know one thing we're not going to do," she says.

She's right. We mustn't have sex. We're both sore, and when we woke in the night and began to make love, we couldn't keep going because it hurt too much. And now we keep toying with each other, even though we are tense, and we must stop. So we dress quickly and leave the house. We get into the borrowed car and she drives. After only ten minutes, we come upon a state park with a lake. Near the parking lot there is an artificial beach that's made up of a long rectangular stripe of gray sand. The sand ends at an inlet, where there are canoes that may be borrowed without charge. We walk toward those canoes, past bunches of children who play in the shallow water.

"This is so excellent!" Katherine says. "Can you imagine? One of the things I really like about America is that we have this sort of thing."

She selects a new canoe. It's green and made of fiberglass, with *Old Town* written across the sides in yellow script. We take paddles and life preservers, but we do not put on the preservers. I get in the back, to steer. She's in the front and I admire the expanse of her shoulders, measured out against the thin straps of her bathing suit. We haven't got any supplies with us, no suntan lotion or water, no sandwiches, cookies, or newspaper. We don't know how much time we want to take.

"Let's get really far away from everybody," she says. We work hard to synchronize our strokes, because we're beginning to feel a real cause and effect. We discuss direction, and we push until we're going so fast that I can see the water part and slide behind us in rolling waves.

We coast until there's no one in sight, past an island, another, through water lilies that are thick as underbrush, through moss and knots of weed that dare to try and hold us. We drag our boat around corner after corner. I tell her to lie down, relax, to put her head back and get some sun. I'll drive. And I do. I work at making my strokes as long and silent as possible. We begin to see a few houses, set back from the water, so we know we have traveled beyond the boundaries of the state park.

She says, "Being with you when we're this way is wonderful, Mike. When we're this way, I feel like it's the happiest I've ever been in my life."

She lays back so her head is on the bulwark. She rolls the straps of her suit off her shoulders and pulls them down below her arms, so she is wearing the suit around her hips and her breasts are visible.

We are filled with the natural sensation that occurs when you can't see any other people, when you suspect that existing in this silence might be the best way to live in the world. We edge around another corner of the lake. There are more houses in the distance. They are big; rich estates on acres of lawn with long docks that stretch out into the water.

We slide along the bank, which seems artificially cut. The grass rolls up to the edge and then drops off into a sheer wall of black earth. We bump against the soft dirt. Katherine has her eyes closed to block the sun. I bring my paddle into the boat and place it on the floor and then I creep forward, just to touch her.

"Careful of the boat," she says. I can't tell whether she is encouraging me to come closer. But she is stunning, with her hair spread out behind her and her whole body wide and open. She sits upright quickly and the canoe rocks.

She says, "I'm going where you can't catch me."

She jumps into the water and then swims around to me. Her breasts bob up, and she grabs at my hand. I can feel myself grow hard for her and then I'm hesitant, because we said we wouldn't.

"Come on," she says. "I'll bet I'm faster than you."

I edge the canoe over until it's stilled under some low tree branches that reach out past the bank. I step out of the canoe and the water is warm and cloudy green, like Chinese tea. I swim to her.

I try to swim fast because I only want to be like a little kid and race under her legs. We move fifteen feet out from shore, then thirty, fifty. I look back toward the boat. It has shifted from where we left it. I begin to swim farther up the bank, to where I think it might stop. And that's when I look up and see the people.

There are two. A man and a woman, sitting in Adirondack chairs. The man wears brown bathing trunks and a seersucker shirt. His feet are at the level of my eyes. He goes over and takes hold of the boat. I begin to swim toward him. Even as I see him, as he is not letting go of the boat, I can hear him.

"Hey now," he says. "Hey now. Get the hell out of here."

I swim closer. He is older, easily seventy years old. He has yellow-white hair that's long and brushed to one side. He is glaring at me. The muscles in his face push his lined skin down toward his jaw. I look beyond him, at a small white house. This is their green lawn. That is their house. I reach the boat and come up and stand beside it in the murky water. But his hand is still on the gunwale. I see the woman's blue sundress, and then I see that she is Sarah Jane Caldwell.

"Let go of the boat," I say.

"We don't appreciate this sort of thing," the man says. "Get the hell out of here."

Sarah Jane comes closer to the man, but she does not touch him. I'm sure it is Sarah Jane. She doesn't look at me. Katherine swims up.

"What don't you appreciate?" Katherine says. She stands suddenly, in what is only a few feet of water, and her breasts show bright white and red in the sun. She reaches for the straps of her suit and covers her chest.

"Just get out of here," he says.

"What's the big deal—we're going," I say.

But the man will not let the boat go. His eyes are black at the iris and pupil.

"Sarah Jane?" I ask. I look at her. Her eyes are red.

"Look at you, trash like you, get the hell out of here," he says. And he pushes the boat forward, hard, and it jabs at me before sailing past. There's a sudden red line on my chest, above my right nipple. I look at the man and he's breathing hard.

"What the hell did he do that for?" Katherine asks.

"This is private property here, Mike," Sarah Jane says, as if we were in the middle of some earlier conversation.

"I don't understand," I say.

"Please," Sarah Jane says, "you're upsetting my father. Take your friend and leave."

Katherine and Sarah Jane stare at each other. Soft mud surrounds my feet and I curl my toes. The canoe makes a slurping sound as it rocks in the water.

"Let's go, Mike," Katherine says. The man begins to breathe hard. He has moved several yards up the bank. He has his hands on his knees and he's glaring at me, and he does not look well.

I turn to Katherine. The droplets of water on her shoulders glitter in the sun. Her hair shoots straight back and it is black and shiny with water. She betrays no expression. Behind us, I can feel the old man glaring. I put out a hand and hold on to the dirt of the bank, to steady myself.

"I want to know what happened," I say.

"Not now, Mike," Katherine says.

But my ribs hurt at the place where the man hit me with the boat. I grab at the grass at the top of the bank and pull myself up out of the water. I struggle and then I stand. There's mud on my chest and legs. The man comes closer to me, but then he waits for Sarah Jane. She is staring. She is at least ten feet away.

I say, "What you told me the other day at the cemetery wasn't the truth. I've got a right. I want to know exactly what happened. I want to know right now."

The old man takes a few steps forward and I just shake my head at him.

"Don't come near me," I say.

The man stops moving but he does not appear to understand. Katherine is still in the water.

"You want to know?" Sarah Jane asks.

"Mike," Katherine says. "Mike, please don't." But I do not look at her.

"Katherine," I say, "be quiet for one minute, can't you?"

I hear her splash her hand through the water.

I say, "My father was in love with you, and he killed himself because you rejected him. He couldn't stand it. That's what happened, isn't it?"

"How was I going to stop him?" Sarah Jane says. "What was I supposed to do, marry him? I did love him for a while, a few months, but then he was always telling me what to do, and that doesn't work with me. So we started fighting. I told him it was over, but I couldn't make him believe me. Then he started threatening me and he kept making mistakes, saying ugly things, and coming after me at the restaurant. You tell me what I was supposed to do."

"My father killed himself because he was in love with you. You rejected him."

The old man only stands there, breathing hard at us all. He doesn't look as if he remembers yelling at me.

"Stop," she says. "That's not right."

"Goddamn you," I say. "Admit that it is right. Say anything different and you're lying to me again."

I stare at Sarah Jane. She bunches the low folds of her dress up in her hands and turns and runs to the house. The old man grunts at me and he comes forward, but I don't think he knows what he wants. Then he follows Sarah Jane.

I come back over to the water and slowly drop down from the bank. Katherine has moved about ten feet away, and I walk through the water toward her. She turns away and ducks down. She swims forward a few feet, five feet, and stays under. I look at the red mark on my chest. It pulses but it no longer hurts. I look back at the house. No one stands outside now.

The water here is low enough so that it is not awkward for us to climb into the boat. When Katherine is ready, I help her get in first. I hold the boat steady.

"You had to treat her that way?" she asks.

"She killed my father," I say. "You didn't like her from the start."

"She didn't kill anybody. I didn't like her because she wouldn't tell the truth. But she was hurt. It would have come out eventually. There was time. He must have been awful to her."

"She could've helped him," I say.

"She did help him. You know that. She probably helped him more than he deserved."

"More than he deserved? I don't know that! I do not know that." And I'm pointing now, pointing at Katherine. "She is not telling the whole story and I don't like you defending her! Don't you get all smart on me now, Katherine. You can't talk about him. I knew my father. You didn't."

"But I know you," she says.

"What? So what—you know me," I say. And I am lunging forward. I've dropped my paddle and I'm lunging toward her and I'm trying to stand in the middle of the canoe. She takes her paddle and holds it up. She angles it straight at my face.

"Sit down," she says.

My heart is beating hard in a way where it hurts. I look down and my skin is cold and bumpy. The red line on my chest is still bright. I sit down. She takes us over to where I dropped my paddle. I reach out to where it floats and I grab it.

The lake must have more ins and outs on the way back, because it takes us forever to find our way. Katherine turns and looks at me at one point, but her look is brief. I can't see her face or her eyes at all. I take the lake water up in my hands and splash my nose and eyes.

"I didn't mean to get so angry," I say.

"No," she says. "You didn't. You're like me that way. These storms of intense emotion are always so brief for me too."

"Good and bad?"

"Yes, both good and bad," she says. She trails her paddle and drops her head down.

"Before, you said it was the happiest moment of your life."

"Yes," she says, "I said that before, but you know how I am. Sometimes I get so excited, and I don't think about the meaning of what I'm saying. Just like you."

Katherine says, "I just can't believe you did that. Didn't you see how ashamed she was?" She bites the inside of her lip.

"You're right," I say. "I shouldn't have done it."

We're standing in the living room and it is nine o'clock in the morning on Monday, the second of July.

Katherine has just come downstairs. I didn't want to see what would happen if she woke up next to me and looked at me like she didn't love me, so I avoided it. I came down early, and I gambled that if she was alone in the morning, she might take time to reconsider us. But I wasn't lucky and I didn't win.

"And in front of her father too? Christ, I was so sure you'd never be like that, even after all that's happened to you. No matter what anybody said. And I wanted to help. But now—I'm going to leave."

I wait and look away, around the living room, focus hard on the floor, at a space between two windows.

I say, "I wish you wouldn't go."

We came home yesterday after our canoe trip and we were quiet with each other. We went to a movie in Red Hook, a big movie called *Strangers in the World*, and it was awful, and we agreed on that. Then, last night, though we both stayed in my father's bed, we were not able to touch each other.

She says, "I'm driving back today."

"I wish you wouldn't," I say. "You were right. I've admitted that I handled everything wrong."

Katherine stands up. She leaves the living room. I look around desperately and wonder if I could just offer her something. Take this bottle of wine, take the food we cooked together, the towels that I used to dry you. Let me sing you a song I learned when I was small, "Blackbird" or "John Henry."

But she goes upstairs to pack. I follow her and stand in the doorway and watch. She did not bring much with her this time, some socks and underwear, a pink sleeveless shirt, her white drawstring pants. Some bathroom things. I would like to be the sort of man who will not stand idly by while he loses a woman. But I do not want to be the sort of man who blocks a door. So I go downstairs and sit in the ugly wicker and leather chair that's nearly black around the edges with age. And then I can't stay in the chair. I go back upstairs and stand in the doorway of my father's bedroom. I watch as she ties up her flaming hair so it stands on her head. Her bag is on the bed and she places her hand on it.

I say, "You don't know what it's been like, not understanding what happened with him. You don't know how it feels."

She turns to stare at me, and then she closes her bag.

"No, Mike, I do know. You forget that I'm working hard to understand things too."

I can't believe that I've forgotten what happened to her, to her sister. But I have. I would leave me too. I feel like a crab, scrabbling around on the floor, trying to grab hold of something that will keep us both safe.

"Maybe I was only doing what your mother asked me to do," I say.

"You think so?" she asks. "Then why couldn't you have done it right, and been gentle, and found out only for you?"

But I can see that it is too late to answer. I look at her and she is crying. Now, with her crying, it is even more impossible to look into her eyes. And if I were to beg her, I would only get a few more minutes with her, a few more stolen minutes; and then, after she gave me those minutes, I would never see her again.

"Mike, look, yesterday was only—it showed that we could really hurt each other. That's all. It wasn't only about your father. I can't help you. You'll have to get over this alone."

She walks out of my father's bedroom and down the stairs. And

I follow her. I feel quite alone, uninhabited, and back to my beginning of years ago with only a dim memory of a curiosity about why we allow the things we care most about to go so wrong. In front of the door downstairs, I cannot look at her. I put my hands on the door frame. I don't move.

"You're not blocking the door?" she asks. She only tilts her head at me. I'm not much bigger than her, but I am in the door, and she cannot get past me.

"Katherine, please. How can you let this happen—we've been through all the hard parts," I say. I feel a pain in my knees, but I do not move. Her bag is over her shoulder and she is staring at a spot on my neck, below my Adam's apple.

"Get out of my way."

"You don't think we can make this work?"

"Mike, we're not going to make it work. It was a mistake. This has been a far too excitable time for each of us, and it should never have begun. Let go of my arms."

"Don't leave me here," I say. I'm gripping her arms, just above her wrists.

"Damnit, he said you might act like this," she says.

I feel a cold line run up through my shoulders and circle around my ears. Then the line flashes in my eyes and everything is white.

"Who said? Who said I'd be like this?"

"Let go of me," she says. And she twists suddenly. Her knee goes up and I am knocked to the side, away from her. She is out and past me, already standing a few steps down the stone path.

"Who said I'd be like this?"

She turns around and says, "Matthew, your adviser—at first he said how nice you are and how much he respected you, but then he started warning me. When he found out about your father, he thought maybe you wouldn't be able to handle being with me, and you know what? He was right."

"You saw him? When have you seen him?"

"See? You don't trust me. And how stupid of me—I was worried about what you'd think because I cared so much about you and I kept thinking that we're the same, me and you. Everybody tells us what to do. And even though I wasn't sure, I kept coming back, but now I'm not coming back anymore."

She goes quickly down the path that leads to the driveway. She stops to get a set of keys out of her bag. I look at her feet, at her funny sneakers that are like spaceships. She gets into her borrowed Subaru and she only looks back at me and shakes her head.

21

Bear comes up at the end of the week. He arrives in a rented car. It's good when people bring these cars. Although walking into town every day keeps me strong, it feels primitive.

We stand on my father's porch and look out at the overgrown grass. I wear shorts and flip-flops, and a red Izod shirt I found in a closet. He's got on black jeans and a long-sleeved plaid shirt. I tell him it's too hot for clothes like that and he looks down at what he's wearing, in surprise.

He says, "Jen and I are spending some time apart. She's up in Canada anyway, wrangling through another of these bankruptcy settlements. This one is a chip maker in Ontario. I guess Microsoft changed their mind about something, and this company ended up with millions of dollars' worth of useless chips."

"How will you decide what you're going to do?" I ask.

"When she comes home, we'll see. She's under a lot of pressure."

"Business is brutal," I say.

"I know—thank God we're not in it," Bear says. "This is a great house. But at the same time, there's nothing holding you to it. I mean, it's not a lived-in place. You don't have to stay here."

"It feels that way because it was cleaned out, right when I got here. It used to have all of his dust and stuff in it, but these cleaners came and sucked it all out."

"Oh, I see. Afterwards. Have you changed anything around?"

"Well," I say, "there used to be more furniture. I think I moved the barbecue."

"Did Katherine like it here?"

"Yes." I wonder if Bear can sniff the sex.

"Does it smell like sex to you?" I ask.

"The house? Well, I'm not sure I could smell sex even if I wanted to, but upstairs it smells very strongly of soap."

"Katherine and I have been wildly solicitous of each other," I say. I do not say that she left me here. I have called her a couple of times and left messages, but she hasn't called back. I'd like to believe that she is taking some time now, to think.

"Who's that?" Bear asks. I look at where he's pointing and I see Richard Ashton, my father's next-door neighbor, walking through the fields. He waves. We wave back. It's hot enough so that his figure vacillates in the air.

"My father's neighbor. He offered his help, but I never did call him. The thing is, just now I need some money, but I don't need any help. There's nothing I don't understand. I just need to pay off twenty-six more years of a mortgage, or extend it, or get another one, or figure out some other solution."

"So you do need help," Bear says.

"Yes. I guess I do."

Bear shakes his head. He takes off his shirt and he's got on a green T-shirt underneath. He looks cooler. It is certainly a hot day.

"What did you do for the Fourth?" Bear asks.

"The Fourth? I stood outside and . . . I think there were some fireworks, over there, in that direction. Christ, my birthday was yesterday, the fifth. I kept real quiet then. My mother called and begged me to leave here. That speech, of course, made me dig myself in a little deeper."

"Your birthday? I didn't know—"

"Forget it. You weren't the only one who didn't call. Suffice to say, I'm happy as hell to see you now."

Bear and I decide to go fishing. There are poles in a downstairs closet that remind me of the bathrobes Katherine and I found upstairs, because they're unused and they must have been gifts, too. We find fishing line in the closet, and some hooks. We even dig up some earthworms from the soft dirt at the sides of the driveway, where Bear notes that he can already see weeds fighting a successful battle to live. They're coming right up where the gravel ends.

"You ought to do some plantings," Bear says with authority, as if either of us has the least idea of how to go about doing plantings.

We drive Bear's rental car through town, and we go slow on Main Street, past Crescent Grange. We park down by the Hudson River, just before the train tracks. We take our equipment and go down to the river's edge. When it's quiet I tell Bear what happened to my father, how Sarah Jane told me about the money and Leonora. Then I tell him about what I said to Sarah Jane.

Bear says, "I guess he was in some real trouble, with both of them. Maybe he didn't want to hurt anybody."

"But he did. He hurt everybody. I mean, he could have worked it out. He could have found some peace by walking in the woods."

Bear smiles and says, "You would find peace that way? Or me? People like us don't do that, Mike. You know that." Bear settles his Yankees cap back on top of his hair.

"He could have dug himself out of it."

"Maybe, maybe you're right. Have you seen Sarah Jane again?"

"No. I think she probably hates me now."

Bear doesn't object to that. We thread line through the rods.

"Do you actually know how to fish?" Bear asks.

I shake my head. We stand close to the water. It's about noon, and I recall that this is probably a bad time to catch fish. The fish are sleeping. The fish are hiding. The water courses down toward Manhattan and the sea, and it looks high, though it is the middle of summer. We fit the worms onto the hooks and we cast. The dissonant sound of nature is all around us, and it's no longer odd to me.

"We might as well yell for them," Bear says after a while.

"We're freshwater fly-fishing," I say. "We need to work on casting."

So we stand and cast.

"These are worms, not flies," Bear says.

"Oh, so that's what distinguishes fly-fishing," I say.

"Maybe we should just get some beer," Bear says. But we don't move from our spots.

"Do you want to tell me about Katherine?" Bear asks.

I hang fire for a long minute, and then I say, "Weingarden warned her against me. I guess they know each other. We got in an argument about Sarah Jane, and she left. I need to figure out how to get her back."

"Do you?" Bear asks.

"Do you know something that I don't know?"

But Bear shakes his head no and says nothing. I walk a few feet down the river from him and try to cast farther out. But I can't get the wrist action right unless I do it very slowly, and that doesn't get the line out far enough into the river. I stop then and watch Bear fish. We talk about the story of the fox.

"I can't really say if it's the truth. I just can't," Bear says. "But I think that me and Jen may separate, just anyway."

"You have no idea what that will mean," I say. "The two of you aren't over. You'll be fine."

"I think," Bear says, "that I may be better off if I leave her."

"Why?"

"Look, Mike, if she can't control herself—it's just like with your dad. If he's going to do a thing like that, then you can love him, sure, but you can't be with him, you know? It's too dangerous. And anyway, I don't trust her." He casts wide, and I can see that he's beginning to find a rhythm.

"But it was me that stopped trusting her, not you. I was wrong.

It was a funny story, and it was about a friend. She did not sleep with a fox in Canada. It's like saying she slept with ghosts in her dreams, don't you see that?"

A motorboat passes, going upstream. Men and women in bathing suits stand at the railings and some are dancing, with drinks in their hands. We can just hear the music over the engines, what must be early Go-Go's, "We Got the Beat."

"I guess I don't need you to reassure me now," Bear says. "How did you leave it with Katherine, exactly?"

"She walked out on Monday morning. Ten o'clock. We didn't say when we'd see each other again. I yelled at her—or no, I didn't yell at her. I argued with her. But we love each other. I'll see her in the city. Or she'll come back here. It isn't over."

I've spoken loudly and I stare down the blackbirds in the trees, glare at the gunmetal canoes out in the water, which bounce in the speedboat's wake. I look at Bear, but he's looking at the river, and I think this spring and summer have been harder for him than I realized.

I go back to casting. We're standing about a dozen feet apart so we won't hurt each other with the hooks. Now would be the most wonderful time to catch a fish. But it doesn't happen. No fish on either of our lines. And we've been here for a while.

"Look, Mike, do you think that maybe you should forget her?"

"I tripped over her. You remember? I didn't mean to fall for her. It just happened. I wasn't looking for anything at all. We got her eyes between us, and then they worked on me. We've never said that we don't love each other. So, no, I can't forget her."

I look up the river. No monsters to reckon with here. And if there were, so what? They'd just be big mute things, terrors of the deep, big nonthinkers. Huge snakes with foot-tall fangs or massive man-eating alligators or snapping turtles the size of tugboats.

We stand alone under drooping trees. Bear casts again, as hard as he can, and his line goes out into the middle of the river. I follow his example and cast big and then reel in slow, let the line drift to the banks. Even if this isn't fly-fishing and we don't know what we're doing. Now I suspect that big fish hang around in the depths beyond the banks and eat the little fish.

"It's the big fish that we want," I say. Nothing could be smaller than the chance that either of us might catch a fish today.

"It sure is nice out here," Bear says.

Bear's line tugs then, and his eyes go wide, but then it stops. He lets it go slack. Then it turns rigid again and he holds it, but he is slow to start reeling it in.

"Maybe you should concentrate on your work instead of thinking about her, at least for a while," Bear says.

"My God, I just remembered . . ." And I realize that I've completely forgotten to go and reread the Song of Songs, and then read Weingarden's paper. The paper is in the house and I haven't touched it. It's unbelievable to me that I'd forget such a duty, but I have.

"What?" Bear asks.

"Nothing. I just remembered something that I promised someone I'd do." And then I can ask him why he said those things to Katherine about me. I can ask him what he meant. Bear bites his lip and watches the river. His line is still taut and he begins to reel it in. I put down my rod and watch.

A flapping brown fish, about six inches long, pops out of the still water and stares at us. For a moment we only look, and then Bear reels hard. He hands me his rod and grabs the fish in his hands.

"You've caught a mudfish," I say, and clap him on the back.

"No, I think it's a perch, or a bass," Bear says. He's smiling so wide that I hug him for a second, across his shoulders. He looks around for a bucket, but of course we haven't brought one.

"I don't want to throw it back," he says. And I agree that he shouldn't, so I take off my shirt and we wrap it up in that.

"You did it!" I say.

"We better get back to your house and cook it," Bear says with authority. But when we march back to the car, he giggles.

We buy heroes from Anthony's Deli, to go with our fish. Heroes and six-packs of beer, some salads, and bags of potato chips. At the house, we find a Fannie Farmer cookbook that looks as if it was here before my father moved in. Bear quickly skins and bones the fish, and fries it. It isn't very big, but it's hot and buttery, and Bear and I only shake our heads at each other in amazement while we eat it.

We spend the afternoon on the back porch, and we don't say much. Bear falls asleep and then I do too. When we wake up, it's nearly seven. We look around and begin to wonder about what we might do for dinner. Then the phone rings.

"Is this Mike Zabusky?"

"Yeah, it is," I say, and I'm already thinking it's yet another solicitor so I'm moving to hang it up, because it's not Katherine.

"This is Mark Staresina. I got your number off the Internet."

His voice is pallid and high. But there's a little of his sister in it. I can hear a little of his big sister.

"Well," I say, "I'm happy to hear from you."

"I want you to meet me in Manhattan. I want to talk about Katherine."

"Yes, okay."

"Let's say Café Cha Cha's on Mulberry Street, around four on Wednesday. That's a good time for me."

"I'll see you there," I say, "and—" But he hangs up.

"Who was it?" Bear asks.

"Katherine's brother. He wants to talk to me about her."

"I thought that guy was some kind of fanatic."

"He is."

"And you're going to see him?"

"Yes."

"What do you think he wants to tell you?" Bear asks.

"Maybe something about how she's a hard person to love, and he knows she left me here, because she tells him everything. Then he'll say he's behind me. He believes we should be together and here's the way to get her back."

"I didn't ask what you wished," Bear says, and smiles.

But I'm quiet. The sun is just hanging on now, in the long summer afternoon, and it looks as if it's gotten stuck up there. In an hour or so we'll be able to hear the crickets.

"When's Jen coming back?" I ask.

"Mike, I may as well tell you—she's in New York, not Canada. I don't know how you saw it when we were having dinner that time, at the Old Walls—but you were right. Jen admitted everything to me. I got angry at you, actually, because of what you saw, but I'm over that now. And I'm going to leave her."

"Fox or frog?" I ask.

"Oh. Fox, not frog."

"I see. You should be angry at me. I shouldn't have done that, and I wish you wouldn't leave her."

Some napkins blow onto the grass. Our empty potato chip bags are already out there. I walk out to get them.

"We've already discussed it," Bear says. "We've been talking about it for weeks. She made me promise to tell you that she still wants you to call her, because she can give you some help."

"That's kind of her," I say.

"It's the least she can do," Bear says. He looks out at me and shakes his head. "I'm sorry that it's over, because we were in love. But I'm leaving her. I don't want to be with her anymore."

22

Mostly, what happens is this: the policies lapse. Health insurance lapses immediately at death. The mortgage needs to be paid, and home insurance bills keep coming. But the rest of it, credit cards and memberships, calls from old acquaintances and solicitations—each time they arise, I just end them. I just let them go. I sit at his desk in the command center and work through all the files again. And then I call Jen. Bear has gone back to the city, but he was emphatic about having Jen help me. He called Jen from here, and they scheduled a time for me to call.

At first, Jen helps me confirm things that I had already suspected. The Big Gamble folder contains letters about a lot of money he invested in a small company that made eyeglass frames for the computers that will have screens that hang in space, which we'll be able to see out of the corner of our eye. MIT's lab endorsed the company, but they came on the scene too early, and though the company still exists, the stock sits at two. We go through other folders and we learn that all of his money was in stock. He kept only about ten thousand dollars in cash. I've spent more than half of that.

"None of these stocks have any value," Jen says. "It looks as if he really was bankrupt."

I put Jen on speakerphone, so her voice fills his study. I tilt far back in his chair and look out the window.

"So what's next?" I ask. We haven't mentioned Bear. I promised him that I would take Jen's advice, and that I wouldn't press her about anything else.

"Perhaps we should be more abstract in our thinking," Jen says. "Tell me a few things about your father."

She waits for me to respond. The day isn't bright, and that combined with the dark paint in this room forces me to turn on some lights.

"It's funny," I say, "I think you're the first one who has asked—not about what happened, but about him. He had one job for his whole life, before moving out here. He was really brought up by this man called Max Asherberg. The moment he got out of Brooklyn College he went to work for him, and that's where he stayed. Then, I don't know. After twenty-five years or more, he leaves, but he keeps contact with Max and his wife, Leonora. Even after Max dies, he tends to some of Leonora's money. He's divorced my mother and he moves up here and he begins to deal with only his and Leonora's investments. He has this huge anger, and that plays a part in all of this. Then he meets Sarah Jane, and he falls in love with her, hard. So the way he feels about her—it takes over. Things start to fall apart—"

But Jen cuts me off there. She doesn't want to hear about what happened with Sarah Jane. That's got nothing to do with his money.

"Okay, you say he was close to his boss, that he'd mentored him, and he stayed in touch with him and his wife. Now if they were that close, there would be paper between them. An old hiring agreement or something."

"So?" I ask.

"So go through the Asherberg files again. Look for old paper."

I go through the files, and back on its own, stuffed in with some long-forgotten business cards that identify my father as a "Junior Researcher," I find an old document, signed by Asherberg and my father and a few witnesses.

"There's something here—it's called the two percent agreement," I say.

"Read it to me," Jen says. Instead, I read it quickly to myself. It says that if Jefferson G. Zabusky stays with Asherberg & Co. for more than ten years he gets one percent of the sale of the firm, if they sell the firm. More than twenty years of service, and his take doubles.

"It says if they sell the firm, he gets two percent."

"There's your money," Jen says. She's speaking fast, because she likes this sort of thing. "If he did his time, then the firm has to honor the agreement. His estate is owed that money, absolutely."

"He's owed it, but they have to sell it first, don't they?"

"Sure, but look, this woman you talk about, Leonora, she could buy him out of that deal—or buy you out, I mean. Sorry. You could calculate what that agreement is worth, null it, and make a different deal for less, or sit tight. There's a thousand things you could do with an agreement like that."

"What if, say, I were starving?"

"Then she could buy you out tomorrow, for that percentage of what the firm is worth on some agreed-upon day, the day when you were starving. Or, since you're starving, she could negotiate you down to a lesser amount."

"So if I get really hungry, I need to see Leonora." I tip back even farther in my father's chair and look up at the beams in his ceiling.

"Have an informal meeting with her, just mention the document. See what she offers. Do not—whatever you do—do not name a figure of your own. You're the ingenue in that meeting. Don't forget that."

"Okay," I say. "I know how to say nothing."

"There," Jen says. "I've helped you, haven't I?" I listen to her stir, as it is time to get off the phone. So I begin to speak quickly.

"Jen, there's another thing, and I need your—your womanly advice on this. That woman I talked about when I last saw you, Katherine, she left me because I've been so difficult because of all of this. But I want her back. What would you want me to do if you were her? Not that you know her, but you know me."

Jen breathes long into the phone. I put the tips of my fingers together and tap them, as if I'm calculated, as if I have some idea of what I'm up to.

"I can't help you with that, Mike."

"What about you and Bear?"

"That agreement should completely alter your financial picture," she says. "I'm pleased that I was able to help you discover it." And then I listen to the clatter as she hangs up her office phone.

———

I walk the four miles into Roosevelt, in search of a Bible. There are two bookstores, one on South Market and another on Williams Road. Both sell an assortment of used books and some new selections. I look in the windows of each while I drink the coffee I bought from the Black Forest Café with my father's nickels and dimes. I eat a chocolate brownie, too, that was half price and is gratingly sweet, now that it is hard and stale.

At the corner of South Market and Main, I drink my coffee and gnaw at the brownie while the cars drive by. Bells ring at the Shell station. The antique stores are open, and people look at the window displays and go inside. I actually wave at Malcolm Willgreve as he scuttles into Northern Granite. He pretends not to see me. I recognize other people too, and I smile at them.

I finish off the milky coffee and walk into the Williams Road store, Ashokan Books, which I've chosen only because it's slightly farther away from Crescent Grange.

Inside the store there's a sweet smell of old dried glue, along with a dusty silence. There are no other customers. I suppose a Bible is kept on a shelf devoted to religion, but this store is so small that there aren't any sections beyond fiction, nonfiction, and new releases. A young girl is seated at the back of the store, behind a big cabinet that's fronted with glass. She's reading a paperback. Her hair is parted down the middle in a perfect white line, and she's absorbed with the book, so I see that I must make some sort of attention-getting noise. I scuff my heel and cough. It doesn't matter. She's bobbing because she has tiny earphones in her ears. There's nothing to do but stand and wait until she looks up and I involuntarily startle her.

A minute later the girl looks up. She pulls out the earphones.

"Can I help you?" she asks. She is the girl from Crescent Grange. The waitress who had to wait while Katherine finished her orange juice, who I also know from the train. I grin with apology. We don't admit that we know each other.

"I was wondering if there's one place in particular where you keep your Bibles?" I shift in front of her, touch the glass countertop. Tiny music leaks from her earphones.

She scratches her chin. She's wearing a purple T-shirt that says *Somebody likes you* across the front, in diminutive script.

"I don't know if we have any Bibles."

"None?"

She stands then and smiles. She's willing to look. I follow her through fiction and around to nonfiction. These are quick trips down little aisles. There's no Bible in sight.

"We've run into each other a couple of times before," I say. "How've you been?"

She glances at me before going back to running her fingers along shelves where a Bible wouldn't be.

"I've been well," she says, "but I'm not finding a Bible here. Wait, let's check reference."

We keep going. There's a small shelf full of dictionaries. We look at a Webster, an abridged Hogarth Press edition, and then there it is, an Oxford Annotated Bible. Small, and only fair in its handling of the Old Testament, but it'll do.

"Are you still waiting tables at Crescent Grange?"

"I am," she says. She's back behind the counter now, and she takes the book from my hands. She looks for a price.

"I'm Jeff Zabusky's son. I'm Mike. You know, I think my dad used to go out with Sarah Jane, who owns Crescent Grange."

She angles her head at me. She's just a high school kid.

"I'm Lizzy," she says. "Oh, yeah, I've seen you. Sure, I know. Your father died in the spring. I'm sorry." She looks down. "That sucks."

"Yeah," I say.

"I can't find a price here." She hesitates. "You know, take it. It was so hard to find. Take it."

"You think?" I ask. I smile and feel the lines at the edges of my eyes crinkle down.

"You want to come out back and smoke a cigarette?" she asks. I look behind me, at the front door.

"It's all right," she says. "We'll leave the back door open so I can hear the bell."

Outside, we sit on some concrete steps. There's a grass parking lot here, with an old Toyota parked off to the left that must belong to her. The woods begin about twenty yards from us, and I settle into the idea that sooner or later an angry boyfriend will emerge from the woods, tire iron in hand. We'll watch him sniff glue, or pop some speed, and then he'll come up and beat me because I'm hanging out with his girlfriend, Lizzy. I'll put my hands up when he attacks, but I won't be able to stop him.

I flip through the Bible. I know the Song of Songs quite well, and it'll be interesting to see how it appears in this edition.

"How did you make it through?" she asks.

"I'm still working on that," I say. I see how she's abrupt, like any teenager. But I'll still need to come up with an answer for this sort of question. Something short and sharp that satisfies people.

"Working on it. Well, what did it feel like? When you found out he died."

I look down. She hands over a cigarette, an American Spirit, and though I haven't smoked in years and years, and I'm sure she knows that there aren't many people my age who smoke anymore, I take one.

I say, "This idea, of somebody leaving and never coming back. You can be angry, you can be sad, you can be happy just to try that feeling out. Whatever you try, it doesn't matter. They're gone."

But Lizzy shakes her head. She knows this is all crap. She wants a real answer. I put the Bible on the step next to me, but I keep my hand on it. I pull in a tiny amount of smoke. The head rush takes me right out of that backyard, floats me up above us. I cough.

"Oh, I guess it just hurts, that's all. Makes you feel more lonely. Can I try something out with you, read you something?"

She nods. She rubs her knees together.

I read, " 'How beautiful you are, my darling. How beautiful. Your eyes are doves, seen through your veil.' "

"Not me—you don't mean me," she says. She smokes, and she runs her perfectly parted hair back behind her ear, and then she touches her finger to the point of her jaw. She smiles.

"Any boys ever write you love poetry?"

"Yes," she says. And I look back out into the woods.

She says, "Tell me how it felt. I know you came out here. I know you had to go to the police and identify him. You tell me how it felt and I'll tell you what I knew about him."

"That woman I had brunch with, my girlfriend, she and I have gotten into some trouble. That's what's bothering me now. I may have lost her. I don't know if I really can tell you how losing him felt."

"Come on. Tell me." She stands. She peeks inside. Nobody's coming into the bookstore. She sits back down with her knees together and her chin on her knees.

"I'm appalled, actually, if you want to know the truth."

"So you're angry," she says quietly. "That's how it feels."

"Well, not entirely. I mean, he was my dad. He did some good things. I think about everything differently now, and I recognize that. But what happened to him isn't like cancer, or a car accident. I think I'm allowed to be angry. But the thing about anger is that it's a dull emotion, and death is dull, too. Somebody was here, now they're not, and you can throw all the words you want at what happened, it doesn't matter." I stub the cigarette out on the bottom of my shoe. I can't afford to get even that high, not anymore.

Lizzy says, "If it helps you any, I think he loved Sarah Jane. That's what I saw. But I also saw that he was driving her nuts. They started out simply enough, where he'd pick her up after work. They looked like they were going to be this really quiet couple. But then she pulled away, and I think it broke his heart. I saw him out back of the restaurant, getting into his car. I read a lot. This spring, I finished *Tess*, and I'm almost done with *Portrait of a Lady*. I took the year off and I may take another year and I'm just reading, and waitressing, saving some money. But what happened with him made me look at people differently. I'm telling you, at the end of winter he walked like his heart was broken. I don't know if that will make you less angry or whatever, but I think it's the truth."

"Don't you think that's a little romantic?" I ask.

"That's okay, isn't it?" Lizzy says. "To be romantic."

I look at her and smile. I can imagine my father walking with a broken heart. I don't think she meant that he sagged down, but instead I suspect that he stiffened, that he would keep going to see Sarah Jane and he simply wouldn't understand that it was over. His back would hurt even more, and he would be clenched, tightened, and then he would hurt. I can see him shaking his head, saying to himself that this was impossible, and then as he realized that it was quite possible, everything would harden inside of him again, as it did when my mother told him to leave, when he began to get rich and when he was no longer able to contain his anger.

I was not there to see these times. But Lizzy saw. Lizzy makes sense. I think that I walk differently too when I'm hurting. And she is right. It is hard to stay angry at someone who was weak.

"But why didn't Sarah Jane love him anymore?"

"Sarah Jane has her own problems. You know what she said to me? That your father, that it was too hard to handle him, because he didn't understand how to be in love. So it's not that she's not a loving person. Have you met her father?"

"Oh," I say. "Yes, I've met him."

"He's got Alzheimer's, and she has to take care of him. I don't think she's very happy. And your father, I don't think she felt like he was that nice about all of that—about how she has to take care of her dad and run her restaurant."

"How do you know?" I ask. I think that this is an awful lot to put on my father. That doesn't make it wrong. It's just an awful lot.

"I don't know for sure. I guess the only person who knows better than me is Sarah Jane. You'd have to ask her."

"Do you like her?" I ask. "Do you like Sarah Jane?"

"Yes, I like her," Lizzy says. "She's a very warm person. And she's given me plenty to think about."

Lizzy smiles and shakes hands with me, without any grip, just the softness of her hand.

"I'll see you around," she says. She goes back inside the bookstore.

———

Leonora Asherberg suggested that we meet in Roosevelt, rather than at her house, which was a relief. I can walk to Roosevelt, but not to her house. We take the window table at the Black Forest Café. It's midmorning and fairly crowded, but there aren't many people sitting. I have a paper cup of black coffee in front of me and she has some hot tea. The round table between us is plywood painted to look like marble, but it's worn and it looks meager and less than appropriate for the elbows of someone like Leonora. I had suggested Crescent Grange, but Leonora said that was out of the question.

"So," I say, "I'm happy to see you again."

She stares at me. Though it is the middle of July, she wears a suit, pale blue, with a gold clasp that closes the front of the jacket. She smiles, but she only looks quizzical.

"You've been staying out at the house. Have you been through his things?"

"Yes. I've read all of the files. Most of it makes sense. He lost a lot of money. But what has been difficult to discern is just what he lost of yours."

"I imagined you'd gotten different reports about that. Less than two hundred thousand dollars of mine was lost under his management, and then I took back the rest. He made a poor decision as far back as last summer on Lucent, and that was it for me. I shifted out slowly. Technology stocks first, of course. We had several phone conversations. I was very worried about him. And he, in turn, was angry with me."

"No margin calls?" I ask.

"Well. Yes, he did call and ask me to cover him for margin, back at the beginning of April, but that's not a good practice. I said no. To me he was like a son, and though it was very painful, I had to put my foot down. Money managers often misbehave that way. I was married to one for fifty-three years, so I'm used to it."

Leonora sips from her cup of tea. She takes the bag out, but then she finds nowhere to put it, so she drops it back in. Someone behind the counter puts music on: *My Aim Is True*. Leonora wrinkles her nose and exhales.

"What a wearing time for us all," I say.

"Yes. Have you been to see Rabbi Vrieslander at my temple? I told him to expect you."

"No, but I've been—I visited the cemetery. I hope you'll call me when the stone arrives."

"I will. I hope that you'll be in touch also. Beyond the money, you know how I felt about your father. I've been very clear about that."

Someone bangs the front door closed and Leonora turns and glares at them. Sleigh bells ring repeatedly when the front door opens. She must not like that, either.

"There was one document that hadn't been dealt with, Leonora. I think it was called something like a two percent agreement."

Leonora raises an eyebrow, and then she bows her head to me. She says, "I thought of that document just the other day." Her gaze is slow. She touches the nail on her pinky to her lipstick. Her eyes do not stray from my face.

"It was the only agreement of its kind that Max ever made. This was so many years ago, when there were only eight people in the firm. Your father was displeased because Max wouldn't let him be a manager, and he threatened to quit. Rather than just give him a raise, or let him get in a position where he could manage anybody else, they wrote out that agreement. Max used to say it was the best negotiation he ever made. The answer is yes. We can try to make something good come of this. We'll structure some sort of deal soon, perhaps in the fall. I'm getting older, and I'll certainly sell the company sometime, or you can let me buy you out. Smart of you to find that paper."

"Thank you, Leonora. This is very kind of you, to show me my options." I smile at her, and finish my coffee.

"It's not about your options. Our firm is still flush, and it occurred to us that if we denied that claim, you could probably sue, and nobody wants that."

"No, of course not," I say. And I see that I am a greater ingenue than I have been instructed to be, because I would not have thought to sue.

"I loved your father, and my husband did too. The fact that he— that he gave himself a terrible winter and spring, this does not make me think less of him, and now, with even a little time gone by, I can already remember only the best parts of him. I feel better. Had you waited a few more months to see me, I might have bumped up the two percent to something outsized, out of a misbegotten sentimentalism."

She smiles at me. She's joking, and she expects me to laugh. But I can't laugh. I can only blink like an ingenue, so that Leonora thinks I'm like her, and that I care about the money as much as she does. She runs her hand over the pin on her chest. I follow, in case she's using pantomime to show me that I've spilled something on my shirt. Then we sit there, with our hands on our chests.

"So I'm not broke after all," I say. "And neither was he."

"That's right. As I said, we'll be able to work something out." She straightens the front of her jacket and gets up from the table.

"Then why did you say all that to me, back at Bard when he died, about him and the markets, when even then you knew it wasn't true?" I ask.

"Not true? Well, it was somewhat true." She shakes her head. I'm still sitting. I don't get up.

"Okay," she says. "Fine. Because this is the way I'd prefer to think about his death. And for your sake, you might think about it my way too."

"But it's not true—it was because of him and Sarah Jane, because of how he felt about her."

"Aren't we done here, Michael? Find a lawyer and have them call me, yes?"

"Two percent," I say. "That could be a whole lot."

23

I don't take anything to New York but my new Bible, Weingarden's paper, and a notebook. I carry these things in a brown leather satchel that I found in my father's bedroom closet.

I phoned the Gouverneur, and I found out that Blake has moved my few possessions to the basement, because he didn't want me to pay for nights when I haven't slept in my room. I spoke to the managers and told them it was time for me to let the room go. They've been extremely kind. They told me that after Asherberg & Co. relinquished the holding, they were never full, not for three straight years. I made a lot of friends there. I paid my bill on time, and they say they never saw a reason to send me on my way.

I ride down on the train and look out over the Hudson. The sun doesn't make its way into the car this early in the day but there's plenty of light reflected on the still surface of the water. I look at Weingarden's paper again, and at the Song of Songs.

Weingarden begins by introducing the *Shiur Komah*—an obscure document that reveals the size and shape of God. He explains why opponents of mysticism felt that it was so awful to try to give proper names to religious fervor: because it is antithetical to traditional Judaism. What is safely poetic in the Song of Songs ("Your hair is like a flock of goats, moving down the slopes of Gilead") is far more massive and unholy in the *Shiur Komah.* Weingarden quotes the great Joseph Dan on the astronomical size of God: "The black in his right eye is eleven thousand five hundred parasangs. In order to understand what precisely are the dimensions here indicated, we have to determine what is intended by the term 'parasang.' In normal usage this Persian measurement of distance means something over three miles, *but not so in the Shiur Komah, which itself includes a definition of the parasang as equal to ninety thousand times the width of the earth.*"

No matter how perfect the calculation becomes, God is still inconceivably big. And then the paper unravels, as Weingarden goes on to viciously attack the Golem. Compared to such a conception, the Golem, given all the benefits of every bit of folklore and explication, is always dangerous and spiritless. A monstrous creature who remains hopelessly mute. The Golem is like a bad love song, poorly contrived even in its conception.

I am reminded of my own transcendent moment, with Katherine's mother, when I had to conjure the massive just to remain calm. Of course, there was no way that any idea I could have would simply come out of the air. And then I see, as the train dips into the tunnel and the blue sky in the window fades to darkness, that I can answer one of Weingarden's questions: what goes on in the monster's head? It dreams of the *Shiur Komah*—which is the only way it knows how to pray. I am struck then by the similarity between us. My hope has been like a monster's—a stupid sort of praying, suffused with the desperation of someone with no soul.

And why would a holy man create a Golem? Weingarden asked me to find the answer to this to help round out his own paper. A holy man creates a monster out of hope, but in the end he tends to his own fate, and his monster destroys him. In all of the medieval legends around which Weingarden centers his studies, this occurs.

I remember Weingarden's party, when he interrupted the conversation I was having with Katherine. The light was just right, and there were candles, and his guests danced in his dining room. He said that he'd enjoy it if I danced with Katherine. And soon after that, we did dance.

———

I take the subway down to Little Italy and loiter for a while in the cool of the station before coming up to meet Mark Staresina. While I walk to where we are supposed to meet, I consider the notion of the parasang. I have never thought of the width of our earth. I can't imagine it. Then, in less than the time it takes to walk one step forward on the street, I feel something that must be akin to bliss when I try to multiply a distance I can't conceive of by ninety thousand. I shake the feeling off, because I don't want this kind of praying to belong to me.

Mulberry Street is blazing hot, and Café Cha Cha's is an outdoor café at the far end. I hear the place first—Perry Como singing in Italian. The garish color of artificial brass is everywhere, and the seats are filled with tourists. Mark is already there. He has a table set next to the curb, and he's straddling a chair, with his legs around its back and the heart-shaped ironwork pressed into his chest. He wears sunglasses, white shorts, and a polo shirt that's the color of a mango. He has woven bracelets on both wrists.

"Hey hey," he says, and he half unstraddles to shake hands. "You're going to love this cappuccino."

"Sounds good," I say.

I let him order for both of us, from an older woman. He speaks slowly and orders a cannoli. He says we should split it; it's terrific, but heavy.

"I'm in the city today to get this Peter Gabriel bootleg," he says, "from a store over on Bleecker, where they know me. When I do something like that, afterwards I like to stop by Cha Cha's. Otherwise, I don't like it here. I can't stand the city."

"Sure," I say. "A lot of people feel that way."

"Not Katherine. She loves it."

In only a few weeks I have grown unused to the heat of city streets. The air around us affects the way we sound, so our voices are not loud, but they are heavy.

"Listen, before we discuss her, I want to be sure I understand— your father killed himself because he went bankrupt?" His tone softens then, and he takes off his sunglasses.

"Not exactly, but if you'd like to think of it that way," I say, "that's fine with me."

"It's not that I like it," Mark says. He shakes his head and looks up and down Mulberry Street. Couples walk by. They admire the T-shirts and white Venetian hats. He takes a gulp of his cappuccino.

"Ah, look—Katherine says she left you because you were acting crazy."

"I've had a hard time," I say. "It's tough to get over something like this."

"Well, I'm sorry for your loss," Mark says. "About Katherine— I can't keep track of her lately. Normally, she calls me. But she hasn't and she's been hard to reach." He frowns as he says this. I doubt it's true.

"You're losing her," I say.

"Losing her? This has happened before." He shakes his head and brushes back his hair. "I'm not losing anybody. Anyway, that's not what this is about."

The cannoli arrives. He motions for me to take the first bite. But I only stare at him. He reaches out and takes some of the filling, and sucks it off his fingers.

"Actually, I wanted to talk to you because I've seen guys fight before, to get her back, and I thought I'd tell you to just forget it, you know? It's like I told you on my father's birthday. She's not right for you. Okay?"

"I don't understand," I say.

"Look, she's my sister and I love her," he says. "I'm in her business and maybe I know her better than you do. So that's it. She's not for you. That's all."

We're quiet. I lean back in the chair and feel the ironwork etch its pattern into my skin.

"Okay. I'll forget her," I say, and smile. But Mark can see that I'm lying. He only shakes his head. He's not eating any more of the cannoli, and I'm not touching it either.

"It's not a pleasure at all, this assignment," he says, and he looks above my head, as if he is only a messenger.

He drums his fingers up and down the back of his chair. His hands are clean. His nails cut. He fingers his sunglasses, but he doesn't put them back on. He takes a toothpick from the shot glass on the table and slides it between his teeth. He checks to see that his bootleg disk is still under the table, and I see him lean it against his ankle.

"Who made Katherine your assignment?" I ask.

"Jesus Christ."

"Oh, right," I say, "him."

"I don't care that you don't believe. I'm just here to make sure that nobody gets hurt. That's all this is."

"If she's not with Adam, how do you know she doesn't want to see me again? She might be desperate for me to see her, and you're telling me to forget it."

He takes the toothpick out of his mouth and tosses it into the street. He points at me.

"You don't know where she is, right?" he asks.

I drink the cappuccino. The hot coffee and the milky foam separate in my mouth.

"No," I say. "But I assume she's at home."

He stops and puts his right hand up and he's gone quite immobile.

He asks, "Would you hurt her if she was with another man? What would you do if you saw her?"

"I would do anything to get her back," I say.

He gazes at me. His eyes are clear blue, and they set off his black hair. His clothes are so clean. They must be new.

"Then you can't see her. I won't let her see you and try to explain what happened. And I won't tell you where she's going. She was right to send me here. Too bad for you," he says.

"Tell me where she is," I say.

"No. The truth is I'm not pleased with the present situation either, and I thought if you were really good—you could save her. But now I see I'm wrong. What a shame. My mother liked you. That's what swayed me. I shouldn't listen to her. The men who come after Katherine are never any good."

He curls his upper lip, as if he's suddenly disgusted that he's allowed himself to talk for so long with someone like me.

He says, "Maybe you never really loved her, and I didn't need to bother to come here today. She's arrogant and sometimes she gets things wrong."

"I don't believe she doesn't want to be with me, even if she did go back to Adam," I say.

"Adam? I don't know why you keep mentioning him. She had me thinking that my coming here would do some good. But I can see that I can't help either of you."

And then he ducks down and grabs his CD. He stands, and he's already looking beyond me. He walks away from the table, toward the subway. I pick up the cannoli but I can't imagine how it would feel to taste it.

In the Gouverneur, I'm given the same room. It's cleaner than I remember. Everything I own is in a wire cage in the basement. My clothes are in boxes, and my books are stacked. My pictures are lined up together and tied. My father's handkerchiefs must be in one of those boxes, and I'm pleased that I kept them.

I go back upstairs to the anonymous room and I know why I liked it here so much. The bed is big and soft, and if I'd been in an apartment of my own for these five years, I would have never bought such a wonderful bed. In the future, I will remember this and not be so Spartan. I lie down on that bed now and rest.

My mother calls in the early evening. She says, "It was that woman, then, who drove him to it? The Catholic?"

"Sarah Jane. She says she's half Jewish, actually. But other people have said she's Catholic, too."

"Mike, after you've talked to her I want you to call me, and let me know what she did to him."

"I saw her a few times," I say, quietly. "It's not what she did to him. It doesn't make sense to explain it that way."

But my mother does not respond. I check my watch. I'm supposed to have dinner with Bear in an hour. He needs to keep busy now that he's without Jen. I am also trying to do activities that don't involve Katherine, so that she has more time before I approach. In the past, I always rushed her.

Tomorrow, I will go and see Matthew Weingarden. It's been difficult to schedule with him. Even though it's the middle of the summer, he's been busy, but he was eager to find time for me because he wants to hear what I have to say about his paper.

"Mom, if you want to think about it less, imagine that he had a broken heart because Sarah Jane didn't want him."

"Don't be ridiculous. Your father couldn't name a broken heart."

And then my mother suggests that I sell my father's mortgaged house for a huge loss and take the few thousand I might get. I'll have some money of my own, and I can walk away clean. I tell her about the two percent agreement and she says she didn't know about it. For so many years it must have been only a piece of paper in a file.

"But Mom, I'm sure he knew he had it. He kept that paper, and he killed himself anyway. It wasn't the money. It was never the money."

It feels funny to say such things aloud. I speak slowly. These sentences are not the kind that I would want to have to repeat.

"Maybe you're right, Mike. A broken heart—my God, I never would have thought of it."

"It's a little bit fantastic, I know, but it could be," I say.

"Yes, it could be."

I stand up. I do want to encourage her to try to find some solace in our conjecture, but I'm conflicted; I don't want to obscure our memory of him.

"Remember how you'd sing with him?" I ask.

"Yes, I remember. It was the seventies, and we were listening to music from the forties. We never got past when we were young, how everything sounded then. But I listen to those singers now too."

"He wasn't violent, was he?"

"You're asking this now?"

I don't speak. I'm all packed. I could move to Roosevelt this afternoon and stay forever.

"Was he?"

"During those last few years we were together he became diffi-cult, yes. We were lucky that we could afford to send you away."

"So that's what he was," I say.

"Don't judge your father. He wasn't a terrible man. He was just angry, and he was not in control. When we divorced, it was be-cause I understood that ultimately I could not change that part of him. He would not change. But I think you knew this about him. I haven't tried to hide it from you. In any case, that's not all he was. Tell me, what will you do?"

I have told my mother nothing about Katherine. I choose not to begin to tell her now. I look out, far past Straus Square, all the way up to Grand Street, where some men have begun to construct a scaffold of steel poles and wood planks around the stone walls of Seward Park High School.

"I'm thinking of living up there, in Roosevelt. I've been seeing this woman in the city, and she's had enough of her job, and that's what we're going to do."

My mother laughs.

"What could possibly make you think that you should live in that house?" she asks. "That's completely inappropriate. You want to live in the country, you go and find your own house."

"But I would be happy there. I know it."

"Why? So you can make what he did there right?" she asks. "He doesn't control your future. Really, you should be grateful that this terrible thing didn't send us all into bankruptcy. It could have, you know."

"It could have, but I don't think he would have allowed that."

"Fair enough—all the more reason to move on. That is not your house."

"Then whose house is it?" I ask.

"Why, Michael, it was his. Now you have to sell it. That's all."

I look around my old hotel room. They have used my absence as an opportunity to paint the walls. The shadows at the edges of the ceiling are gone. Now that I'm looking, I realize that the venetian blinds have been replaced, too. The bedspread is a lighter blue now, and the carpet is a rich yellow.

"I'm not ready to give up that house," I say.

24

"Mike, it's good to see you," Weingarden says. "I am sorry about what happened to your father. That must have been very hard and I won't try to console you with common phrases." He nods his head slowly, and his hair falls forward.

We're sitting in the Jewish Theological Seminary's misshapen courtyard. It is so hot that steam seems to rise from the dirt encased in the seams of the courtyard's slate walkways. Weingarden has switched from his familiar clothing palette of charcoal and black to one of cream and white. He leans back and lets the sun bathe him. He's just the sort of man who looks comfortable in leather sandals. I'm in blue jeans and a T-shirt that's the color of tar. I sit across from him on a bench made of stone slabs and I sweat.

"Thanks—I think I'm going to be okay," I say. "I read your paper. And I was fascinated by the *Shiur Komah* and your argument. I see why you used the Golem as a foil. Only, there are some things you left out."

"Go on," he says. He shoots his legs out in front of him.

"Well, there's two things, actually. One is that the Golem, or any monster—you asked me what they dream about, back in the spring? The thing that pulls your paper together is this: they dream of the *Shiur Komah*. If that's what you were looking for from me, then you've got it. It's all already there. Now, I can easily work out the connections through close readings of the Golem myths and through the descriptions in the Song of Songs. When I read it, it was as if you had the connection and you just weren't letting it click."

"Yes," he says quietly. "Yes, of course there's a link."

He smiles. There's no need for him to make a note, as he'll remember my idea.

"Then there's something that I think you may have forgotten, about the Golem and its creator—about how their story ends."

"The Golem destroys the creator," he says, and nods at me. "Of course I hadn't forgotten. I'd been avoiding that part of the story because I didn't find it wholly relevant."

"It matters. I think you have to mention it."

"I'm not sure of that," he says. And then he begins to talk about his correspondence with a man named Martin Stone, a man who wrote the definitive exegesis on the *Shiur Komah*. Weingarden wants to refute his analysis. He goes on about the *Shiur Komah* and how little has been made of it, how it's going to really belong to him. He gestures with his hands at the ideas behind the measurements and how excited he is—how different this is from more conventional mysticism.

"I don't see the point in your argument if you have to lop off the end of a myth to make it work," I say, but I'm only trying to interrupt him.

"What—Mike, I don't understand," he says, and squints at me. He brings his legs in then, and crouches forward, so he's looking up at my face.

"Why did you speak against me to Katherine?" I ask, and I believe I sound quiet and calm. I don't move. I watch him draw back and relax.

"I hope you're not angry with me," he says, and smiles. "After all, when the subject is as delicate as a woman like Katherine, well, I'm sure you agree that I did the right thing?"

I look through the tall windows on the second floor, at the entrance to the seminary's library, where a girl places books into a metal receptacle, one at a time. She has the flushed look of an undergraduate who has just completed a long overdue paper, and now she's returning all the books she's had to read. She drops them in, throws them away. It's an exhilarating feeling she's having, and it represents the opposite of the place where I have just arrived, within the moment when I hear Weingarden acknowledge that he's been in contact with the woman I love.

"Katherine," I say carefully, though I can hear the cracking in my voice. "Why would you turn her against me?"

"She's brilliant, isn't she? Really, she's quite something. A lovely sort of intellect on that one." He shakes his head, and it's clear that he does not intend to answer my question directly.

"So you've seen her?" I ask.

"Yes, we've had things to discuss, what with her involvement with Adam Savioli and all that's followed."

While I let what he's said hang between us, I force all of me to sink down, and I hope that by doing so, I've slowed my heart. Then I say, "Your friend? The married man? Has she gone back with him?"

"Back with him?" Weingarden says. "I should hope not. But then again, with her, who can know?"

I find that I cannot release my grip on the stone bench. I slowly bring my legs apart and lean forward.

"Why would you hope not?" I ask. "And why won't you answer me? Don't you understand? She left me, and she said you encouraged it."

The undergraduate walks past us. She's done for the day, perhaps for the summer. Weingarden looks at her too. When she disappears we are completely alone. He looks up at the sky and begins to hum a piece of classical music that I do not recognize.

He says, "I love it up here. The students are sweet, but it's a shame how conservative the institution has become. Thank God we're all down at CUNY. Anyway, yes, Katherine. I didn't warn her against you. When she came to me, I only suggested that you might behave badly."

He shakes his head and smiles. "I remember back in the spring, Adam begged me to invite her to that party so they could get some time together, and then, the moment they were in the same room, they were in a fight. I enjoyed meeting her. More recently Adam's been making plans to move with his wife and child to Berlin. He's going to rebuild a company over there, and he'll do the necessary work to make his marriage survive. Far greater traumas than one broken heart in that city. I'm going there myself in a few days, for a conference. What a party that was! We all watched her wrangling with Adam. And from there, you swept in and took her off where no one could see. It was brilliant. Too bad for him. And quite a surprise to me, really. I misjudged the situation. I didn't think you had that sort of thing in you."

"I know about the party," I say. "What happened after that?"

"Don't you see? You can be a bit of a monster yourself, so I had some reason to be concerned about Katherine. I'd been helping you through your work with the Golem, but you kept circling the same ideas, over and over. You were obsessed, and when she came to me, the first time, that's what we discussed."

"But that's not true. That's not what you said in our meetings. And I'm not—"

"And then your father committed suicide. She had me worried that she would bear the brunt of your grief, and by then—I was convinced. It doesn't matter now anyway. She certainly broke old Adam's heart, and that was damned sad. If it's been the same way with you—I'm sorry for that."

"So she's not with Adam now," I say.

"Thank God everyone's come out okay," he says, and he stands up to leave. I watch as he glances toward the arched doorway at the bottom of the Kripke Tower. And I do not correct him. I do not mention that, in fact, my father was hurt. And I do not say that Katherine and I are not done.

"Really," he says, "thank you for everything, Mike. It was your obstinacy that kept the Golem at the forefront of my mind all this time. I had to have something to play the *Shiur Komah* against, and now, thank the Lord above, and thank you, I've got it. The frustrated monster of Judaism against the *Shiur Komah*. And the idea that the Golem dreams of measuring the size of God? It's too brilliant. As you know, other religions have monsters that are far less tortured. But you have done such wonderful work at—dare I say?—putting our ideas into practice."

"But I haven't done anything like that," I say.

I stand. I say, "I'm not putting any myths into practice and you didn't create me. If you did, if anything you're saying is true—I'd be furious and I'd be mute, and I would destroy you right now."

He laughs and says, "Then what a relief to be wrong. Perhaps it's best that I left that part out of my paper, yes? I'll be in touch with you in the fall, although I may not be on campus too often. But we can continue to work together—if you still want to."

He moves quickly then and walks away from me. Though it is still early in the day, there are passageways at the sides of this courtyard that are shaded over and dark. He waves at me and walks into one.

"Good-bye, Professor," I say. I look after him, but it's impossible to find his figure in this sudden gloom.

———

Katherine's roommate, Leah, is a black-haired woman. She has long eyelashes and slight lines on her face that turn down from the sides of her nose to her mouth. She wears black pants and a black T-shirt. It's Sunday morning, and she must have been out late the night before. I haven't been up to much, besides waiting to see Katherine. I've called her only once, but there was no answer, and I chose not to leave a message.

Because I sat down on the stoop after I rang the bell, I'm looking up at Leah. I rest my elbows on my knees. She closes the door behind her. She has on white flip-flops. Her toenails are painted red. Slowly, while holding on to the railing, she sits down next to me.

"Katherine isn't here," she says.

"Where did she go?" I ask.

Leah opens her mouth, but then she only whistles, low. There are no more people between Katherine and me. I need to see her, and I am prepared to wait. If we are the same, then she is ready for me now.

I have come with nothing in my hands. I'm in khakis and a shirt of my father's, a green striped button-down, and I've brought nothing but everything that I've memorized. All of the Song of Songs. Every myth and story that I know. I was going to say some of these things aloud to her, or I was only going to think them, while I asked her to come and live with me in Roosevelt. She was going to be enraptured by my fervor. But I still don't know where she is. And Leah isn't telling.

"You write songs?" I ask. "You're a songwriter?"

"Yeah, songwriting. That's what I do. I used to sing in bands, but now I just write songs. I've sold a few, and I'm living off them."

It's just before noon. Now that July is nearly over, the searing heat is leavened with light winds. I wonder what Adam Savioli's wife and child are doing right now.

"I'm sorry about what happened between you two," Leah says. "She said you loved her."

She stretches out, so her legs reach far down the steps, and she closes her eyes and yawns. The skin on her forehead is almost translucent, and I see a tremor pass over her brow.

I look at the windows above us, but Katherine is not looking down. Perhaps the door isn't locked, and I could run upstairs and find her. Or she's gone somewhere, on retreat, and she has left a note asking for me to wait. Or even an object meant to reassure me; some piece of her clothing, or the green leaf in the lump of glass. I look at Leah and her eyes are closed, and suddenly she looks much older than she could possibly be.

"Are you okay?" I ask.

"No, not really. I was up late last night," Leah says. "I was coming home from watching my friend's band play at the Big Room, and my cab was hit by this guy in an old truck. He was delivering newspapers. He'd fallen asleep and he just slammed into us. Right in the cross section of Flatbush and Atlantic. We spun around one and a half times."

"Did you go to the hospital?"

"No," she says. She rubs her temples, and I look at the place that she's touching. When she takes her fingers away, her skin is mottled and red.

"I didn't have to go. He banged into the trunk of the cab, and I had on my seat belt. So we spun out and I didn't bounce around or anything. I just knocked against the door and then we stopped. It was one of those things, though: four feet to the right, or one quarter of a second, and that truck would have killed me."

"It's good that you're okay," I say. She nods and pouts her lips. She appears to be testing them.

"Me and the cabdriver got out and hugged each other. I started praying, so he did too, and normally I don't do that. The cops drove me home. I'm supposed to go over to Downstate Medical later if I feel funny."

"You should go. You should have them take X rays."

"Yeah, I probably will," she says, and closes her eyes again. She places her hands over her head and she begins to rub at her skull.

"I don't think you should rub there," I say. "Not until after a doctor sees you." She turns then and looks at me. She stops rubbing.

"You think I have a concussion?" she asks.

"It could be," I say.

"The only reason I'm up and dressed is that the police said they'd send somebody by around noon, to take my statement, because I couldn't do it last night. So I had to put myself together."

"I'm lucky to have caught you," I say. "And I can sit with you until they come."

"Thanks. I'm sorry about Katherine. That she's not around."

A woman comes up the street and I look at her quickly. But she is dressed in a white suit for church and she isn't Katherine. Another woman follows her. I lean forward, my arms folded hard into my stomach, but this woman isn't her, either.

"You can make great songs out of being hit by a car," I say.

"I know. It's callous, but that's exactly what I've been thinking," she says. "I've been up all morning, drinking black coffee and writing lines about spinning out on Flatbush. And all those newspapers, they came out of the back of the truck, and that's a good image, you know? Flying newspapers. But at the same time, I'm glad I'm alive." She shakes her head and laughs.

"Where is she?" I ask.

This time, Leah speaks quickly. "She went to Berlin with somebody called Matthew Weingarden."

I can feel a sudden wetness in the interstices between my fingers. There is nothing to strike at, and that feels like a blow against me, that I can look ahead and find nothing to attack. He lied to me and I let him go. I reach out with both hands and grip the iron banister to my right. I can feel the grit of the rusty black paint. The surface peels off in my hands, and I do not open my eyes and I do not let go.

Leah says, "She said he was relentless with her, and that she couldn't help it. She fell in love with him. She said that you knew him and that it was a problem. Is it?"

I don't say anything. I open my eyes. I taste my top lip and it is cool and dry, as if no blood is flowing there.

"Shit—maybe I shouldn't have told you," Leah says. "I thought you had a right to know, but it looks like you shouldn't have found out." She opens her mouth wide and begins to sing up the scale, "Ah, ah, oh . . ." But then, as she goes higher, there is a quaver, and she stops abruptly.

"Well," I say through the cold in my mouth, "it's not a good idea to try to sing right now. You've been hurt."

At that moment an unmarked police car double parks in front of us. Leah watches the car. The window goes down and there's one policeman, who looks up at us.

"Let me help you," I say, and I stand and give Leah my hand. She leans into me and slowly gets up. We go down to the police car.

"Make him take you to the hospital first," I say, "before you do anything else."

"Okay," she says. "That sounds like the right thing to do."

I open the car door and Leah steps in. I close it lightly after her.

After Leah is driven away, I don't stand still in front of their house. I walk quickly off that street, taking long strides, because I'm in an unexpected rush. I arrive at Flatbush Avenue and keep going.

25

It's late August and I'm pulling my rental car out of the lot behind the Gloria Lawson Real Estate office at the north end of Main Street, in Roosevelt. I'm finished with her team for the day, and they're ready to take over the sale of my father's house. I drive down Main, to Crescent Grange. It's about four-thirty now, and I'm sure that Sarah Jane must be getting ready for Friday dinner. I just want to go in and tell her that I'm sorry, and maybe get something to eat before I drive back to New York.

I'm tired out from wrangling with the real estate people, and from talking with Malcolm Willgreve at Northern Granite, who has promised to do whatever he can to help with the sale. I find that the reality of all of this is such a lot of work, and nothing like my studies.

I take off my blazer and throw it into the back of the car. Lately I've been behaving like a businessman, and feeling like one has confirmed what I already knew. I don't want to be one. But I don't think I want to write a dissertation now either. So when fall arrives and I'm finished taking care of my father's affairs, I will look for some work while I reconsider what sort of dissertation I need to write.

When I come into Crescent Grange, I find Lizzy alone in the dining room. She's setting the tables for dinner. Tall stalks of fall grains have been placed at the corners of the room, and there is a large display of flowers between the two doors to the kitchen. The crescents that fill this place seem less prominent than I remembered. A few candles have already been lit. The white ceiling makes the room feel light.

"Hello, Mike," Lizzy says. I come and stand by her.

"I can't really stop what I'm doing," she says, "because I'm behind schedule, but it's good to see you. Are you going to live up here?"

"I don't think so, not in my father's house anyway."

"That's too bad. Sarah Jane and I thought that you might be going to. People have seen you in town lately, so we'd been wondering."

"I've had a lot of business to handle," I say.

She nods at me and keeps at her work, setting the silver cutlery into patterns.

"Sarah Jane's in the kitchen," she says.

I go through the swinging doors. Sarah Jane has her back to me. She stirs a pot of what could be broth. She is alone. The air in here makes me dizzy—it's thick and warm. I've brought a hint of the fresh flowers in, and I'd like to believe the flowers mix with the good smell of the stove.

"Sarah Jane, I need to talk to you," I say.

I watch her back as she breathes in. She doesn't turn but breathes deeply, until she's still, and then when she is ready, she faces me. I have not seen her since I was in the water and she was on the bank, and that was a long time ago. She looks at me and blinks, to cool the heat in her eyes.

"What can I tell you, Mike?"

She finds a lid and places it carefully over the broth. She puts it on at an angle, so steam rises at the edges. Then she simply gazes at me, and leans against the counter behind her.

I say, "You don't need to tell me anything. I know that my father must have been horrible and abusive with you and I'm sorry for it, that it happened."

"Strange. I was just thinking about you and now here you are," she says.

I say, "Well, I'm here to say that I'm sorry. I want to ask you to forgive me, for how I acted in front of your father. I had no right to yell at you. My father died of a broken heart because you wouldn't be with him, and I'm working on understanding that."

"Let's go outside," Sarah Jane says. She takes up her apron and dries her face and neck. Another woman comes into the kitchen and Sarah Jane motions for her to take care of the broth. She walks with me through the dining room and then down the front steps, out to the street. Though it is not yet dusk, the light is low.

"He didn't die of a broken heart. You're wrong to think that," she says.

"I'm calling it by the wrong name?" I ask.

"No—this is my fault—I've been slow to explain. I could never see your father as much as he wanted. He was so lonely out here and he refused to admit it, and he put everything on me. He attacked me one night when I was late to come meet him because there was an emergency here at the restaurant. He threw a chair at me, and then we fought. That sort of thing happened a few times. When I told him it couldn't happen anymore or I would never see him, he went cold. But he did stop. Then, in the winter, he started to say that he didn't want to be alive if he couldn't be with me, but that's not what he meant. He didn't want to be alive unless I existed only for him. And that is impossible for me. Of course, I didn't believe him, and I stopped seeing him. I used to have Lizzy tell him to go away when he'd wait out here in his car. I wanted to hide all of that from you, but I guess I can't. So, there's no need for you to ask me to forgive you. If that's what you want—I forgive you. But I could ask you for the same thing."

I look away from her. It wasn't money and it wasn't the broken heart that I've been using for consolation. It was just him, furious and unable to control what was happening. I look down Main

Street, toward the river. He's suddenly familiar to me this way: angry, and entirely himself.

I say, "I'm going to sell his house. There's no reason for me to stay there, and I could never really afford it."

"Where will you go?"

"Oh, I'll find an apartment in the city. My studies are moving too slow, so I need to look for work while I pursue them."

She runs her hands through her hair. A woman drives by and honks, and Sarah Jane smiles and waves. She reaches down and picks up some paper that's caught in the grass at the side of the curb.

"Do you forgive me?" she asks.

I look behind us at the parking lot and I can imagine him idling the engine of his Cadillac, waiting for Sarah Jane. Lizzy would come out and tell him that she wouldn't see him, and he'd drive back home, and there would be nothing to do there, and nowhere else to go.

"Yes, of course I forgive you," I say.

"What about your girlfriend?" Sarah Jane asks.

"She left me," I say. And now it's my turn to shake my head. A small breeze comes up and I squint my eyes.

"I was being difficult," I say. "And it was all too much for her, so now she's on to the next thing."

"I'm sorry for that. Do you want to stay and eat an early dinner with us?"

"Yes," I say, "I'd like that. I'll just stay for a little while and then I need to get back."

"Go inside and have Lizzy set you a place. We can all eat to-gether before the dinner crowd comes in."

Later that night, back in the city, I wait while the woman at the Budget Rent a Car outlet puts my bill together. I watch as she counts up the days I've used the car and combines them with the deluxe insurance package I took. She has big brown eyes and a great mass of brown hair, and she wears the company blazer over a soft white blouse. We're the only ones in the checkout station and we can hear the lights buzz above us. Cars creep down East Forty-ninth Street, but this is not a busy neighborhood on a Friday, not at this time of night. I get out my wallet and hand over my credit card. While we wait for the card to be accepted, her cell phone rings. She takes the call.

"Come on, I can't talk now—I'm not finished working," she says.

She glances at me, and then turns to her right so she can look through the big window that separates us from the garage where the rental cars are parked. I turn too. There's only a few left, as most have been taken out for the weekend. I find that already I can't pick out the one I just used.

"Stop it, stop it," she says. "Yes, I'm coming home after work. Yes, I promise." Then she breathes in. She says, "Yes. I swear to you."

She puts my papers down and goes to stand and finish her call by the back wall. When she gets there, she holds the phone out in front of her and looks at the sound of an angry voice. Then she brings the phone back to her ear.

"Please," she says. "Charles, please stop."

She turns completely away from me and faces the back wall of her station, where there is a brightly colored map that shows all of the Budget locations, all over the world. There are thousands of them. If I combine them with all of the other car rental agencies, and all of the other places to get cars, and all the other ways to travel—well, it is beyond my capacity to conjure even this minor calculation. How many locations that must be, how many thousands of places, and then all those places, all our places, in turn, making up a world, which is then multiplied by parasangs? How can it be? I can't conjure it.

The woman's left hand is clenched tightly in a fist behind her back. It's a fantastic map that she's facing, with lots of primary colors and outlined states and countries.

I look through the window and a man in the Budget uniform

comes and gets into a car that I might have used. He drives it up a ramp. The noise the car makes is muffled by the glass, so that the car's engine sounds like crashing waves.

She comes back and hands over the bill and the credit receipt. I carefully sign the receipt. She knows that I have heard her on the phone. I look up at her, and she stares back at me.

"My stupid boyfriend," she says, and shrugs her shoulders. She nods at me. "Is there anything else I can help you with today?"

"No, I'm set," I say.

She takes the receipt from me and hands me a thin sheet of paper that came out of the printer.

"It's hard to deal with someone when they talk that way," I say.

She looks up quickly and leans forward, as if she wants to be sure she heard me correctly. She glances at the phone beside her, then back at me.

She says, "Come on now, you don't know the first thing about it." She cocks her eyebrow and waits for me to say anything more.

"You're right," I say, "I don't. But at least I can try and begin to understand."

She doesn't say anything in return. I pick up my father's brown bag. I look once more at the fantastic map behind her, then push open the glass and metal door. I begin to sing to myself. Behind the counter she watches me as I start down the street, singing as loud as I can.

Acknowledgments

Most of the ideas about the Golem and Jewish mysticism that I've written about here can be found in a much expanded and clearer form in Gershom Scholem's *Major Trends in Jewish Mysticism* and *On the Kabbalah and Its Symbolism*. For comprehensive scholarship about the Golem, I used *Golem: Jewish Magical and Mystical Traditions on the Artificial Anthropoid* by Moshe Idel. For insight into the monster's character, I relied on Gustav Meyrink's novel *The Golem* and *The Golem: Legends of the Ghetto of Prague* by Chayim Bloch. I found many modern ideas and arguments in Elliot R. Wolfson's *Through a Speculum That Shines: Vision and Imagination in Medieval Jewish Mysticism*. Dr. Elsie Stern of Fordham University, Jonathon Kahn of Columbia University, Dee Cohen, and Shannon Hill of the Network for Women's Services gave me ideas and advice. In chapter 23, I quote directly from Joseph Dan's excellent and all-but-unique article "The Concept of Knowledge in the *Shiur Komah*," which can be found in *Studies in Jewish Religious and Intellectual History Presented to Alexander Altmann on the Occasion of His Seventieth Birthday*, edited by Siegfried Stein and Raphael Lowe.

ACKNOWLEDGMENTS

I am grateful to the MacDowell Colony, the Ledig Rowholt Foundation, and the Writers Room. Finally, I thank Richard Abate, Jennifer Braunschweiger, Lee Boudreaux, Daniel Menaker, and Danzy Senna for their invaluable help with every stage of this book.

ABOUT THE AUTHOR

Ben Schrank is the author of *Miracle Man,* a novel. He has written for the *Financial Times, The New York Observer, Vogue, O,* and *Seventeen,* where he was the voice behind the fictional column "Ben's Life." He lives in Brooklyn, New York, where he grew up.

ABOUT THE TYPE

This book was set in Sabon, a typeface designed by the well-known German typographer Jan Tschichold (1902–74). Sabon's design is based upon the original letterforms of Claude Garamond and was created specifically to be used for three sources: foundry type for hand composition, Linotype, and Monotype. Tschichold named his typeface for the famous Frankfurt typefounder Jacques Sabon, who died in 1580.